THE MONEY RUN

E. R. Wytrykus

ISBN: 0-9742216-5-1
ISBN-13: 978-0-9742-2165-6

Visit www.booksurge.com to order additional copies.

>>ONE<<

"The End"

After I finished with the body I hiked home, stripped off my clothes and put them into the washer, started the machine, then walked naked through the house into the bathroom. I showered with the hottest water I could stand and shampooed my hair for five minutes. I stepped into sweats, poured myself a cognac and put on a cd of Dvorak's 'New World Symphony.' But I'm getting ahead of myself; I need to go back a few weeks.

>>TWO<<

"A Few Weeks Before"

It was a Saturday morning, not that it matters what day of the week it was. Several varieties of birds were chirping in the backyard trees and the familiar chattering of squirrels joined the chorus. It was shortly after six o'clock but once it gets light I'm awake. I got coffee started and Bret and I went out front to pick up the paper; at least, that's what I went for. Bret went for his morning constitution and to smell around to see what critters had been out and about during the night. The lawn was covered with shiny dew, the walkway with raggedy strips of silvery slime. It was time to feed the snails. A slight mist hovered as the morning fog fought a losing battle against the sun. Bret sniffed several plants, chose one, and watered it.

The paper in its plastic bag lay at the bottom of the driveway. I went down to get it while Bret wandered over to the neighbor's to check on the odors on their lawn, to see if anything more interesting had gone on there during the night. I opened the bag and sat on the top stair and kept an eye on Bret, though he was good about not roaming too far away. The headline was nothing of consequence but the picture on the front page caught my eye. It was a picture of the president of the United States flanked by two Army officers. In the background were people seated in bleachers. The caption said the president had been giving a speech to some military group in Hawaii. The soldier on his right I recognized as my cousin Rick. That was not a big surprise; I knew Rick was stationed in Hawaii. I had been there a couple months ago to visit him and play golf. His job required Rick to travel all over the Pacific countries and just a few days ago I had received a postcard from him, posted from Sri Lanka. The postcards had become a way of keeping in touch; he would send them from exotic places and mention that he was having a wonderful time or some such drivel, though I knew he was on a supposedly sensitive mission for the military. So I thought he was still out there in Asia or India or even China, for God's sake. I read a few sentences of the story but it wasn't anything earth-shaking.

I went down the red brick stairway so as to keep a better eye on Bret. At the sidewalk I looked around the cul de sac and for the umpteenth time wondered why so many people left their cars on the street overnight rather than park them in the garage or at least pull them into the driveway. Miles above me the sky was a dazzling azure with splatters of white, as if a blue canvas had been hit with a shotgun blast of white paint. It would be a beautiful day and maybe a little warm. I turned to gaze at the mountains that dominated the skyline of Madre Hills, the village I and Jane and Bret lived in. There were nigh onto ten thousand people in our little burg, and many people wanted to keep the official tally below five figures, thinking that a lower population gave us a better claim to the desirable description of 'quaint, peaceful village.'

Bret began to amble back towards me, stopping several times to smell something or mark a bush. Opening the paper to the sports section I scanned the stories and the scores until Bret nuzzled my leg, his way of saying he was ready to go in. More surprising than the picture in the paper was when only a few seconds later I heard the phone ringing inside the house. It is usually not good when the phone rings before seven in the morning. I said, "C'mon," and Bret followed me into the house.

Normally I don't answer the phone until the caller starts talking. My friends know that so they will speak up, often impatient with the message machine. But this early on a Saturday morning I figured it wouldn't be a sales person or a fund-raiser so it would be safe to answer. It was Rick.

"Like my picture?"

"Hey, yeah, well I thought you were still traveling."

"I am. I'm here, in California."

"No kidding? Well, where? You coming by?"

"Just wanted to make sure you had some coffee on."

"Hey, how'd you know I already saw your picture?"

"Just been waitin' for you to come outside."

"What? Where are you?

Just then there was a tap on the front door. My phone went quiet as Rick shut off his cell phone.

"What is this?" I said as I opened the door to let Rick in. "You spying on me? And when did you get here, I mean, this picture, it's recent isn't it?"

"You ever hear of jet travel?"

"Smart ass! Come on in, the coffee's brewing. I'll tell Jane you're here."

When I returned to the kitchen Rick had helped himself to coffee and was looking around at the kitchen and family room.

"This is a nice place. Must be worth a bundle."

"When we bought it, it was a stretch. But the way housing is around here, Rick, it's just crazy. We fixed up a few things: flooring, air conditioning, re-modeled the bathrooms... and with the equity I have now, I'm technically a millionaire, can you believe that?"

Rick nodded, saw the paper I had placed on the counter and picked it up. He smiled at the picture on the front page of the newspaper.

"So did you fly out right after this ceremony?" I asked.

"Actually, no. I'm still there, in Hawaii."

"Ah, okay. And you are what, a clone?"

"Let's go on the patio and talk, Kit."

Bret was standing at the pantry door which was a signal that he wanted his morning biscuit. I tossed one to him and grabbed the coffee cups and followed Rick out the back door. Bret followed me, biscuit secured between his teeth.

In the backyard Bret, our buff-colored English Cocker Spaniel, lay down on the lawn, held the biscuit between his paws and took a big bite. The biscuit crunched and crumbs fell into the grass. Rick glanced up at the trees and down at the flowers and we were just getting seated on the patio when Bret began his tour of the yard. This consisted of running through the shrubbery to stir up and chase off any birds that dared to land on the ground looking for seed or a wayward worm. Bret worked his way through the bushes on a path he'd worn from the countless forays searching for lizards, moles, or any other many and sundry creatures. More than once he'd snared a lizard, though usually all he'd end up with was a piece of its tail. One day he burst in through his doggie door proudly displaying a lizard that stuck out several inches from either side of his mouth. It was alive; probably in shock! I told him he'd better get that thing out of here before his mother saw him. He was hurt, just as he'd been the time he brought in a dead bird and laid it at Jane's feet, and she'd screamed and tossed the bird in the garbage. The conversation of the squirrels in the trees caught the dog's attention and he bounded back and forth across the lawn, his remarkable optimism that this was the day he would finally catch one of those creatures once again on display. For all his success in catching lizards and birds, so far no squirrels, thanks be.

"Is this going to be serious? I mean, you're not here to play golf, I gather."

"This may sound crazy to you. And normally I wouldn't be telling a civilian half of what I'm going to tell you. I swore if there was anybody in this whole wide world I could trust it would be you. But even so you have to give me your word that what we talk about now you will not repeat to anyone."

I looked at him, sipped my coffee, tried to read through the tiny grin on his face.

"You are serious. The last time you sounded so serious you enlisted in OCS, if I recall."

"That and when I got married, but you're right. So, just so you understand, no coffee break talk about this, okay?"

"I'm retired, Rick. I don't take coffee breaks."

"That's right, I forgot. So how's it working out? Bored yet?"

"No way. I've done lots of odd jobs that had been piling up just waiting for some attention. I'm trying to improve my golf game, we've taken a few trips, and I'm even learning how to use that freakin' computer for fun, not just work. Hey, the days just fly by."

"I'm not sure I'd know what to do with myself if I didn't have to go to work in the morning."

"Well, in the morning Bret and I sit outside and I read the paper with my coffee. In the late afternoon I sit outside with Bret and read a book or magazine with a glass of wine. Or, if I want something a tad stronger, a shot of Laphroaig."

"And in between?"

"In between I work the yard, I run errands, I visit friends, I golf, I read some more. I've read all the

Hillerman mysteries, in sequence, all the Ian Fleming James Bonds novels—most are better than the movies, and not to forget, *The Decline and Fall of the Roman Empire*, and a little Shakespeare on the side."

"Just to keep your mind sharp, eh? And a crossword puzzle once in a while?"

"Oh, yeah. A crossword puzzle a day keeps Alzheimer's away!"

"Not playing too much computer solitaire, are you?"

"Ha!" Kit laughed. "No, no; you can't win, anyway."

"Seriously," continued Kit, "I like not having to go to work. I guess it's different for some people but I find plenty to keep me busy. It's not like I was doing anything so important that the next guy in line couldn't do it."

"I suppose that's true for most of us."

"I know you don't want me to ask, but really, what the hell do you do, Rick?"

Rick gave Kit *the look*, the one that said, 'why are you asking what you aren't supposed to ask and I'm not supposed to answer'. But then he did answer.

"Stuff, I do stuff that I'm not suppose to talk about."

"Why?" Kit asked. "Because John Q. Public isn't able to handle what it is you do or because you are ordered not to tell?"

"Mostly the latter, though you have to admit, the average person in this country is not exactly cued in on current events. Hell, it's a miracle if fifty percent of the voters show up for an election."

"That's true. But would it make a difference in your job if more people voted."

Rick laughed, a guffaw, to tell the truth. "No, it wouldn't. Jesus, Kit, I'm dealing with people from different cultures than us; different perspectives. Not necessarily bad people; they are politicians a like our politicians. We deal with them but so much is under cover. If the truth comes out they will deny or stonewall. And we do the same thing. It can get bizarre at times."

"I suppose your work now is tame compared to commanding a tank brigade in the Iraqi desert."

Rick nodded. "For sure, but this job has never been boring. However, sometimes I get to wondering whether what I do matters."

"I know the feeling," said Kit.

"I'll have to try retirement some day. But anyway, some business first, before Jane gets here. I don't want to worry her."

"Are you playing with me? Is this some kind of a candid camera gig?"

Rick looked over at the dog and watched Bret as he sniffed the yard, wagging his stump of a tail continuously.

"Is this something dangerous?" I tried to sound lighthearted, still not sure how serious he was. I had often joked with Rick that if he ever needed help on one of his jaunts to an exotic isle, he could call on me.

"Are you finally going to send me on some secret mission? Just so I don't get killed! Jane's too young to be a widow!"

He paused, and then said, not, I thought, totally convincing, even to himself: "I wouldn't have agreed to this unless I was assured there was no danger. You just need to meet a guy you once knew, try to build up an acquaintance and get him talking about something you and he have in common."

"Meet a guy? Who?"

"He calls himself Tony Abbott, but you would have known him as Tony Abazini when you served with him in 'Nam."

I almost spit out coffee. "Are you kidding? In Vietnam? Whew, you are going back a few years. Yeah, I knew him for awhile. We called him 'Abz'; that might be the guy you mean. He arrived after I was already there, so we were in the same unit for only a short while but we got along okay. We did work in the same hooch for a few months. But he wasn't a guy I kept in touch with after I got out of the Army. It's not like we were real close buddies or anything."

"That's fine. But if we bump into him today, and you can act like you're interested in talking to him and maybe arrange to meet him for lunch again, then you'll just need to go along with where he takes the conversation. We expect he'll lead it and you'll just need to go along and mostly listen."

"Talk about what? Vietnam?"

"No, don't worry about it. You'll have a device and we'll be able to hear your conversation. We know what we want to get from him, and if it doesn't work out with you, well, at least it's a chance we'd like to take."

I was afraid to ask who he meant by 'we'.

I'm not one to sit and dwell about the Vietnam War. Oh, I get teary-eyed when I see a program about it, or when I've visited the Wall or other memorials. I don't *think* about it, but I'm reminded of it every time I see or hear a helicopter, which is almost every day. I wasn't *in* combat, just *around* it. I spent many sleepless nights on the base camp perimeter guard duty, trying to stay awake and alert in case there was an attack. Tony Abazini was one of the guys I knew, and like most people you know for a short time in a place and time that is cut out of your life in an unusual way, once the experience is over you don't have any contact. I understand that for people who shared blood and guts and constant fear of dying and the guy next to you getting blown up a more intense relationship develops; I understand that. But Tony and the other men I knew did office work. Our Vietnamese version of an office was a hooch constructed of two-by-fours, sandbags and a corrugated metal roof. The walls, such as they were, consisted mainly of screen stapled to the boards and when it rained, and it rained very hard at times, the noise as the water pelted that roof was so loud you literally could not hold a conversation. When I look at the pictures I brought home I remember some of the guys, but I only stayed in contact with two of them for a while after it was over, and even those relationships ended years ago. My best friend from the Army days was a guy I met before being assigned to Vietnam, when we were stationed in Washington, D.C. We got separated when we were sent overseas, ended our service at the same time and got an apartment together after we came home. We now lived several states apart but still kept a communication going. But Tony Abazini, I couldn't even picture his face, as I explained to Rick.

"No problem. We can arrange for you to see him, accidentally on purpose. You just act like you remember him well, fond memories of those days, yeah, yeah. Go for coffee, a beer, whatever, shoot the shit."

"So is there something from back then that you're trying to find out about? You know, we were just stationed at some itty-bitty finance company, nothing big happened there."

"You handled the money from the guys coming through Bien Hoa, didn't you?"

I nodded, remembering those bags and stacks of dollars, the cash that soldiers had with them when they arrived in Vietnam. The money was no good there, on base or in PXs, though quite valuable on the black market. Cash was turned in for Army script and the real dollars we packed up, after accounting carefully for every George Washington and Andy Jackson, and transported to Saigon. We were well armed for the truck ride to Saigon as the enemy would have loved to get their hands on several millions dollars of American money. I always thought that if we were attacked I would have gladly given the money away as long as they'd let me go! A real hero, not. Of course, when the attack did come, well, there was no time to do anything, heroic or otherwise. But that's another story. Was that why Rick was here?

I asked him as I went inside to refill our cups. By then Jane was up and she and Rick greeted each other with hugs and the usual verbal exchange of friends who hadn't seen each other in a long time. Jane and Rick had met a few times before and I was glad they hit if off well as Rick and I were close; had been since we played together as five-year olds, got lost and had the cops looking for us when we were ten-year olds, golfed when we were college age, then went separate ways for jobs and homes. The birth of e-mail, as for many others, allowed us to more easily stay in touch; electronic words eliminating the need for the drudgery of actually writing out and mailing a letter.

"Nice surprise, but why didn't you call? You'll be here a while or what? You can come for dinner tonight?"

"I am on duty, and yes, dinner would be nice. Oh, Jane, don't say anything to anybody about my being here."

"Well, hush-hush, eh? Who would I tell, anyway? Go on with your business then. You staying here or do you have a place?"

"Thanks, but I've already got a room at the Embassy just a few miles away."

"Did you check-in last night?"

"Yes, very late. Then up early to come here for the fine coffee. Of course the Rick Walker on the passenger manifest is not an Army general, so I'm not really here."

"Yeah, you've already told me," I said. "So, how long are you *not* going to be here?"

"Two days, maybe three; okay?"

I nodded, "Affirmative, general."

For the next hour we continued to drink coffee, rounded up some bagels to toast, and talked about everything else but what Rick came here for. He told me what he could about his visits to Korea, Vietnam, Myanmar, Australia, and few other places. Not about his work, just the sights. My cousin was in 'Special Forces,' which doesn't tell you much, and anyone who wanted to stay friends with Rick knew better than to ask about his work. Even his kids and wife, now ex-wife, didn't know exactly what he did or, often, even where he was. He did tell me that the postcards he sent me were often mailed either before or after he had actually been in that place. I laughed out loud when he told me of his procedure.

"You guys, you and your secret agent shit. I should have known." Actually, I've long felt that most of the secrets our government feels they need to keep from the civilian population could be readily revealed without compromising much. But I didn't want to hurt Rick's feelings by saying that. Besides, what would all those thousands of spooks who work for all those alphabetically named intelligence agencies do for a job if they didn't have secrets to generate and guard from us incompetents?

We talked about families, his four kids, our one.

"Chris moved out a while ago. He's an engineer, lives in the Bay Area. Has a nice girl. We expect wedding bells soon. What about your gang?"

After a brief recap of the whereabouts and doings of his brood, Rick went back to the subject he was here to discuss. "You have time this afternoon to meet Tony Abbott?"

"Do I have a choice," I said, in a soft, conspiratorial voice.

"Yes, you do. Of course, I'd have to kill you now if you refuse to cooperate!"

"Tough guy. Yeah, I think Jane is going to work with her friend Cindy on their pamphlets project so I guess we can go out spying."

"And—seriously now, for a moment—don't call me *general*, even in joking, and also don't make any jokes about spies and such. I don't want anyone to overhear anything like that."

"Getting back to the money trucks in 'Nam. Is that what this is about, all these years later?"

Rick shrugged. "Abbott wasn't even on that run, the one when your truck got hit."

Yeah, I thought, then: "Hey, how in the hell would you know? Why would that particular little episode from all the years that war went on be something that would come to your attention now?"

"If I told you then you'd have my job and I'd be spending my days soaking up the sun on the golf course."

For a few seconds, or maybe it was as long as a minute, I was remembering bits of information long forgotten consciously, but not totally eliminated from the memory banks. Something screwy here.

"But why is it that today of all days your picture shows up in the paper?"

"That, I swear is a coincidence." Then he stopped and was thinking something.

"What, Rick."

"Oh, you know, even I can be fooled too. I wouldn't be surprised if 'they'—the people who order me around, planned specifically for me to be in the picture after it was arranged that I'd be coming here. I'm not sure why, probably just one of those many precautions they like to take. But as far as I know, it has nothing to do with you and me and what we're talking about."

"Rick, you know I'm happy to help, since it's you, and only because it's you. But are you sure this is something you want a civilian to get involved in?"

"It wasn't my idea. It seems a reference to a Tony Abazini came up in a CIA investigation."

"Oh, great, I should have known!"

"Somebody at the Defense Intelligence Agency heard about this—probably a spy spying on the other spies—and this name raised a flag regarding a possible MIA situation. One thing led to another, one name to another is more like it, and then some sharp sergeant figured out that among the people who knew Abbott when he was Abazini in Vietnam was a cousin of mine. So, that's how it started. But at first I was supposed to completely snow you. There I balked. No way was I going to bring you into this without giving you some idea of what's going on."

"But you haven't told me much of anything yet."

"You know, Kit, this isn't my usual line of work. However, Special Ops has in the past been involved in attempted MIA recovery operations, so my boss, General Lytle, gets flagged when an open case like this pops up. I've been volunteered, too, just like I'm getting you to do. I'll tell you more when I can. But first you need to see if you can get Abbott to talk to you. If he won't, your part is over, that's it, done deal."

"Okay, but your Mom, and my Mom, would be pretty peeved at you if you let your favorite cousin get hurt."

"I'll be careful. Now, we think we know where Abbott, or Abazini as you knew him, will be today around lunchtime. You and I will be there too. I'm going to go back to my motel for some things and then I'll pick you up in about an hour, okay?"

Kit said, "Sure", as if he truly understood what the hell he was getting into.

>>THREE<<

"Later the Same Day"

We went to a sports bar called 'Sports 'n' More', in the Glendale area. It was not busy as the lunch crowd hadn't gathered yet, but there were several baseball games showing on the TVs, which hung so that at least one was in view from any spot in the place.

I couldn't help but look around for a familiar face, though I was having a tough time recalling what Abazini looked like.

"He's not here yet," said Rick. "Let's order a beer."

We sipped beer, ordered sandwiches and watched the ball games without much talk. The backdrop hum of the customers increased as the bar filled up and an occasional yell told us that something had happened in one of the games.

"Maybe this will be the year," Rick said.

"The Cubs, you dreamer?"

Rick laughed, "Just one time I'd like to see them get to the World Series; just one time."

Then he was all business again. "He should be here soon, but I won't point him out at first. I want to see how well you recognize him."

"It's been a lot of years. I may not know him at all."

"How much do you remember about the time your truck was attacked and the money stolen?"

"So it is about the robbery!"

"Kit, even I don't know much about this. I told you this isn't my line of work. I'm sort of helping out, you know, other duties as required."

"Yeah, right", I said, with a smirk that meant, 'I don't believe you.'

I searched my memory, the vague recollections of bouncing along on footlockers filled with cash, my rifle in hand, then slipping back to the present.

"Well, I made three or four of those money runs but obviously this one does stick out in my memory more than the others. And Abazini wasn't on this run. He and I were on one a few weeks before; I think that's when we met. It did give us some sort of a connection, but that connection didn't carry over into a lasting friendship.

"Now on the day of this particular run he was sick, I think. There were two other guys with me in the truck, plus the driver. He got killed. I wasn't hurt, other than pushed around, and neither were the other two. In fact, I think it was shortly after that they were transferred, and so was Abazini."

"So did you make any more runs after that?"

"One more, if I remember correctly. Then I wasn't assigned to a run for several weeks, and just before a run was due I went on temporary duty to a unit in Long Binh. Actually it turned out to more than temporary because that's where I finished up my tour. You know, I hardly remember seeing those guys that were with me after that incident. Howard and Jenkins; I just remembered their names."

"It's like you all were separated?"

"Maybe; I didn't think of it at the time. The three of us talked about it a bit, had to make reports, and even went to Saigon. You know, there was about four million bucks on that run. Enough to make some general worried, I would imagine. And the way they questioned us, I think they were suspicious that one of us, or all of us, knew something about it. First they questioned us together, then individually."

By now the place was crowded and very noisy. I scanned the room and tables and the guys standing at the bar. Nobody looked familiar to me at first. Then I noticed someone at the bar, his back to me, who was tall and thin, as I remembered Abazini, with dark hair, thinning and gray at the sides.

"Is that him, the guy in the yellow shirt?" I nodded towards the bar.

"See, you recognized him right off."

The man in the yellow shirt turned just enough to reveal his profile and I saw nothing that was definite. "Maybe. He sort of looks like the guy but as I remember 'Abz' had a long nose and thick eyebrows. This guy's nose is too small."

Rick said, "That's him, I've seen him on film and I have a good picture of him with me that I didn't want to show you yet. Of course his hair would have thinned and we think he had a nose job."

"Alright, if you say it's him, I believe you. So what do you want me to do?"

A few seconds later I realized that Rick was being honest when he said he didn't know everything because he was clearly as surprised as I was when Abazini, or Abbott, or whoever he was, came up to our table and greeted us.

"Excuse me...Walker, isn't it?"

"Oh, yeah, that's me," I replied. "And you...you do look a little familiar," I said, trying to not overplay my part.

"Abazini. We were at that finance unit in 'Nam. Am I right?"

"That's right, 11th Finance Unit." Now I could act like I remembered him, though straight on he didn't look like the Abazini I could picture in my mind.

"Yes, I'm Kit Walker. I remember you. We called you 'Abz', didn't we?'

"Yeah, yeah, that's right. I changed my name to Abbott. Too many misspellings, and I didn't like 'Abz' after I got out."

"This is my friend Rick; Rick, Tony…it's Tony, isn't it?"

He nodded and reached out to shake hands with Rick.

"Tony and I were in Vietnam at the same unit for awhile," I said to Rick, as if he didn't know already.

"Counting money and stuff. Hey, weren't you one of the guys on the truck that got robbed? I could have been there too, but I was sick. Man, I was never so glad to be sick. I sure felt bad for the guys that got in on that mess. And what's his name, the guy who was killed; it could have been any of us."

"Yeah, he was the guy we called Tater, the driver. I don't recall his real name. That was sad. I didn't know him well, but still… never did figure out why they shot him, unless he was reaching for a weapon or something. At least the rest of us didn't get hurt. Hey, you want to join us?" I offered.

"Just for a bit; I met some other guys at the bar. So, do you come here often to watch the games?"

I shrugged, stole a glance at Rick, who said nothing. "Not too often. Rick is visiting; we haven't seen each other for awhile so we're just catching up on things."

"So where are you from?" Abbott asked, turning to Rick

Without a blink Rick said, "Illinois. I'm in tool sales."

"So what do you do, Tony?" I asked.

"Oh, man I have done a little of everything. Took me awhile to get going after the Army. Wasted a couple years just hanging out and doing odd jobs. But I went back to school and finished up. Only had a year to go. Got a Business Management degree and I went into sales, too," he glanced at Rick.

I was afraid he would try talking shop with Rick, but I figured Rick had a prepared storyline in case that happened. To my relief Tony continued on with his own tale.

"I got into the management end at a heavy equipment company and did that for the next twenty-seven years. Now I'm just doing some part-time consulting and I'm in this area for a few days. Funny thing running into somebody I knew back in 'Nam. What about you, Walker?"

"I stayed on the finance side of things. Just retired a year ago so now I'm catching up on house repairs, trying to play golf, that kind of stuff."

"Sounds great. Hey, you want to get together some time for lunch? Maybe shoot some pool and swap war stories."

"Yeah, sure," I said, surprised again at how easy this was.

"How about Monday? We could meet here if you want, unless you know a better place."

I looked at Rick for help. "Ah, well, I think Rick might still be here."

Rick shook his head. "No, I've got things to do. Go ahead, make your plans. Don't worry about me."

Tony took that as a confirmation. We shook hands and then Tony saluted me and laughed as he headed back to the bar. "See ya Monday, about noon".

I waited for Rick to say something after Abbott was gone. Rick was looking towards the bar, maybe watching who Abbott was talking to. He seemed to be thinking about what had just transpired.

"Now I'm confused. It's almost as if he was looking for you to bump into."

"Yeah, I didn't have to do anything. It's almost like he wants to talk to me, instead of me trying to get him to talk."

"I have no reason to think that. We were supposed to get you to encourage him to talk about himself, but he just walks over and chatters like he was trying to make a plea-bargain. Beats me."

"Okay, but why? If it has something to do with the money run robbery, he wasn't even there that day. And what could have caused that robbery to be an issue now, over thirty-five years later?"

"Like you said, Kit, four millions bucks can worry a general."

"You, *general?*" I asked, in a whisper.

He didn't say anything but downed the last of his beer. "Let's go, I need to make some calls."

As we drove away, he suggested that maybe I didn't want to meet Abbott again after all. "Seems that I'm—we, are getting into more than I know about, and I don't like that. And I don't believe a word he said about being in heavy equipment. He's lying, but I can't say why I feel that."

"Would it be a problem for you if I refused to meet him again?"

"No, don't worry about it. Let me drop you off at home, then I'll meet you there later for dinner."

"What am I supposed to tell Jane? I don't want to pretend there's nothing's going on."

"I agree. And since obviously *they* haven't been upfront with me, some bets are off. For now, just tell her you ran into a guy you knew in 'Nam, and don't mention yet that's the reason I'm here. When I see you later I'll figure out what we can say."

"Come anytime, we'll be there."

All Jane asked me was where we had gone, no particulars. So I made it sound very casual and told her that Rick would fill us in when he returned, but that he thought I could help him with something. She gave me a strange look, as if saying, what goofy things are you boys up to?

That afternoon I looked through my pictures from Vietnam. I had shot slides and since then had scanned them into the computer. There were pictures of the guys I'd known there, many whose name I could no longer remember. I did pick out Howard and Jenkins but had no pictures of Tony Abazini. There were pictures of the Vietnamese children who worked in our compound, filling sandbags or doing other odd jobs. We all took turns monitoring them and I think they liked it when it was my turn because I didn't make them work hard. I felt sad that they here at all, working instead of in school or out playing somewhere.

There were several pictures of aircraft, helicopters and even the U-2 spy plane. We had been warned not to take such pictures and to destroy them before leaving 'Nam but I and plenty of other people kept them. I remembered that as we were lining up to board our 'freedom bird' we were sternly warned that this was the last chance to rid ourselves of forbidden items. No drugs, guns, knives, etc. A large box was situated where we passed on our way to the plane and by the time I got to it I was amazed how full it was. Enough weaponry to start yet another war!

There were pictures of my R&R in Japan and a few of visits to Saigon, including some from the Bob Hope show. One picture was of three guys I had known there, one of them Curtis Howard, standing in front of a sign that said 'FTA'. When I returned from Vietnam and showed the slides to my family, my mother asked what 'FTA' stood for. Without missing a beat I said, "Fun, Travel and Adventure". I was sure my Dad wasn't fooled.

A picture of me and the guy we called Tater, standing in front of a truck, had been taken by someone else with my camera. I wondered if this had been taken just before that fateful money run but I couldn't remember.

There were also pictures of the endless mountain ranges of Alaska that I took from the plane on the homeward bound journey. We had flown from Saigon to Tokyo to Anchorage to San Francisco, a flight I swear included two sunrises and sunsets, several meals and several naps. As I looked at the slides I began to remember more about the months I spent in Vietnam over thirty years ago. And the more I remembered, the more mysterious Tony Abazini became. He'd been an elusive character; never said much about himself or where he had served before. He didn't talk about his plans for after the Army or what kind of work he did in civilian life. And why Rick would be involved with Abazini made no sense to me at all.

Rick returned with more news than I had expected. We were in the backyard, with the grill heating up and each of us savoring a glass of wine.

"Did you notice the bandage on Abbott's arm?" Rick asked.

I had to think; "Yes, now that you mention it, why?"

Rick shook his head slightly. "I don't know, just wondered how he got it. Looked like a serious cut, that's all."

I didn't see the significance of the cut on Abbott's arm nor understood why it bothered Rick. I guess he was just more observant of such things.

"Kit, I spoke to my boss, General Lytle."

"So even a general has a boss, uh?"

"Hell, it seems I have more bosses now than ever. He's got three stars to my two. But hey, I've got a reserved parking place at the PX and I can get a tee time whenever I want, as you found out when you came to Hawaii.

"General Lytle and I have been through some battles together—both figuratively and in the field– that has built up a trust. He wouldn't try to con me about this. He says he received information he didn't have when he and I first talked. As far as he knows, all you are being asked to do is meet with Abbott and let him talk as much as possible about whatever he wants to talk about. We'll meet with the people from the Defense Intelligence Agency. They've got a bug you'll wear, and the people who will listen to it will figure out if there's anything on it to help them do what they want to do. And the general agrees--because now I pressed him on it—that I can confirm to you that yes, this definitely has to do with four million dollars that's been missing since 1969. Tada! No surprise to you and me.

"But, I reminded him, Abbott wasn't there. And the general says yes, and that's part of somebody's suspicion. Why exactly, he couldn't, or wouldn't, tell me. Also, and this I didn't know until he told me just this past hour, the serial numbers on some money the CIA recently located in a deposit box in some Swiss bank match the numbers from the money stolen on your money run."

"That's incredible! I figured that money had either deteriorated to dust by now, or was still floating around Southeast Asia."

"Maybe most of it has. Supposedly the box *only* contained a few tens of thousands of dollars."

The grill was hot enough so I put on the steaks and waited for Rick to continue. "Is this what they call a pregnant pause, or are you done?"

"There is something that's even more startling."

Again he stopped, took a sip from his glass of wine. "Nice. What is it?"

"It's a syrah, from the Los Olivos area, not too far from here. It's my current favorite wine. So now what's so startling?"

"When I spoke to General Lytle he tells me—and Kit, believe me, if I'd known this before I would have contacted you even if I hadn't been ordered to…"

"All right, you've startled me. Should I have something stronger to drink?" I asked.

"Maybe. This is a part you might have to decide on how much to tell Jane."

"The steaks are almost ready. So tell me right now or wait till after dinner."

Rick lowered his voice. "General Lytle tells me that shortly after those serial numbers were identified a man died in a robbery attempt in Michigan, and another one was almost killed here in southern California in a hit-and-run. He swears he didn't know about this until a few hours ago, though both incidents occurred about three weeks ago."

"And these incidents are connected somehow to, what, the truck robbery, Abbott, or all of the above?"

"The two men were Curtis Howard and Bill Jenkins," Rick said. "Howard was badly hurt in the hit-and-run, Jenkins killed in an apparent robbery. The hit-and-run car was stolen."

"No kidding? So this is considered related, how? I don't get it."

"Don't you see? Those were the two guys with you; then the money shows up, those two are attacked, and now Abbott beats us to the punch in setting up this meeting with you."

"So you think he set us up, instead of the other way around?"

"Could be. When I suggested that the general agreed. He himself thinks we aren't being told everything. "

"So am I, or Jane and I, in danger, you think?"

"I honestly don't know Kit, but I don't think so, not yet, anyhow. But if Abbott was looking to talk to you, it might be good that I am involved in this. At least we can be on guard."

Rick sipped his wine, his eyes starring out at nothing, the wheels turning in his head. "Since the Howard and Jenkins 'accidents' were over two weeks ago, and nothing's happened to you, maybe it wasn't Abbott who caused those accidents, assuming they were caused, and that whoever did doesn't know that you were on that money run, or can't find you, or doesn't care about you."

"But aren't you thinking it's more likely that it was Abbott who killed Jenkins and tried to kill Howard? And before you answer, remember, I don't hang out at that bar we went to today, so if Abbott was trying to meet me, that meant he must have followed us. Which might mean you didn't do such a great job of covering your tracks, my dear general!"

Rick slowly nodded. "All that has occurred to me. The DIA people I'm dealing with say Abbott has been going to that bar every day for almost two weeks, and I just got into town last night, dear cuz."

The conversation was fascinating, if a little scary. Steaks were ready and we took them to the table as Jane appeared with the side dishes. The conversation turned more mundane while we enjoyed the food. By this time I felt the need to let Jane in on what we knew so far. Telling the story, which also involved a short version of the money run robbery, took us through the meal.

Jane sat quietly, and I sensed she was having a tough time curbing her urge to speak up. I figured she'd be upset or scared. Both, she finally said, which is why she tried to cover up by saying, "This sounds like a good time for us to get away on a nice long, ocean cruise."

That lightened the atmosphere a bit. "Maybe Cindy can help," I said.

As we began to clean up the table Rick asked me to again tell the story about the robbery. I gave him an abbreviated version.

"There's another possibility. It could be that whoever attacked Jenkins and Howard—and it probably was Abbott— cares enough about your safety not to take you out, too, because there's something he needs from you."

"Oh, well, that's nice," said Jane. "But what happens when this person doesn't need anything from Kit anymore?"

Having no good answer, Rick ignored Jane's comment, wishing he could think of something to say to alleviate her fears.

"I read the old reports that were filed back in '69. But they were summaries, not verbatim. I need details. So don't skip anything. A while ago I had the feeling you were downplaying the danger you were in at that time. But tell me everything you can remember, not just the events but what you saw and thought and felt, right down to how many mosquito bites you got."

So to the taste of an old cognac and the sounds of Wes Montgomery's guitar on the stereo, I took myself back to those humid days and sleepless nights in Vietnam, those days of dust and the all-pervasive sound of helicopters, of earth-shaking B-52 strikes, of jungle-rules volleyball games, of bad food and cold showers, of too much noise or too much silence, and of riding herd on millions of greenbacks.

>>FOUR<<

"Vietnam, 1969"

Since I had been on guard duty all night I was supposed to have the morning off. But Abazini was sick so Sgt. Graham asked me if I would take Abz' place on the money run. He promised me I could have the entire next day off to catch up on my sleep.

"That's a deal, Eddie," I said. "What's wrong with Abz?"

"I don't know. He's at the clinic over at the air base. Thanks, this helps me keep things on schedule. Stay loose. You've got Howard and Jenkins with you."

"Jenkins? Gee, thanks. Does he know how to use that rifle? All he seems good for is doing his laundry."

"Well, you shouldn't have any trouble. You know, I've been here seven months and we haven't any problems on this run yet."

"Yet. You'll owe me big if we have trouble on this one. See you later."

Bien Hoa airbase, a stone's throw from the finance unit I was assigned to, was the busiest airport in the world round about 1968, '69. This was mostly due to jet fighter activity, but Bien Hoa was the welcoming base for thousands of troops coming into Vietnam for their tour of duty. They came with lots of cash, none of it legally useful. Among the duties my unit had was to exchange Army script for this cash, prepare the paper work to account for it, pack it up in wooden footlockers, and truck it to Saigon, from where it was, I suppose, repacked and shipped back to the States. A run would consist of several footlockers loaded with three or four million dollars and three scared-shitless finance clerks to guard it against an enemy attack. In reality the route from Bien Hoa to Saigon was a well-traveled and well-protected busy highway, Route One, and the two runs I'd made already had been uneventful. I expected this one to be no problem and for my participation I would get a day off.

I had landed at Bien Hoa myself recently. Some things the military does with such precision and so well organized that one can only stand back in awe. Then there are other things they do that make one ask, 'Is anyone in charge here?'

That's what it was like when I and a couple hundred other newbies climbed down after a flight that had stopped in Hawaii, tempting us to stay in the hotel bar rather than return to the plane once it was refueled; in Guam, and again at Clark Field in the Philippines.

You'd think there'd be someone to tell us where to go and how to get there. Maybe a sign spelling out 'Da Nang', or 'Saigon', or '11th Finance'. But it was two hundred guys bumping into each other trying to figure out where to go. As it turned out I was in rock-throwing distance of my destination; I just didn't know it yet. Finally, I bumped into a guy who called himself Tater who had a jeep and was looking for lost souls like me. He took me to my new base, a quick five-minute ride that kicked up enough dust for a brigade of tanks.

11th Finance was a rinky-dink looking collage of huts and wooden walkways connecting the various buildings. The wooden planks that made up the walkways would come in handy now that the rainy season had begun.

It was September when I arrived, a time when the dry season was ending and the monsoons began to kick up. There were many muddy puddles now, potholes filled from a recent downpour, but when it was hot and dry the ground was a dusty yellow and gray composite. The sky a beautiful blue; too beautiful, it seemed, for a place of such chaos and death.

Tater guided me to a Sergeant named Eddie Graham who said he was expecting me and welcomed me like a long lost son. He showed me the desk where I would be working and told me to take the day to get oriented and he'd see me tomorrow. Tater showed me where I would live and took me to supply. I was issued a blanket and pillow, a mattress thinner than a pancake, a rifle, flak jacket and helmet. The latter three items I could have done without. I mean, this is a finance company, isn't it? What the hell do I need a rifle and helmet for?

The next day, before I could report to Sgt. Graham, I was informed I first had to practice at the firing range. First with my rifle, then a machine gun, then a grenade launcher. I did okay; in basic training I actually had been one of the best sharpshooters, a feat I feared might send me to the infantry.

The company had a captain, but I think I only saw him once or twice. It was a lieutenant who ran things. I saw him almost every day, and sometimes he was sober. Then there was a master sergeant who thought he was the Army's answer to Captain Queeg and had us out on Sundays building up the berm that surrounded the base. Fortunately he left shortly after I arrived and things settled down to a nice, easy pace.

This morning I was stone tired, having been awake nearly the entire night on guard duty at the berm. It had been raining for several days and the ditches surrounding our camp were head-deep in water. To get to the perimeter bunkers we'd had to wade through the ditches. So at five o'clock yesterday afternoon I was soaked to the skin, and I stayed that way until eight this morning. Usually two of the three guards would stay awake while one caught some sleep. But soaked to the skin as we were made sleep impossible. Fortunately I'd had time to change to dry clothes and grab a quick breakfast and, thank you, it had stopped raining.

My plan for the morning had been to sleep three or four hours, then, depending on the weather, dash over to the swimming pool the engineers had dug out for the local units. Mostly it was for the use of the grunts coming in from the field. Here they could relax in the sun, take a dip in clean water, and try not to think about going back to the fire zones for a few days. For those of us lucky enough to be stationed in the vicinity, it was an unexpected luxury. Occasionally, as I sat there soaking up the rays and reading a book or dozing, helicopters would whirl overhead. They carried soldiers, wounded ones, laid out on stretchers attached to the 'copter. Some of the poor slobs likely expired before medics or a mobile hospital could be reached. The sight caused a tinge of guilt to seep in and usually I'd stay away from the pool for a week or so until I'd forgotten about it. It wasn't until years later, when the television show M*A*S*H was popular that I recalled the scenes, almost exactly like the opening segment of the show.

Our driver was the guy called Tater, from Idaho. He was a sergeant again, having been busted down and promoted up more times than even he remembered. With a military driver's license and contacts in the motor pool he was constantly going places he wasn't supposed to, when he wasn't supposed to. And sometimes he got caught. But he knew the streets of Saigon like a native taxi driver, so when some visiting officer needed transportation likely as not Tater got a stripe back and the job of ferrying the brass around. Having an experienced driver was some compensation for having to sit in back with Jenkins.

Jenkins was quirky. He spent all his free time doing his laundry and polishing his boots. He starched his fatigues until they could stand at attention and polished his boots until they shone like the morning sun twinkling off the still waters of Crater Lake. Many a night I awoke to see him using his cigarette lighter to inspect his boots and melt the polish into the leather.

"Kerist, Jenks, go to sleep already," someone would yell.

In the morning Jenkins would awake with smoker's cough, reach under his bunk for the first of his two dozen a day cans of Coca-Cola, take a swig of the warm liquid, cough some more, and light his first cigarette of the day. Still, to talk to him he seemed like a normal, sane person. He was just a fanatic about his clothes and addicted to nicotine and caffeine. To tell the truth, I didn't know what he might be like in a stressful situation—a combat situation, but because of his weird habits it was assumed he wouldn't be much help. Then again, I didn't know what I would do either.

We were finance people. Our unit was the 11th Finance Company and if I never had to handle a rifle or duck for cover it was okay with me. But the first day there I was given my rifle, my flak jacket, helmet, and other gear, *just in case*, I was told. Also, I soon found out, we were expected to handle the perimeter guard duty at night and assist in case of enemy attack at any time.Being in the shadow of the air base and of a brigade of the 101st Airborne put us in the line of fire for the frequent Viet Cong artillery and mortar attacks. Our main concern was for short rounds, those that didn't quite make it to the target. And, if the VC did break through our perimeter they could, theoretically, sneak around and attack the air base and its valuable jets from point blank range. A turn on this all-night duty came around about once every five nights, and lasted from five in the afternoon until eight in the morning. There were always three of us to a bunker so you could get some sleep, depending on the noise level. We were well armed with an M-80 machine gun pointed out our bunker across the field and with boxes of ammo and grenades, plus our own rifles. Wire fences and a minefield made it unlikely anyone would get through, but better safe than sorry.

Commercial jets bringing in new blood often landed at night, coming in over the field that sprawled between 11th Finance, the air base, and the village of Bien Hoa. To make it difficult for those nasty mortars to spot them the planes kept their landing lights off until the last possible moment. In our bunkers we could hear them (I think they were stretched 737s) as they came in for a landing. But we could not see the planes until they suddenly turned on their lights, just about the time they swept over our bunkers. They soared in so low over us I know positively I could have hit those planes with a rock if I tried. Between those planes and the roaring F4 Phantom fighter jets it was too noisy to talk to your buddy until late into the night, and then it could be deathly quiet until near dawn, when the jets awoke and screeched off on their way to early morning action.

There was a string of about a dozen bunkers around our camp. Most of the action was when monkeys or pigs scurried around in the field looking for food. The initial noise always gave us a stop—was there anyone out there? Eventually a grunt or a screech would identify the intruder. Worse, and scarier, was when one of the animals got close to the fence and set off a mine. If one of us did hear or see (or think we heard or saw) something out there we were to call it in to the Tower guards and request flares to light up the field. (We had enough ammo to start a new war but we weren't trusted with flares). One night one of the guys a few bunkers down from mine was sure there were enemy soldiers crawling through the field coming right at him. Those of us in the other bunkers listened in on our radios to his conversation with the Tower. His request for flares became more frantic. The Tower was reluctant, probably because they knew a plane full of newbies was due in and they didn't want too much light on the area.

"Are you sure, Bunker 5? You know there are pigs out there."
"This ain't no pig, Tower! I can see something, about a hundred yards out."
"Bunker 5, I doubt you can see a hundred yards out in the dark."
"Well, then they're even closer! Give me some light!"
"Negative. Give us a chance to survey the area."

This went on for several minutes while the rest of us strained our eyes to see if we could spot any movement in the darkness. It was a relief when the Tower guard came back on.
"Okay, Five, we will set off a flare over your area."
"Oh, man, we're all dead already!"

Well, it was nothing. In fact, the only time we ever had any excitement was when I heard movement outside our bunker, in *back* of us. Rifle in hand I cautiously looked out and spoke the password. I think it was 'Good' and the proper response was supposed to be 'Ugly'. I didn't get any reply except a groan and a cough. I saw something move and called out, "Drop your rifle!" My two partners were alerted by then and we all aimed at a shape that we could just barely see in the dark, a shape that seemed to tumble over as we approached it. Fortunately the intruder meekly lay down his gun. Then he puked. It was one of ours; some guy high as a kite and stumbling his way towards the minefield. Turns out he was a short-timer; only a couple days from freedom and he'd begun celebrating with booze and pot. We called the MPs and our prisoner was taken away to sober up.

Far more often than the one day in five of bunker duty were the times we were rousted from our cots in the middle of the night to hunker down in the crude shelters within our base camp area. This happened whenever there was enemy artillery or mortar action. Often we spent the rest of the night in these trenches, not much more than sandbags piled up with a metal roof and wooden benches lining the inside. We'd try to sleep sitting up while we waited for the all-clear signal. After a few weeks a soldier could tell the difference between the outgoing shells of the artillery unit that guarded the air base and incoming rounds fired by the Viet Cong. Those of us who had learned this would be out of bed and grabbing our boots and helmets even before the warning siren went off. By morning we would be both tired and high; there were always a few guys who decided this was a good time and place to suck those reefers. In the confined quarters the sweet scent reached all of us. So all in all, we were tired most mornings whether we were on guard duty or spent the night in a bunker or in our bed in the hooch. If it wasn't roaring jets it was thunderous rain. If it wasn't rain it was the thump of mortars. Most days our hour and a half of lunch break consisted of a quick bite and then a nap.

Right after we finished our regular workday, for those who didn't have to head to the bunkers for the rest of the day and night, there was basketball and volleyball. Jungle volleyball, we called it, because there were very few rules to consider. None of this pansy stuff like you couldn't touch the opponent while blocking his shot. We would play until about a half hour before the mess hall closed, then dash over for dinner. If it was still light after we ate we might play some more. At night there were often first-run movies, although if there was any sign of potential enemy activity nearby we couldn't have movies because the lighted outdoor screen was too big a target.

So it's March, 1969 in Vietnam. I've been here seven months already and spent Christmas playing volleyball and enjoying a steak we'd bar-b-qued using an ammo carrier as a grill. A bunch of us did manage to see the Bob Hope show with Ann-Margret last week, and then snuck over to the USO for a dinner slightly better than we got in our own mess hall. Because of the less than brilliant talents of our cooks, a bunch of us would get together on weekends and purchase steaks from the mess hall and cook them ourselves. Somebody– Tater was a good bet– obtained charcoal; that and a few cheap beers made for relatively pleasant Sunday afternoons. The poor steaks would otherwise have been either burned to a crisp in the mess hall or ended up in the officer's mess.

But today it's the money run, and I'm sitting on top of more money than I knew existed, and probably more money than I'll ever be close to in the real world as long as I live. The back flap of the truck is open so as we barrel down the highway we can look back and see what we've passed. Small farms and hovels, oxen, people working in rice paddies and kids playing in the dirt or chasing chickens, the road busy with natives on bicycles and Americans in jeeps and trucks. I start to get sleepy and began to doze off even as we bounce along, sitting on our fortune.

Normally the run is smooth and uneventful. Once we deliver the strongboxes of dough we hit the USO for a beer or two, maybe catch some dinner at a local restaurant. The food is palatable; chicken, I think, I hope not dog, and vegetables and rice. At least here it doesn't smell as awful as the lunch of the kids and women who work around our compound. The smell of fish heads and rice cooked in some kind of gluey fish oil is enough to make one swear off seafood.

And again, normally, we have an officer with us on the run. Lieutenant Walsh was on all of the runs that I knew of, but in this case instead of riding in the truck he was well ahead in a jeep and planned to meet us in Saigon. On the previous runs I participated in he rode up front, with the driver, and after we were finished with business he would treat us to the first beer. It depended on the time; we needed to leave early enough to get back to Bien Hoa before dark. Traveling along the highway after dark was even money for an ambush.

On my first run, which I thought would be my last, we left early, had time for drinks and a meal after delivery, and climbed into the truck for the return trip. Tater was the driver then, too, and even with a few beers in him we felt confident he could find his way back home. Just head down Highway One. But the damn truck wouldn't start. I'm not mechanically inclined, so I was no help then and even years later I can't remember what the problem was. Generator, alternator, who knows? Tater knew who to contact for help but it was too late in the day to get the part and make the repair. So we had to find a place to hunker down for the night.

This night was the only night of my life I slept with a rifle by my side. It's easy to say, yeah, a night on the town in Saigon, with all them pretty oriental ladies eager to please. But we'd heard too many stories of GIs who simply disappeared, were mugged or drugged, or, maybe worse, contracted some sort of disease that nothing, not penicillin or anything in our medicine cabinets could combat, and who were listed as missing in action and kept as virtual prisoners on some remote island in the Pacific. Now for the most part we didn't believe those stories, but as it got later and darker, the noise of the drunks, the occasional gunshots, and the screams made us clutch our rifles in an almost paranoid bonding in our musty hotel room. More than once someone would pound on the door, yelling, "Hey, GI, number ten mamasan! Good nookie! Only two dollah!" And we would yell back, "Diddy Mao!" or other equivalents of "Get the hell out of here!" in English, French and Vietnamese, fearful that at any second a grenade would come crashing through the window. It's not that any of us feared getting laid, we just feared getting dead.

Well, we all survived the night, but no one slept much. We got the truck fixed in the morning and laughed about our adventure all the way back to Bien Hoa.

About twenty minutes out the traffic is less dense and Tater yells back to us, "Detour, guys". The truck slows, almost stops, then turns and clatters along an obviously inferior road. I stretch to look out the back but can't see what caused the detour. We are only going about ten miles per hour now as we seem to hit every pothole, splashing water that had accumulated from yesterday's rain.

"Hey, Tater, take it easy, you're killing us back here," yells Howard.

"Sorry guys", Tater yells back, "bad road...shouldn't be much longer."

The three of us have just enough time to glance fearfully at each other for less than an eye blink after we hear the 'Whoomp!' 'Whoomp!' of mortar fire. Then the explosions, one on the right, one on the left, straddle the truck and knock me onto the floor. Tater struggles to keep control when a third explosion hits in front and the truck careens off the road into a ditch.

I'm sure I wasn't unconscious for more than a minute. When I awoke Jenkins was dragging one of the footlockers, urged on by three Vietnamese soldiers with their rifles pointed at him. When they noticed I was awake they babbled something at me and pointed with their rifles for me to help Jenkins. Howard was starting to stir and one of the soldiers poked him with his gun. I didn't see our rifles anywhere so I assumed the Vietnamese had quickly gathered them up. Not that I was planning to play Rambo or anything.

"Are you guys okay?" I asked. An outpouring of harsh orders, now in heavily accented English, told me to shut up and move the boxes. We did so and as we heaved them outside the truck I saw there were four more armed Vietnamese. We are definitely outnumbered, I thought, glad that I could now truly justify not trying anything heroic. And, about fifty yards away, there were two other men dressed in jungle fatigues and holding BARs. They were taller than the average Vietnamese solider, wore jungle hats pulled down to cover their eyes, and stood motionless as they watched. They said nothing. For looking at them I was pushed and told to get another footlocker out of the truck.

"You think they're going to shoot us when we get all the boxes out?" whispered Jenkins.

"I doubt it," I said, though I didn't doubt it; I just didn't want to panic Jenkins. I figured I would panic myself soon enough anyway.

Just as we dragged the final footlocker out we heard a shot from the front of the truck. Howard started to go there and was warned to stay away.

"No! Now load!" The soldier pointed with his rifle to the footlockers on the ground, then towards a truck, a beat up but apparently serviceable flatbed.

So now we had to lift the boxes of Uncle Sam's currency up onto the flatbed, wondering all the time what had happened to Tater.

When we finished, a soldier poked his rifle at us and we were told, "Go now, walk back." One of the soldiers pointed with his rifle towards the way we had come down the detour road.

First I walked to the front of the truck and looked in the cabin. I could see Tater's head down over the steering wheel, blood dripping down the side of his head.

"They shot Tater! Why'd they do that?"

I was grabbed and pulled away and pushed down to the ground. I cut my knee and later would joke that I should put in for a Purple Heart. "No talk! Walk on," we were ordered.

We heard truck noises and Howard dared to look back. A bullet splattered at his feet and kicked up dust.

"No look, walk on!"

For the next hundred yards we could hear each other's hearts pounding as we expected a shot in the back at any second. We heard what sounded like the soldiers struggling with the footlockers, securing them tighter in the back of their truck. We were afraid to run for fear of being shot, and afraid to walk too slow and give them a chance to change their mind about letting us go.

There was the sound of a truck starting up and I turned to look. The flatbed was bouncing down the road away from us, kicking up puffs of dust in the dry spots and splattering mud when it hit a low spot filled with water. It was only a short distance before the road and the truck disappeared into the thick jungle. All the footlockers, along with four million dollars of Uncle Sam's greenbacks, were gone.

We ran back to our truck to check on Tater. There was nothing we could do for him. The radio was smashed so we had to walk back to the main highway. We didn't see any sign of the detour. We waved down the first American vehicle that came by and told our story. In a short time a helicopter had picked up Tater and a jeep had sped us back to our base. The rest of the day was spent telling our story to the MPs, and the next whole day (my day off), was spent in Saigon telling it again to the brass.

"You really owe me, Eddie", I said to Sgt. Graham when I returned that evening. "I'm going to bed now and don't wake me until tomorrow, if then."

>>FIVE<<

"In the Jungle"

While Walker, Howard and Jenkins were hoofing back to the main highway, the truck with the stolen footlockers crashed through the jungle brush faster than it was safe to do so. After several miles the truck came to a sliding stop on the shores of a river. There the Vietnamese soldiers hurried to unload the money from the footlockers into dozens of canvas bags, which were then stored aboard a scow tied up to a rotting pier. The two taller men stood by watching, smoking and occasionally whispering to each other. When the transfer was done one of the soldiers held on to a canvas bag and spoke to the tall men.

One of the men shook hands with the soldier and nodded his head. The Vietnamese nodded in return and called to the others. Like phantoms they disbursed into the jungle and disappeared. The two taller men climbed into the boat, started the outboard motor and with a sputter moved down river into even thicker jungle.

"You gave them too much."

"We promised them cash for their part. Don't worry, Antonio, they won't get far before they are arrested. They'll get a grilling about the truck robbery, probably get blamed for it, but so what do we care? Could lead to that break in black marketing operations we're trying for, right?"

Antonio, as Kegler called him, and said it with a sneer, had used so many names even he had a hard time keeping track of them. He was tall and thin, owned a dark complexion and what some would call a Roman nose. At the finance unit to which he was assigned—and to which he was not planning to return– he was Tony Abazini. To Kegler he was a swarthy wise guy of Italian ancestry who worked for the CIA as a free-lancer. To Kegler, a career agent, Antonio was a leech, a mercenary; someone never to be trusted, whether out of one's sight or near at hand. Kegler had accepted Antonio's role because he knew two men were needed for this phase of the project. What Kegler didn't know is that Antonio, baptized name Francisco Antonio Abazini, was a link to a contingent of CIA agents who ran wildcat operations, those 'off the books', so to speak, and not officially budgeted. The lack of legal funding called for inventive ways to provide the financial resources the wildcats needed, such as robbing their own government.

Antonio had done some minor work for the Agency in a clean and professional way, which brought him to the attention of Karl Volkers, who approved the plan to hit the money run truck. Volkers was a former field agent, very experienced, but now he was 'Management", i.e. a high echelon suit in Virginia who worked two sides, the legitimate CIA, and the wildcats, and did it in complete confidence that these extra-legal operations were needed if the CIA was going to do its job properly, the legalities aside. One advantage for a mercenary like Antonio—for mercenary is certainly what he was—is that the *real* CIA, the one with all the red tape, literally did not know he existed. Somewhere, surely, someone, probably Volkers, kept records of the wildcats and their operations, code names, real names, contacts, etcetera, etcetera. But when it came to people like Antonio who had long ago lost their original identity in the maze of lies and false documents, even the unofficial operations of the CIA couldn't keep up with their trail, if they didn't want it followed.

Kegler was not yet privy to the wildcat operations. Not that he would mind, but circumstances had simply not occurred yet in a manner that endeared him to those who ran these off-the-books projects. If he performed well here, that could change. As far as he knew, this job was a legitimate one being used to break the large black marketeering, smuggling, and counterfeiting operations that were running rampant in Southeast Asia. He'd convinced himself this was the case but any fool should have wondered about the legitimacy and danger of hitting a United States Army truck full of money. One of Antonio's secondary objectives, he'd been advised, was to consider whether Kegler was a good risk to be brought aboard, that is, once the money was secure, to explain to Kegler that this money was for special projects. Antonio didn't have any interest in that, but he'd implied to Volkers that he would keep the notion in mind.

The official Army report would be that the Viet Cong had attacked the truck; official CIA would know nothing about it; the wildcats would use this money for their own operations. People like Kegler could be brought into the wildcat operations because he had cover from his own section chief. Antonio, being a free-lancer, would disappear into another identity as smoothly and silently as the jaguar dissolved into the misty foliage of the lush Southeast Asian jungles.

What Antonio did know – and of course Kegler was unaware of Antonio's real intentions – was that the Vietnamese soldiers they had just left behind would be ambushed before they were a mile down the trail. They would not be arrested, but eliminated, and the money recovered, a minor portion of the stolen millions, just enough to show that it was a VC operation and divert thoughts of any other explanation.

Anyone who has ever planned anything, from a high-tech jewel heist to a family picnic, knows there are plans, and then there are the things that happen that the best-laid plans do not foresee.

In this case the plan was that Antonio and Kegler would float down the river a few miles to where other hired mercenaries, who thought this was a legitimate, combined CIA/Army Intelligence operation, would transfer the money to a small plane. It would, supposedly, fly to Bangkok. These men would get a little cut and go their merry way. By this time Kegler would have been apprised of the wildcats' plan to use the money for their private operations. What Karl Volkers, an assistant director at CIA headquarters in Langley, former field agent with the Office of Strategic Services and with the Central Intelligence Agency, disgusted with the regulations that tied the hands of the people who knew how to get things done, and second in the chain of command of the secret wildcats, suspected when he planned the money run hit, based on years of working in a cynical industry, was that the free-lancer known as Antonio, or sometimes by other names, had made his own plans, far different than what Volkers expected. So Volkers' plan wasn't exactly what Antonio believed it to be, and vice versa. These two would prove there really is no honor among thieves.

Antonio's plan involved paying the Thai agents a little extra to ignore their original orders, and to plan on one passenger, himself. Kegler's plans, well, whatever plans he had, maybe just a hot shower and a cold beer in the near future, never got more than a few minutes down the river. The bullets hit Kegler when he turned in response to Antonio's voice, and came from a captured VC rifle Antonio had hidden in the boat. Kegler was a goner before his brain could begin to assimilate the information of the gunshots, the bullet holes, the falling out of the boat. He never even knew he hit the water because he was already dead.

Antonio continued to pole the boat down the river, as oblivious to Kegler's demise as he was to the occasional screeching of the jungle birds. He did let his mind wander to the plans he had made, starting over a year ago when he was hired by Volkers for some espionage work in Saigon. It was here that he learned about the money runs and for several months he could not rid himself of the idea that this was the gold mine he'd been looking for. He wasn't the only one thinking such thoughts.

In Bangkok, six months ago, he sat and listened to Volkers complain about how he never had enough money to fund necessary operations. The government expected him to gather information about enemy whereabouts, plans, armament, but never gave him enough agents or money.

After quietly nodding and agreeing while he sipped his drink, Antonio said, "I've heard that sometimes you run your own ops using, let's say, 'found money'."

Volkers, a plump man, white haired and well tanned with age lines decorating his round face, looked at Antonio and twirled the ice in his drink.

"You do pretty much everything in your line of work, don't you?"

Antonio shrugged, took a deep swig of his gin.

"How'd you like to join the Army?"

For a man who didn't shock easily Antonio was taken aback, his mouth gaping half open.

"A man like me? You can't be serious."

"It would just be for a short time. And, it could make you three hundred thousand dollars for a few days work. Interested, or is that too small a take for a big shot like you?"

Antonio stared angrily at Volkers. A veteran field man like Volkers knew damn well that even for someone like Antonio three hundred thousand was an exceptional amount of money. It was an amount that could keep Antonio happy for many years.

Volkers won the battle of silence. Antonio finally said, "Go on, I'm interested."

"It wouldn't be too hard to get three or four million dollars, US cash, mostly small bills. And it's right in front of us."

"Please, go on," Antonio said, almost inaudibly, not wanting to reveal that he'd already been thinking along the same lines as Volkers.

On hearing of the plan Antonio was enthusiastic. It sounded doable and he began thinking of a 50-50 split. Two million would be enough for him to set himself up in some small village, maybe in Greece or Italy, with a nice stash in a Swiss bank to be used for his travels and pleasures. Volkers wouldn't even consider such an outrageous demand; he needed this money for important operations. He offered ten per cent.

"Not a chance," Antonio said. "I have to plan it and I take most of the risk; it's my neck, so I want half," figuring he'd start high and give a little.

At first Volkers wouldn't budge. "It's too big a risk for *me* to give you the lion's share. Besides, you make it sound so easy. Where else would you get a salary of three or four hundred thousand for a few hours of work?"

"Don't piss me off, Karl. It'll take a lot more than a few hours to set up something like this."

The CIA agent relented a little, as he knew he would: "Okay, half a million, my best offer, you set it up, tell me what you need."

Confident that he could pull one over on Volkers and cover his tracks indefinitely, confident that he could still make his share more than what Volkers intended, Antonio nodded agreement.

"And another round, on me," he said with a smile. For a split second Volkers saw treachery in the smile and thought, no way he'd try to screw me, would he? Volkers felt confident he was more than capable of staying a step ahead of a man he considered barely a notch above a common criminal.

Antonio's calculation was that Volkers simply wouldn't have the time or staffing, or money, for that matter, to go after him. Volkers couldn't possibly let too many people in on this kind of operation. Two, maybe three others. And he would have no basis for going after Antonio using legitimate resources. By the time the operation was over Volkers would be back in Washington without the slightest idea where Antonio was. With Kegler and the driver out of the way there'd likely be no one else in Southeast Asia who knew about the money run operation. Even if Volkers could get one of his cohorts on the trail, Antonio would have a big head start. In fact, it might be several weeks before Volkers even knew he'd been had. And by the time this stupid war was over Antonio would be well hidden with a new name, maybe a new look, and plenty of dough.

Of course, killing the driver might be a give-away. But he needed a good driver—someone easily persuaded– to make the plan work, and didn't intend to leave him around to squeal under interrogation. That part of the plan Antonio hadn't discussed with Volkers—the less the CIA man knew of the fine points the better. The sap Antonio found was perfect: a wheeler-dealer always on the look for a way to make an easy buck or two. And the missing finance clerk, Abazini, might cause someone to start adding two plus two. When the Army did get around to examining Abazini's personnel file and eventually checking with his home town—because AWOL soldiers, even in far-away lands, tended to return home or at least contact people at home—they would find that no such address existed, and that no such person as Aloysius Alejandro Abazini existed. For that he had to thank Volkers. Once he was in Thailand on the next leg of his journey, he would be a respected Italian businessman, Santini Bruzzi, with a perfect passport and business papers, needing to deposit a large amount of cash to be used for a major electrical engineering project. But, he will unexpectedly be called back to Athens for urgent business, so will leave the plane when it stops in Bombay. From India he would hop on a freighter to Djibouti, then a flight to Cairo, another freighter to Rome, and the train to Geneva where he will meet up with his money which by now has been wire transferred. Santini Bruzzi would no longer exist and all the papers Antonio had related to that identity would be burned. In Geneva he would assume the identity he had quietly established many years ago and which had never been revealed to anyone. Volkers, no one, would ever find him. Antonio smiled inwardly at his cleverness.

"You know, I saw you there, you and the captain," Antonio said, as he and Volkers were preparing to split, having agreed on the principles of their caper.

Volkers looked at Antonio, not understanding.

"On the bridge. It was a few years ago, but I'm sure you remember. The captain gave you something, a brief case or a file of some sorts. It was thick, brown color; he shoved it into your belly. I was watching through my telescopic lens. I got some nice pictures."

"You were there? You took pictures of us?"

Antonio nodded as a satisfied grin spread across his face. "Still have them, too."

"Why were you there?" Volkers asked, not totally accepting what Antonio was saying.

"Actually I was originally a back-up, then was told I wasn't needed. I got paid off and was told to keep my mouth shut. Well, of course, I'm good at that. But I was curious, and I wasn't far away so I thought I'd come into town and see the show, see what went down. Didn't expect to see you and the captain there."

"Antonio, don't think you are immune from repercussions. You don't have anything that anybody wants, and a few pictures wouldn't prove a damn thing. So be careful. You may think you are so smart, but you aren't shit once you're not needed."

Antonio didn't reply anymore but he was sure that a seed of concern had been placed in Volkers' mind.

The river narrowed and the overhanging flora blocked most of the sunlight. A bird cackled in the trees and a ripple in the water revealed a long, thin snake. Antonio saw the encampment as he neared the next bend in the river. He cleared his mind of the daydreams and came alert for any danger, anything different than what he expected. The boat glided to shore and Antonio picked up his rifle, poling now with one hand and scanning for movement. Two men appeared out of the brush. With their brown skin and Army fatigue clothes they were almost impossible to detect if they had not moved. It was okay; they were his agents. So far, so good. But he <u>had</u> miscalculated.

As smart as Antonio thought he was, Volkers was smart enough to not totally trust him. When he thought about it later, Antonio realized he was probably lucky to be alive, that Volkers had actually stuck to his part of the bargain, the half-million, sort of. The two men who met Antonio had been turned, easily enough by hard Yankee cash. Antonio would get his share but the rest was flying away. With an automatic rifle pointed at him Antonio was tied up and advised, nicely, that he would find his share in a Swiss bank deposit box, in three months. The sacks full of the cash he'd taken from the money run would be leaving with these two men. The thumping of helicopter blades startled Antonio but the other men were expecting it. Antonio watched as they loaded the bags of money unto the helicopter. As the whirlybird lifted off a small package was tossed at him.

"You can look at this after you untie yourself. We're sure a man of your talents should be able to free himself shortly."

That was true, and Antonio had freed himself and was cursing at the helicopter before the sound of its rotors had dissipated. The package contained food and water and a typewritten letter, from Volkers, Antonio knew, though it wasn't signed. The letter stated that the money, as the two men had just told him, would be available in three months at a bank situated in a town near Geneva. It said that just before the three months was up he would be contacted and given the information he would need to access the bank box. The note went on to remind Antonio that sufficient resources were available to eliminate him if the mercenary tried to get at the money before he was contacted with the information needed to access his share, or if he tried to gain revenge. Though Antonio doubted it would be easy for Volkers, he realized that the CIA had its ways and maybe he'd better back off. Antonio had underestimated Volkers but he couldn't feel too angry because he also appreciated the shrewdness and planning that had gone into the caper. He'd wait three months, get his money, and later, maybe much later, he'd find a way to get even with Volkers. If he felt like it.

Antonio wouldn't have quite as much money as he'd hoped, so he'd have to find work sooner than he'd anticipated. For now, his immediate dilemma was to get off this river, back to Saigon, avoid the MPs, and get to his stash so he could buy his way to Thailand. The last thing he wanted now was to get nabbed as an AWOL.

A week later Karl Volkers was in Switzerland for a meeting related to the economics of the Cold War; a junket, to tell the truth. He arrived a day early and visited a branch of one of Geneva's largest banks, a branch in the suburb of Annemasse. Three of his people met him at the bank. In the name of the Columbia Consortium, Volkers opened three accounts and a safe deposit box.

There is a lot of misunderstanding about the nature of Swiss banks and a mysterious aura about so-called numbered accounts. Yes, numbered accounts exist, but only to make it difficult for anyone outside the bank— and most bank employees—to know the identification of the person whose account it is. Someone, a very high-ranking and very discreet bank official will know. Generally both a valid identification (most probably a passport) and the code, if the person wishes to add that layer of security, are needed for access. Of course, some accounts and safe deposit boxes exist for years without anyone ever appearing in person to access them. Transfers and deposits by wire into accounts may occur, and with proper paperwork and codes transfers out can also occur, just as in any normal bank used by everyday people conducting normal bill paying and other bank activities. However, it is also true that a person might show up with a proper passport and the proper numbered code and gain access to an account or a box that hasn't been visited in person for many years. And no one at the bank could say for sure that the person here now was the same person who was here, say, fifteen years ago. If they have proper identification and know the code or have a key they will likely gain access.

But the secret bank vaults that can be accessed by someone who walks in off the street one fine day, possessing a secret code and with fingerprints matching the most sophisticated system ever devised, or maybe even requiring scanning of the iris, but without providing any photo identification or other proof of identity; it's all make believe. Of course, passports or other papers are not particularly difficult to forge, something that banks are keenly aware of. It must be understood that there is only so much responsibility the bank can accept when people set up accounts this way.

Papers to transfer money from a bank in Bangkok were ready; also needed was for Volkers to make a telephone call with the identification codes to make the transfer to the Swiss bank. The accounts were numbered; into one he deposited a half million dollars. The code to access the funds and the passport being used now by one of the agents, in the name of Antonio Abazini, would be delivered to Antonio in about ten weeks. The instructions reminded Antonio to have his own picture replace the one in the passport. It was assumed he had connections that could do this bit of forgery in a way expert enough to preclude any question as to the legitimacy of the passport. If Antonio couldn't accomplish that, well, that was his tough luck.

Into another account Volkers deposited two and half million dollars and into another a quarter million. The latter account was also set up with instructions to pay the various administration fees for as long as the accounts remained opened, and for the deposit box, into which he loaded several hundred thousand dollars of cash, his emergency slush fund for when quick, liquid payments were needed. And last, instructions were made to make rental payments for a box in a bank in Washington, D.C. He anticipated that this last arrangement would be needed for only a few months, but should continue until he or one of the officers of Columbia ended it.

The three agents and Volkers prepared the paperwork and provided their passport identifications. They were in the names of the four officers of Columbia Consortium: Karl Volkers, William Jenkins, Kit Walker, and Curtis Howard. Passport identification plus the proper numbered code would be required for any of the four officers to access the accounts and to make withdrawals or deposits. Naturally, Volkers arranged it so that only he knew the numbered codes. He also arranged that access to the safe deposit box was available for one Preston Volkers, upon identification and with a key.

The agents were reminded that they were never, ever, to speak of this errand, under pain of consequences no one cared to think about. The passports they had used to identify themselves as Howard, Jenkins, and Walker, were retrieved by Volkers. He retained the booklets for possible later use after peeling out the photos and destroying them. The three agents, when they returned to their offices would find they had been transferred, one to an obscure outpost in Africa, one to an equally dire location in South America, and one to a desk assignment in Saigon.

Volkers also had an appointment with a doctor who had been recommended to him by his personal physician.

By the time he'd returned to Washington, D.C. the diagnosis was 99% confirmed: inoperable lung cancer already spread to the lymph nodes. In his obsession with his job he'd ignored the coughs, the pain, and his doctor's pleas for tests. Karl Volkers thought he was too young for anything this serious, but now he knew his time was passing. Amazing what such a diagnosis will do to a person's perspective. Wildcat operations weren't important anymore. Nothing about his job was important anymore. The money in Switzerland, Antonio, the money run operation, none of it mattered. A divorced man with no children, Volkers' closest relative was the nephew, Preston, who was just starting college. Preston's parents had died in a plane accident and Karl had taken in his late brother's only child. There was money for school, but Volkers knew he'd never see his nephew graduate.

One afternoon shortly after his return from Switzerland Volkers surprised his staff by leaving earlier than usual. He didn't tell them he was going to a baseball game. Amidst the noise and excitement of the game he would be alone to think. He found himself thinking of Alice. Volkers' wife had tired of his long hours at work, his secretiveness, and the many days and night away from home, her not even knowing what country he was in. The divorce left Volkers angry at first and then depressed and with only two interests: his work, and as a hobby, baseball, though his work prevented him from following the game as closely as he'd like to. When they divorced, Alice stayed in the house and Karl got an apartment. Before long his ex re-married—too soon, Karl contended– and Alice was gracious enough to let Karl keep the house. Her new husband was wealthy and she didn't need any money from Karl. As much as he appreciated the gesture, Karl often felt lonely in the house so he buried himself in work.

This would likely be the last ball game he ever saw. The Washington Senators were playing someone. Karl sat in his third base side box seat for several innings in thought, not paying close attention to the game, not hearing the crowd or the crack of the bat as the Senator's slugging outfielder hit a blast far into the left field upper deck to add to his impressive early season home run total.

The next several evenings Volkers worked late in his office. He cleaned up the files of the agents he had used on wildcat operations and destroyed what papers were too damning. He did keep one special file for himself that described a variety of wildcat operations but with the names of the agents he had used deleted. Some of the ones he'd used had never known the operations were unsanctioned. For those others who did know, and had not already been transferred from their latest postings, Volkers wrote orders to transfer them, none together, to other locales and operations and sent each a coded message informing them that the wildcat operations were permanently disbanded. This would break the chain between the field agents and Volkers' superior, who was not privy to the identity of any of the people Volkers was using on the wildcat operations. Karl felt a discomfort suggesting he should own up to what he'd been involved in, but at the same time he did not want to take down any others involved. Best, he reasoned, was to end it without drawing scrutiny and suspicion onto everything he and the others had accomplished with the Agency. When Volkers died, as he now accepted would happen shortly, the wildcat operations would also die with no record of their existence, at least, none that Volkers knew of, except for the notes he intended to leave with Preston. But it would also be foolish to leave all that money locked up in bank accounts or boxes without anyone knowing. He needed to figure out how to leave a message without incriminating anyone else. He would then take a few days off to clean up personal business, update his will and spend time with his nephew, and bring him up to speed on some facts of life and death.

The one matter than bothered him more than others was *The File*, as he could only think of it. He hadn't thought of it in years but remembered the day it was given to him, by Capt. Cushman.

He was standing by the railroad tracks surveying the scene. He didn't quite understand what was supposed to happen, but then he hadn't been in on any of the details. He was just supposed to be there to meet someone. He hadn't been told who, or even when, just to be there by noon and wait.

When he saw the captain, good old Walter, he knew this was his contact. As the captain neared him Volkers heard sirens wailing, increased traffic noise, screams, and more sirens. He still wasn't sure if he should do something when the captain reached him.

"Take this, Karl," the captain handed Karl a brown file folder tied securely with twine and tape. Karl still thought of Walter Cushman as the *Captain*, his rank when they knew each other in those last days of the war, and in those years as neophytes for the Office of Strategic Services.

"What is it? What's going on here?" Karl pointed towards the traffic below them.

"Don't worry about it. Just take this file and put it where no one can find it. Don't even tell me where you put it."

"What is this?" Karl knew it wasn't a question he should ask, or that Walter would answer, but he was suspicious.

The captain stared at him and pushed the file into Karl's hands. "Don't ask, don't tell. Don't ever tell. And don't look."

"Why not just destroy it? Do you want me to?"

In charge or not, Walter didn't want to make that decision. "I can't tell you to do that. I just don't want to ever hear about it again."

The captain quickly turned away and left. Karl was stunned for a moment then just as suddenly turned the other direction and ran off down the steps and to the car he had parked there. He drove prudently to the airport and was lucky to get on a flight leaving for Washington in twenty minutes. He went to the men's room and stalled there for as long as he could before boarding the plane just as the last boarding call was given.

Back home Karl slumped in his chair in front of the fireplace and dropped the file onto the floor. It hadn't left his hands since the captain had shoved it there, other than when he was in the men's room, and even then he kept it between his feet. He was quite sure what was in the file but was no more eager to read it than the captain had been to deal with it.

Karl built a fire, turned on the television and watched the news, but soon shut it off and went to the kitchen to scrounge up something to eat. He hadn't eaten since a donut and coffee this morning but hadn't noticed any hunger until now. He fixed a bowl of soup, took it back to eat in front of the fireplace. The file lay there where he had dropped it. It would be easy to throw it into the fire; who would blame him? Who would ever ask him? That, he realized, was what frightened him.

Walter did not show up in the office for several days and when he did, he acted and spoke to Karl as if they had never discussed any brown file. It was business as usual. And business as usual kept Karl busy and gave him an excuse to not think about the brown file. It now sat, innocently, on a shelf in his closet. Maybe, Karl thought, it's just as safe there as it would be in some foot-thick vault.

Eventually Karl tired of seeing the file every day when he went into the closet. No matter where he put it he thought of it. A year went by, with the file being moved from place to place; the kitchen pantry behind cans, the bathroom, under the towels; Karl even carried it in the trunk of his car for several weeks, until he thought of the disaster it would be if he were in an accident and the file went flying into the street, or if the car was stolen.

One Saturday he decided. He moved his bed, rolled up the area rug, and pried up several floorboards. Then he smashed down onto the concrete. It took him what seemed like several pints of perspiration and several hours of hard work to knock out a space a few inches deep and wide enough to lay the file flat. Still never having opened the file, he now wrapped it in a thick rag, then put it into a metal box he'd purchased at the hardware store. The hole he covered with a piece of plywood cut to fit snuggly. In the kitchen sink he mixed a small batch of quick setting concrete and slopped it over the plywood. When the patch had set he replaced the wood boards, being careful to avoid scratches that might reveal anything had been pried loose. The rug was rolled back, as was the bed. Now, he told himself, thinking he was making a clever joke, I can sleep on it.

The illness attacked Volkers more viciously and quicker than even the most pessimistic forecast. A hacking cough turned to pneumonia and weakened him to the point he could not get to his office and wrap up projects he was still involved in. He had not even informed his superiors of his illness, a definite lapse of protocol that would not make the Agency happy. Checking up on him one morning, Preston had called his uncle's office, and was told he was not in. He went to the house and found Karl Volkers tossing and coughing in his bed, too tired to get up but too sick to sleep. First Preston called an ambulance, and then he called his uncle's office again to inform them.

With the siren already audible outside the bedroom window, Karl motioned to Preston to come closer.

"There's a box of stuff you need, I have the…" a cough broke him off. "The key…" Another powerful cough racked Volkers and he gasped for breath.

"Don't try to talk now. Rest, an ambulance is here and you're going to a hospital."

"Probably…too late," Karl spat out. As he faded Volkers remembered there was one other note he was supposed to leave for Preston. Well, maybe he'd have time to do it later. And Antonio…I forgot to send him his code and paperwork.

The 'cleaning service' from Volkers' office arrived at his home before the ambulance and was still there after it left with the patient. They would cover with a fine comb, whether anyone objected or not, the entire house. Files, closets, storage bins were opened to be sure that a high-ranking employee had not, purposely or forgetfully, brought home any documents that shouldn't seen by just anyone. Funny how things work, though; they'd missed a key tucked in Volkers' shirt pocket. It fell out in the ambulance and when retrieved was given to Preston. He stuck it in his pants pocket and that evening threw it with spare change into an ashtray on a coffee table in his apartment. The cleaning service had already been there too, and gone, with little evidence that they'd been through every drawer and every conceivable hiding place for anything that anyone might want to keep hidden. Perfectly normal procedure.

Volkers was right: it was too late. The ailing Volkers survived a few more days but was mostly unconscious. He never finished telling Preston what was so important. The day after the funeral Preston gathered up his change and the key from the ashtray and put them in his jeans pocket. Later in the day he noticed the key, couldn't think of where it came from and tossed it into a drawer in the kitchen to join other keys and mysterious objects that get picked up here and there in the course of a person's day and lay around until the drawer is finally cleaned out and the stuff is thrown in the trash. Now with keys, people are wont to throw them away, even when moving. The thinking is that this key goes somewhere and as soon as I throw it out, I'll find I need it.

When news of Volkers illness reached him, Walter Cushman felt a tinge of fear. He ordered Volker's office sealed and when he had the chance went through the file cabinets and safe with an eye for anything related to the wildcat operations. He found nothing, as he had hoped and expected. Volkers was good, too good to leave anything around, too good to leave anything that would incriminate himself or others. The way it was set up, only Volkers knew the agents he used on these operations, and none of them knew who else besides Volkers was involved. They shouldn't even know each other's real names. Even if later, after a few drinks or cozy in bed, they talked about things they weren't supposed to talk about, there would be no evidence, no corroboration. Volkers was good that way, and if he had been as good as the assistant director thought, any agents he was running would know that upon Volker's death or retirement, any and all operations ceased immediately. The cleaning crew had found nothing in Volkers' home and the office inventory did not list a brown file.

>>SIX<<

"Francisco Antonio Abazini"

By the time the 21st century had begun, whether you believed that it was on January 1, 2000 or January 1, 2001, the man known as Antonio, or Santini Bruzzi, or Francisco (only his mother had called him Francisco), or Abz, or by many other identities, was bored. He had lived an active and for the most part, a comfortable life; not filthy rich, but never lacking. He could have become wealthier had he wanted to, but he firmly believed that people who did the type of work he did lived on borrowed time. As one got older it was easier to make a mistake and harder to concentrate. So for several years he had been more or less retired, enjoying the sun and the beaches, or the fresh air of the mountains, traveling quietly around the world for weeks at a time, always returning to his modest cottage in Tuscany.

He wasn't a young man anymore and didn't need to pretend to be. Now in his mid-60s, he was still a handsome man, despite that his face showed the lines of weariness from long nights in the cold and damp, or the sun and heat, waiting for someone or for something to happen. The mental scars from years of looking behind to see if anyone was following had also tired him. He wasn't bothered by the lines or the gray hair he now possessed. More important, he figured it changed the look that most people he had encountered in his younger days knew him by. With tinted contacs and minor plastic surgery to his nose, he was not likely to be recognized by those he had worked with in the past.

Alphonse Antonini was known to his neighbors as a peaceful man who kept mostly to himself but was friendly and took part in local events, always contributing some time or money, or at least his company. Virtually everyone assumed he was a European, born and bred. In reality he'd been born in New Jersey, of Italian immigrants and raised in an Italian immigrant's neighborhood. He'd never even come to Europe until he was a young adult. He could speak English and Italian fluently, and in his years traveling and working in the international field of a hired strongman had become reasonably proficient in French, German and Spanish.

This man of many names was at an age when a person looks back and wonders if he could– or should– have done some things differently. Would one's life have been better if I'd done this or that, instead of the path I chose? Ah well, Antonio, living alone these days, had many hours to think on what he had done with his life. To be honest with himself, he wasn't proud or particularly happy, but he'd didn't have enough of a conscience to feel regret, either. Who's to blame? After all, he grew up in a neighborhood where petty crime was rampant, and it was easy, and profitable, for a smart young man to move on to bigger criminal activity. And as a young man it was easy to convince oneself that after there was enough money, one would quit the streets and the shadow life and become respectable. Somehow, that never happened.

Many of the people Antonio had known who lived similar lives as he had were now gone. None were ever friends; he had no friends; no one he could trust. He had memories of great adventures and exciting and dangerous escapades which at the time were so exhilarating that no thought of a quiet, peaceful way of life could ever have replaced the drama and fear that gave his existence meaning. Sometimes now, though, he wondered.

As a child his mother insisted on calling him Francisco; he preferred to be called Tony and introduced himself to everyone that way, irritating his mother. His development from a typical energetic kid playing hard in the streets of the several cities he'd lived in on the East Coast, to a neighborhood enforcer was quick and logical. He was a natural leader, tough, well liked, and enjoyed being a kingpin, albeit a big fish in a little pond. His father had died when Tony was seven, and his mother when he was twelve. An aunt tried to take care of him but the lad was difficult to discipline both because he was likable and because he was so seldom around. He actually did well in school; he was smart and the lessons came easy for him. But with his aggressive nature schoolwork alone was not enough to keep him entertained. He was always on the edge of trouble, usually for bullying, and was suspected of several thefts of small amounts of money from other students and even once from a teacher's handbag. But nothing stuck.

It was a few years after the war had ended. Many of the soldiers had returned from Europe and gone back to work, gotten married, and built houses. One such ex-soldier, a man known as O'Shea, appeared in the neighborhood one day, several years after the war had ended. It was said that O'Shea lived a few blocks away before the war and was thought to have died, since he did not return when the other soldiers came home. The new rumor was that he had worked as spy after the war; yet another one was that he had been captured by the Russians and forced to work in a labor camp. Whatever the truth, he soon took over several small time rackets in the part of town that Tony called home. Protection, numbers, a little blackmail or extortion, whatever he could get away with. His glib talk and shiny new car impressed a youngster like Tony, the kind of kid who without much discipline was ready to fall one way or the other: the high road or the low road, depending on where the strongest influence came from.

Before long the young teenager was running errands for O'Shea, such as collecting money, and soon he was skipping classes and dodging the truant officer. He frequently worked out in a gym O'Shea had taken him to. When he did come to school he had actual paper money in his pockets that he flashed at the other kids to show off. It helped too, that a growth spurt gave him the appearance of someone a few years older. By fifteen he was shaving regularly and the muscles he built up from working out gave him a formidable look even to men several years older. And as O'Shea's reputation grew, Tony's did by mere association.

Ironically, it was O'Shea that cracked down on Tony's truancy and encouraged, nay, even insisted, that Tony finish high school.

"People respect a person who speaks well, dresses nicely, talks and acts politely. You need to learn this and even the cops will be more respectful to you, Tony. It's taken me a long time to figure all this out. So the deal is, you keep your grades up, finish high school, or you can't come to work for me. But if you hang in there, I'll have a job for you that will keep you in fancy cars and fancy women."

A smart kid like Tony quickly saw that this was a no-lose proposition for him. School was easy, if boring, and he could still make money working for O'Shea on weekends and in the summer. And the more he learned the less he would need O'Shea in the long run.

In due time he made the irreversible step from local muscle to murder. It wasn't supposed to happen; O'Shea was adamant that no one was to be hurt so badly that their life was endangered. Tony saw it differently. If the people who gambled and then couldn't pay their debts knew they would only suffer a few bruises, then what was the sense of trying to collect at all? What he didn't know was that for extreme cases O'Shea had other methods to employ, those that involved experts from other parts of town, or better, other towns, who saw to it that examples were made of anyone who tried to welch on O'Shea. The neighborhood knew when someone was in arrears, and it became common knowledge if they couldn't pay or refused to pay. And when that person was no longer around, they knew they would not be coming back–ever.

This poor slob was one who constantly owed money. More than once Tony had had to rough him up. Still, the man didn't learn, and the debts piled up as he begged for more credit, sure that the next tip would be the one that made him a winner.

"I know a guy at the track, Tony."

"You always know a guy, Freddie. And they give you tips, the horse loses, you owe more and more money. No more. Pay up."

Tony got a percentage of what he collected so there was little benefit and much danger to claim someone hadn't paid up or had paid less than what was owed. Tony had graduated and needed only a little more to get the new car he had been eyeing. His share of Freddie's debt would give him what he needed. By next week he'd be careening around town in a new convertible that would be the envy of the neighborhood. Tony didn't know that O'Shea was planning to surprise him by giving him a bonus, enough to buy the car. But Freddie couldn't pay; he simply didn't have the money.

It was after midnight and Tony had taken Freddie for a long walk out to where the scows loaded crates and bags of garbage to be dumped. The air was damp, the ground stank, and the oily water lapped up to a rotting pier.

"Let's take a walk, Freddie, on my pier."

"Ha, Ha, Tony, what a joker; your pier! You're funny, kid." Freddie was getting just a bit scared now. He remembered that the last time he was late in paying Tony had busted his lip. "I don't think this pier is safe, Tony," Freddie suggested. The frightened man didn't have the strength resist as Tony grabbed hold of his arm and steered him onto the planks.

"Watch your step, Freddie, I wouldn't want you to fall in and get your nice overcoat all dirty and wet. You'd never get the stink off. But you know, you might not need that coat if you can't pay me."

"Whaddya mean, Tony? I'll pay ya, I promise. Tomorrow, after the feature race. I can really feel that this is the big one."

Tony wasn't a killer, not yet anyway. He only wanted to scare Freddie; unfortunately Tony pushed just a little too hard. A rotted plank gave way and Freddie flipped over and down into the dark, stinky waters. At first he dropped all the way under, then his head bobbed up and water sprayed off his face and spat out of his mouth.

"Tony! I can't swim…ah," he went under again.

Tony didn't want to dive into the dirty water and he couldn't reach Freddie.

"Wait, Freddie, I'll get a stick, or a rope." He ran off the pier to look for something to use to try to reach the panicky gambler.

"Don't leave…" and down under again. A frantic grasp as the drowning man tried to grab water in his hands.

Tony disappeared into the dark as Freddie thrashed around, crazy with fear now as he swallowed whole mouthfuls of the black water. The drowning man felt a spark of hope when Tony reappeared, carrying a board he had found on a pile of wood someone had dumped.

"Freddie, where are you! Freddie!" There was no answer, only ripples. Tony waited five minutes than tossed the board down and ran off, not stopping until he was out of breath and barely able to stand.

O'Shea was furious. It now became necessary for Tony to escape to greener and newer pastures where he was not known by the local police. O'Shea found Tony a place to lay low with a colleague, as it were, in the Philadelphia area, with a new name and protection from the police. There was no solid evidence against Tony and soon he could operate in the open again. Using gentle persuasion O'Shea later arranged for Tony to travel to Europe with him and meet people there who would take him in as a trusted comrade.

While O'Shea was thought of as a small-time hood controlling two-bit numbers games and protection rackets in the ethnic neighborhoods of New Jersey, this was maintained as a front for his more lucrative activities.

While they were in Europe O'Shea introduced Tony to others like himself, people whose work could never adequately be explained to someone outside their sphere of interests. People O'Shea had met in the war or shortly after; people he had worked with those years he was thought to be dead or in a prisoner of war camp; people he still had associations with, ones who moved around a lot and always seemed to have money. People who were secretive, knew other people who could acquire things that weren't purchased at the corner grocery store, or knew people who could get documents that made travel and identity changes a part of every day life. Many were people who could never acclimate to the changes in the world after years of depression and then years of warfare.

With his quick mind Tony soon learned to speak and act like a European. When he worked it was hard and dangerous. But it was an exhilarating way of life, one with no scheduled hours, no long terms plans, no regular boss, and work that required an alertness that put excitement into living.

So for several years Tony lived in Europe, traveling to wherever the need and the money took him. Many of his jobs simply required a gentle threat, some called for theft or industrial espionage, sabotage or trading of secrets between governments. Rarely–but if necessary he could do it—the job involved the elimination of a person who had become too much of a bother or a threat. All his orders came from a man related to O'Shea, known as Uncle Sean. This kindly old Irishman seemed to know everybody and got invited everywhere. It was at a party at an embassy in London that Uncle Sean introduced O'Shea and Tony to two men who worked for the United States State Department. One of them, a man named Walter who possessed a head of bright red hair that he self-consciously kept running his fingers through, didn't remember O'Shea. But O'Shea knew him from the late days of World War Two and those early days after, when Walter, then a captain, and O'Shea and that wonderful sidekick, Karl Volkers, were trying to figure out what to do now that the legal killing was over.

O'Shea's sly chuckles and innuendos were all Tony needed to know that the State Department gig was a cover. "During the war the captain worked with the OSS on certain projects and later he helped start the Central Intelligence Agency. Remember I told you about him and Karl, who I knew from the war? Karl and the red headed captain had been good friends, and I did hear that Karl stayed with the Agency and was working out of Washington. Probably for the red head, Walter...I can't remember his last name. So, they are still in the spy business, it seems, just like us, only with the legitimacy of a government position. They might be useful people to know."

Tony was aware that O'Shea was apprised of all the jobs Tony did, that he received a percentage of the payment, and that he was expecting Tony to return to the United States to work for him. But Tony didn't want that. He wanted to be independent and in fact had already done some work on his own. He was worried that Uncle Sean or O'Shea would find out and insist on a cut of Tony's earnings. So when Tony heard that Uncle Sean had died, while Tony was away on a job, he did not return to the village. He lay low for over a year, and then returned to the United States on a perfectly forged passport in the name of Tony Abazini. For several days after his return he quietly followed O'Shea, whose habits in the old neighborhood hadn't changed at all. The aging Irishman had become careless and overconfident. One evening he took his dog for a walk. Turning a corner he came face to face with his protégé. O'Shea held the dog leash in one hand while the other hand was in his coat pocket holding a gun, which he was never without. Because he recognized Tony he hesitated, a mistake.

"Tony…why are you back?" Even as he hesitated he felt the first icy ripple down his spine.

"O'Shea, thank you, and good-bye, I don't need you anymore," said Tony.

Owen O'Shea was found a few minutes later, dead on the sidewalk, the dog sitting nearby and whimpering. Tony Abazini was long gone.

Francisco Antonio Abazini was always careful to leave no clues as to his true name or family or origin. As a mercenary who hired himself to many different employers he always tried to use different names and different guises, never letting anyone know any other identity. At least he hoped he had succeeded and after several decades it appeared he had. Until one cloudy

Tuesday morning while he sat with his hot chocolate and newspaper in his adopted village of LeDione.

This is how he spent most of his mornings; sipping his hot drink—usually chocolate but sometimes mixed with coffee—and reading the International Herald Tribune or one of the London or Paris papers. While fluent in several languages, he didn't care to get his news in other than English.

When he was younger and an active participant in the field of espionage, Antonio would never have frequented the same place day after day, forming a habit. Isn't this what retirement is supposed to be about, he thought? So most mornings he walked into the village from his cottage and before he had spread the paper out a waiter, almost always Geraldo, had brought him a steaming cup of chocolate and a freshly baked pastry.

Weather permitting, Antonio preferred to sit outside, letting the early sun set on him and warm him. He was an early riser and his days began when the morning air was still chilly. It was invigorating and only rain would push him inside. Some days, if good conversation with other locals developed, he sat here for hours, to the point where he had to switch to a cold drink as the day heated up.

A man, an American, had appeared in the café sitting at one of the sidewalk tables. He was quiet and Antonio immediately felt shivers run up his arm. He realized he had become lazy to not have noticed this man sooner. Had he been an assassin Alphonse—for he now thought of himself by that name– would not even have seen him or heard the bullet. Alphonse could tell he was American just as he knew the man could tell that under his guise Alphonse too, was still an American, albeit one who fit snuggly amongst the natives of this village. Alphonse knew, with a deep gut feeling, that he had been found. But for what? Not revenge; he would have been dead already. For a new job? He was not considered active in the community of mercenaries who were willing to perform virtually any assignment. So it must be a job for someone with special skills, or a special knowledge, maybe related to a past assignment.

Alphonse relaxed a bit, felt safe again. He could say no, he was retired. He could refer the man to someone else, someone active, younger, stronger, and especially, more interested.

>>SEVEN<<

"Jones"

The man was named Eddie Jones. Not Edward, but Eddie, at least until he became old enough to realize he didn't to have fill out paperwork with his name as Eddie. So he became just Ed, just plain Ed Jones. Why he was in this Italian village fifty kilometers from Florence was a mystery even he was confused about. A few mornings ago shortly after he'd arrived for work in Langley, Virginia, he'd been called into Syd Swanson's office. Syd was standing at his desk engrossed in reading something and nodded at Jones to take a seat.

"Got coffee?" he asked before he noticed that Jones had brought a cup with him. "Just a sec, Jonesy."

Jones looked out the window at the green lawn and blue skies and thought that this would be a good day to quit early and do something outside– like golf, or sitting in his backyard, nodding off as he read through a pile of magazines. He also thought that his boss was not going to let that happen this day.

In a minute Swanson walked over to the coffee pot and refilled his cup. He began to talk as he walked back to his chair.

"You ever hear of a guy named Karl Volkers? He worked here some thirty years ago."

Jones' eyebrows rose and he shrugged his shoulders. "Hell no, why would I have ever heard of him?"

"Eh, no reason I guess. He was fairly high up at one time. Got cancer, I've been reading, and died rather young; never even had a chance to retire."

"Tough," Jones said, and meant it.

"Kind of odd. His nephew used to work for our buddies at the Bureau. He left a few years ago to go out on his own. Got tired of the bureaucracy, can you believe? Went to work for some security consulting firm and now he owns the company. Good guy, I've had contact with him several times. He called me the other day about some files that his uncle, this Karl Volkers, kept in a safe deposit box. He says he got a call from the bank about this box that's been sitting there for over thirty years. Now the nephew, Preston, says the box is in his and/or his uncle's name, but he never knew about it.

"How was it paid for?"

"He wondered the same thing. Turns out a payment is made every year from some bank in a suburb of Geneva, Switzerland."

Jones' eyebrows arched.

"But the bank here in Washington is reconstructing its vault and needs people to claim their goodies until they can get the work done. So they called Preston. But he can't find a key. The bank says they can probably let him in once they have ascertained his identity. So he fills out a ton of paperwork, gets a notary, fingerprints, the works. In the mean time he starts digging through junk he has at home. He remembered something his uncle had said to him just before he died. Mumbling about a box, or a key. So he digs around, finds an old key that looks just like a safe deposit box key, and returns to the bank. Sure enough, it fits. So he brings home the stuff."

"You are sure about this buddy of yours?" asked Jones, a hint of disbelief in his tone.

Swanson grunted, "Yeah, he can be trusted. He's not a buddy, really, I just know him from when he was with the Bureau. We actually had to work together one time, if you can believe us and them working together. In the course of events I found out that his uncle used to work here and was a semi-big shot. Anyway, he shows me all this stuff. Well, of course I can't be sure he showed me everything that he found in the bank box.

"Included was a letter from Karl Volkers, Preston's uncle. I won't read it to you now, but there's a copy here in this file. Basically it says he didn't get to do all the things he wanted to do, blah, blah, same thing I guess we all feel. Or will feel when we know we are dying."

"Wonderful," said Jones. He went to the window, looked outside. "Like wishing I could have an outdoor job on beautiful days like today?"

"Yeah, you and me both. There are papers regarding an account he had set up for his nephew, worth, Preston said, far more money than he'll earn in several years."

"I sense a rat," said Jones. "This guy Volkers had that much money to leave?"

"Well, remember, he set this up in the '60s. Apparently he didn't have any kids of his own; he and his wife were divorced and she had re-married, Preston tells me, and Volkers had no one to leave his money to. So from then till now is lots of time for the account to grow. But the part that brings us in is notes he left about some operations he and some other guys were running, on their own, sort of; that is, not legit."

"Sort of? Yeah, I hear about those things all the time. You think they still go on, after all the bad PR the Agency has gotten over such programs?"

Swanson lowered his voice, looked serious; "Well, Jonesy, if I knew I couldn't tell you, could I?" They both laughed.

"But yes, I've heard there were a lot of these off-the-books operations in the sixties. Some of them the Agency isn't too proud of now. It got to be epidemic; circles within circles, guys working secretly in a small cabal of other agents, then working against this same group in another circle. Very confusing, very crazy actually. And virtually all of it illegal. I don't think our current fearless leaders want to start another round of investigations."

"Who were the other guys besides Volkers?"

"Doesn't seem to say, at least from what I could find. There isn't much detail; more of a confession, but not naming any others. Didn't want to be a fink. You'll have to read all this before you go and maybe you'll spot something I missed."

"Go? As in *go* somewhere? Like where?"

"Hold on, you might like this. One of the notebooks references yet another bank box, this one in a bank in Switzerland, and several accounts. It's probably where the payments for the box here in D.C. come from."

"I knew it, numbered accounts."

Swanson shrugged. "I suppose so. One page even has what can only be called very bad poetry. And it also refers to a guy Volkers apparently used for some off-the-books ops with so many aliases I can't keep track of them all. But Volkers calls him Antonio."

"So my job, should I accept it, is…?"

"Go to Switzerland, see what's in this box. Preston has given us permission– as if we needed it– as long as he can go along. The box here in D.C. that Preston got into included his uncle's notes and another key, this one for the box in Switzerland. The notes say that the key and proper identification by Preston will get him into the box. Then see what it leads to. You might have to find out if this guy is still alive, the one Volkers called Antonio."

"So this nephew, when do I meet him? And do I really let him see what's in the box?"

"Oh, yeah, he's okay. And he's the one with the key so I think he'll insist. I've arranged us to have lunch…at the golf course."

In Annemasse, Switzerland, Preston Volkers and Ed Jones walked into the Cite Geneva bank and tried to act nonchalant. Veteran intelligence agents or not, visiting a strange bank in a foreign country hoping that by using a series of numbers or a key they will gain access to someone else's safe deposit box was a bit bizarre. But admitting persons to bank boxes that haven't been opened in decades is not unusual in the culture of secretive international finance. It is not uncommon for someone to set up an account or rent a box, have the fees paid automatically, will the contents to a son, or even a grandson or granddaughter, and never enter the bank again once the account has been opened. And if the person who has the code gives it to someone else, and that someone else has identification the bank considers proper and legitimate, they can gain access, even if the stares are a little disconcerting.

The key from Volkers' Washington box, along with Preston's credentials, did allow them in and they took the box—it took both of them to carry it—to a closed room in which they were told they could take as much time as they wished, up to closing time of four p.m.

"Here goes," said Preston.

The lid opened with a squeak and let in light for the first time since 1969.

"Holy Moses!"

The first thing to greet their eyes was money, packets of twenty and fifty and one hundred dollar bills, each packet sealed tightly and wrapped with a rubber band. Many of those had broken.

"It will be interesting to run these serial numbers," said Preston.

"Damn, Preston, you could have just come here yourself, never told us anything, and had all this money for yourself," said Jones.

"Don't think I didn't consider coming here alone. But I really didn't expect cash. You know, he left quite a portfolio for me. I told Swanson about that but I didn't feel a need to show him the details. There were dozens of stock certificates Uncle Karl had purchased in the 60s, some worth many times more than when he bought them. Of course, there were also a few for companies that long ago went belly up. So I figure most of his money went into investments. This, well, I'm almost reluctant to find out where it's from."

"Yeah, you know, a guy doesn't like to want to find this out about somebody they care for, but those notes about some free-lance operations doesn't sound good."

"I know, I know. Let's see what else is in here."

A notebook gave information about what Volkers knew about the man he called Antonio and about operations Volkers had used him on. Later, when they had time to read through it, they would learn about the robbery of a truck full of money in Vietnam in 1969. But there didn't appear to be anything that would gain them access to any accounts in the bank.

"Hmm. I don't get it. He says he left the account codes, but I don't have anything like that," said Preston.

Jones thought that sounded like an honest statement. Besides, why would Preston lie now after all the other information he'd revealed?

"Volkers' notes say there are three accounts, each with a numbered code. And they've existed since before your uncle died."

"That must be money they were using for the secret operations Uncle Karl mentions. I wonder why three accounts?"

"What I wonder is how to we get into them. Me or you telling these people here that the accounts might have money that belongs to the United States Government isn't going to get us any sympathy."

"Maybe we'll have to look more closely at the papers he left in the Washington box. Maybe there's something there that can help us."

Preston had brought the notebook found in the safe deposit box in the Washington D.C. bank. Eventually they got to the page of bad poetry.

In extra carefully printed block letters, it read:

One # is the small bear's
Another, the big man in town
And the third is the phantom's

Beneath this was written, in what looked like the same handwriting they'd seen in the notes Volkers had apparently written, the following:

'Preston: By the time you are reading this my funeral should be over and you'll be getting on with your life. At the time the others and I were involved in planning our own operations we honestly felt it was the right thing to do. That the ends justified the means. I haven't got time to argue it now, but we were probably wrong. I won't name anyone else; there were only a few of us and I am ending all aspects of it that I know about. There is still a lot of money that needs to get back to where it belongs. The little ditty above is only to make it difficult if for some reason anyone other than you gets this. Otherwise just use the account code numbers and your passport. Technically the other officers, besides me, can access the accounts. But the others don't know the codes, and have no knowledge that they are listed as officers of Columbia Consortium, the name on all the accounts. All you should need to access the box is your own ID (passport) and the key.

More important is 'the FILE'...if you still have the house, you have to decide whether you want to look for it…it won't be easy…and all you might do is stir up some ghosts that might be better left sleeping…I leave it to you.'

"Can you make anything out of this clue, if you can call it a clue? 'The small bear', and 'the big man in town'. Who's that, the president?"

"And who's the phantom? Sounds kind of silly, coming from my uncle. He was generally a serious guy. Of course, when he wrote this he knew he was dying. Maybe that affected him somehow. Maybe trying to reconcile things in his mind made him a little screwy."

"Well, he was your uncle, so whatever you say. Anyway, it wouldn't be unusual for a trained field agent. It seems that whatever he was involved in, he didn't want to leave any clues as to who the other people were. So he probably figured the one person he could trust was you. And if somehow anyone else got into that box, he didn't want to make it easy for them."

"But all this time…that I don't get. Why didn't he tell me about the bank box before he died?"

"You tell me. Do you recall what happened?"

Preston shrugged, trying to remember back to when his uncle had died. He clearly remembered the last days, and rushing his uncle to the hospital, spending most of the next few days there. But more specific details didn't come to him. The two agents decided to leave the bank. They left the money after writing down a few of the serial numbers. They also had copies made of every page of the notebook, then returned the original to the box.

Over lunch Preston began to talk about his uncle, trying to jog his memory.

"Tell me how you remembered about the key to the bank box in Washington," urged Ed Jones.

"You know, that's it," said Preston. "When the bank called me and I went to find out about the box, I started

84

to remember. I looked through some old junk in the attic and found that key. I told Swanson that I recalled Karl saying something to me at the time I found him home in bed, when I called the ambulance. What I'm thinking now is that Uncle Karl meant for me to know about all this before he died, but he didn't get the chance to tell me. He lost consciousness and remained semi-comatose until he died. Who knows what else he meant to do with those accounts."

"When we get back to our hotel I'll contact Swanson. See if I can get him to fax me those notes about this guy Antonio. Find out what he wants me to do next."

"What about this mention of a file, in capital letters? It seems like it might be separate from the other hints he left. And he says it's more important."

"Maybe that's where the bodies are buried. Maybe it's the file that names names and gives the raw details. Nothing like that in the D.C. box?"

Preston shook his head.

"He also says, 'if you still have the house.' Meaning his old house?"

"I suppose," answered Preston. "I inherited his house, rented it out for awhile, but Meg and I have lived there our entire married life. She loves that house as much as I do. We did some work on it– put in new plumbing and electrical– but I never came across any old files."

"Maybe it's not hidden that well, just not noticeable."

Preston thought on it a moment, shook his head. "There's a footlocker in the attic with some of Uncle Karl's old things. But I've been through them; that's where I found the key. There was no file or briefcase that I noticed. I'll look again when we get back."

By the next day they had read all the notes Volkers had left regarding Antonio, and more, they had the story of the money run, laid out by Volkers as if he'd been writing a field report.

"This is truly incredible, Preston. That uncle of yours had some imagination."

"Don't rub it in." Preston was embarrassed, though he need not feel responsible for the crimes of a relative. Still, it had an impact on him.

"He became like a father to me; seemed like an honest guy."

"You know, Preston, he probably was, except in this one thing. And maybe the system drove him to it."

"That's a good reason, even if not an excuse," cut in Preston.

Jones was given his marching orders: try to track down the man known in Volkers' notes as Antonio. There wasn't much to go on: a brief physical description, with the caveat that Antonio tended to disguise himself from one job to another, personal habits, places he tended to visit, prior associates, more, actually than Antonio ever realized Volkers had accumulated, but still, very old and stale information. Jones' first step was a predictably futile search in the local database, but the international link indicated that the European Section had some fairly current references.

>>EIGHT<<

"Tony and Jones"

Jones didn't approach Antonio that first time in the café. But he let his quarry know he was being watched, without, Jones hoped, making it seem overly obvious. Keep him wondering for awhile. It had only taken a few days to get a scent of the man called Antonio in Volkers' notes. There are only so many world-class mercenaries, and even the ones who are virtually retired are still known within the circle of people who frequent this exclusive club.

Patterson, of the CIA's Rome branch immediately came up with a lead.

"I've heard for years that there was a guy called Antonio who used to be very active, and extremely good, but who is apparently retired. We haven't kept tabs on him in long time since he settled down in some little village called LeDione."

"You have file on him?" asked Jones.

"Yeah, Alphonse Antonini is what he goes by, but we think he's used Antonio at times. Hard to know for sure about these guys who were active years ago. The information gets stale, people die, and pretty soon no one remembers."

The file showed no entries for over a year, and then there was one that simply said that the man known locally as Alphonse Antonini, an alleged for-hire free agent who would do most anything for money, including kill, showed no signs of being an active participant in the field of espionage, intelligence gathering, or any other of the secret arts practiced by the people who like to keep secrets.

"But he could move in and out quietly at times without you knowing it, couldn't he?"

"Sure, we've got better things to do than watch old, washed up free-lancers. Now, if you've got something on him in particular, we could push him a little, or check with some of our active contacts."

"No," said Jones. "Don't do anything yet. I'll go to LeDione and check him out myself."

"This must be a real old case, right? I'd hate to think that something's happening in my own back yard and Washington isn't letting me know."

Jones shook is head. "I don't blame you, Patterson. But this is old, old, old, and we aren't even sure what we are looking for. And I don't even know enough to keep secrets from you anyway!"

"Alright, but keep me appraised, okay?" Patterson was polite but he meant that as an order, maybe even a threat.

"I will, I promise." Jones wasn't sure he would but figured he might need more assistance so for now, be nice to fellow workers who might be useful later.

Eventually Antonio did what Jones wanted him to do; make the approach himself.

Antonio politely asked if he could join Jones, who nodded an affirmative.

After ordering a refill of his morning hot chocolate, Antonio spoke.

"At first, I was a little concerned. Then I realized you wanted me to know you were watching. Not too obvious, you're a good spy, I think, Mr.....?"

"Jones. Really, it is Jones. I always feel I have to confirm that."

Antonio chuckled. "And when you check into a hotel with your wife? You, what, make up a more complicated name?"

Jones shrugged and smiled back. "Names are funny things. Some people have one simple name. Like Jones. Others have many names. Sometimes they can't keep track of them all."

"Maybe I should just do that, use a name like Jones, or Smith, instead of … well, other names."

"So you can call me Jones, what should I call you?"

"Alphonse will suffice. For this meeting, anyway."

"Is this a meeting?" asked Jones

"Maybe it was impolite of me to approach you. I thought maybe you were too shy. Or maybe my curiosity got the better of me. Since I first saw you here I've learned many things about you, Mr. Jones."

"Oh? Such as?"

"For one, that you are an agent of the CIA, which I figured in the first place. I know you have been to the bank in Annemasse, that you work for a Mr. Syd Swanson, and you've never killed anyone."

"You've been around a long time if you have connections that can give you such information."

"You wouldn't have stayed in this little town for so long unless you wanted me to know who you are. You've done nothing else except either sit here or take walks in the park. But that's alright. I like you for allowing me some time to learn about you. I must admit, after all these years, I never thought I'd hear of this matter again."

"What matter is that, Antonio? I'm sorry, Alphonse"

"Oh, come on now, I thought we were developing a relationship. Don't treat me like this or you'll ruin a budding friendship."

"Okay, you're right. But I must admit you've got an edge on me, for I really know very little about you. Other than the information that Volkers left us."

Even though he was beginning to suspect that Jones was here related to some long-ago, near-forgotten escapade, the mention of the name Volkers still stunned Alphonse, just enough for Jones to notice.

"So you can be surprised. I was beginning to think you were on to me all the way."

The slightly European accent disappeared from Alphonse's voice now, and this time Jones was surprised.

"I haven't forgotten about him, but I never thought I'd hear of him again. He cost me a lot of money, something I'm sure you must know, if you've been to the bank. But that was long ago, Mr. Jones, and I don't think even the CIA can make trouble for me now. Especially since I never got any money from him for that job."

"Really? Well, I must say that does surprise me. But then, maybe not, if Volkers was as sly as I'm beginning to think. Still, four million dollars went missing, at least two people ended up dead. It's not something easily forgotten, even after all these years."

"So is it the money you want, or revenge?"

"Look, you're right, we aren't likely to do anything to you. But we'd like to know what you know. Even after several decades there could be people or operations going on that we should know about. And the money gets a little bit more important, too, when you think what three of four million dollars invested in 1969 could be worth today."

"Hmm, yes, or even $500, 000," said Alphonse.

"Was that your cut?"

Alphonse looked at Jones for several seconds, then motioned to a waiter to bring him another hot chocolate. "Do you like stories, Jones? I'll tell you one, and you tell me what it might be worth, that is, if it were true."

So over coffee, hot chocolate, and several pastries, enough to destroy whatever diet Jones may have been trying to maintain, Alphonse told a story, a theoretical one, if you may. As he spoke Jones realized that Alphonse, or the fictitious Antonio character in his story, never got his cut from Volkers because Volkers died before he could send Antonio/Alphonse the code he needed. Jones might have felt sorry for him if it wasn't for the fact that Alphonse himself was a double-crosser, a murderer, and a thief. And that if Jones could find proof of his crimes, he would bring Alphonse in, no matter what promises were made.

"So you see, a man like that, who worked free-lance, he wouldn't know anyone else. Wouldn't know about any other operations. Wouldn't know what happened to all the money."

Jones believed him. It made sense based on the box in the Swiss bank. "The attack on the money run truck is not a fiction. It happened. One man was killed during the robbery, and later a CIA agent was found dead."

Alphonse shrugged, "Well, I don't know about that."

"Do you remember any of these names?" Jones said as he slid a piece of paper across the table.

Antonio shook his head after scanning the names. "I can guess who these are, but I never heard of these people," he said as he memorized the three names on the list.

Jones took the paper back without saying any more about who the names on the list were supposed to represent.

"It's always a good day when one learns something new, wouldn't you say, Mr. Jones? Now I realize something I didn't when we first began this pleasant conversation."

Jones waited quietly.

"This morning I have learned that you can't get the money, can you? Volkers died, shortly after the, ah, the so-called raid on the money truck you spoke of. And as you said, four million dollars invested for over thirty years, yessir, that's something worth bringing skeletons out of the closet."

"Alphonse, Antonio, or whatever you're name is, I can't say what you'd get if you can help us. Certainly you won't get $500,000 that Volkers may have promised you for being involved in a theft of United States Army money. But there may be an incentive. How much I can't say."

"As I said, I was only telling you a story. And if I did know how to get that money, wouldn't I have done so by now?"

"Maybe you have been getting at it, little by little."

Alphonse sat silent for a moment, thinking. So all these years the money has been sitting in a Swiss bank. When Volkers died his operations must have automatically shut down. No one else at the CIA probably even knew about the money run robbery. And now they can't find the codes to get into the accounts. Amazing. And even worse, right now I haven't got a fucking clue myself how to get that money.

He rubbed his nose, something he did when deep in thought, ever since he'd had the plastic surgery. He remembered that the driver of the truck was in on the scheme, which was why he had to be eliminated. But what of the others? Did they learn something? Were they in on it? Seems impossible.

"Why can't we work on this together, for a fee, of course?" Alphonse suggested

"A fee, of course," Jones agreed.

"I think three million would be good."

Jones gaped. "You are out of your ever-lovin' mind. No way we'll pay that much."

"Are you good with math, Mr. Jones?"

"If we are friends, Alphonse, you don't have call me Mister."

"Ah, yes, of course. Well, you do the math on what the money is probably worth today. Three million isn't too much to ask."

"And what do you think you can find out? You already told me you, or whoever might have been involved, wouldn't have known any more about Volkers' operations or his other agents."

"I won't try to snow you. Off hand, I haven't the foggiest idea where to start. But I know a lot of people. And I've met a lot of people in my days. Would your people be interested in knowing who else was running secret operations with Volkers, even after all these years?"

"Maybe." Jones knew the true answer was a solid "Yes".

"Or would you like to know about the operations themselves, the ones that your people would like to keep buried forever?"

Jones made no answer.

"I'll start asking around, see what comes up. But first you get your people to agree to my cut."

"I'll see what I can do. Nice chatting with you. I will definitely be in touch." And Jones abruptly stood up and left.

Antonio was surprised by Jones' sudden exit and he sat for several minutes thinking on what had transpired. He decided it wasn't likely that Jones, be he CIA or some other agency, was going to part with more than a pittance unless Antonio could prove he had relevant information. Maybe, just maybe, I have one last game in me, the weathered mercenary mused. Pondering what steps to take next, Antonio made a mistake a younger and more active agent would never have made.

When the waiter cleaned the table and brought the cups into the kitchen, Jones was there. For twenty dollars he bought a hot chocolate- stained mug.

Back at his cottage Alphonse—already starting to morph into his American identity of Tony Abbott—sat and remembered. He let his mind wander back many years to when he first met Karl Volkers, and even further to when he first heard of him, that time in London with O'Shea.

It was a couple of years later—O'Shea was dead and Tony moved like a cat from one identity to another, from one continent to another, from one job to another. In Europe he was known as Antonio, in the United States he was Tony Abbott. The encounter in London had led O'Shea to contact Volkers in Washington, and to let him know that if he ever needed a good field agent for something that he didn't want his regular agents to handle, he had a good one in Tony Abbott. Nothing developed immediately, but then there was the time Tony saw Volkers, after O'Shea was dead, and it couldn't have been a coincidence.

From his vantage atop the building Tony studied the developing scene. On the overpass he saw two men and as he focused his zoom lens he recognized Volkers. The other man looked like the redheaded captain he'd met, though wearing an unflattering wig. Tony began to click away. The latter handed Volkers a packet or thick file. It could have been a briefcase. Volkers looked at it, appeared not to want it. They spoke for several seconds. The impression Tony got was that Volkers was reluctant to take the package; that the two men were arguing. Eventually the man with the bad wig won out and Volkers took the package. The two men quickly walked off in opposite directions, Volkers breaking into a trot as he climbed down the stairs and was gone from Tony's view.

Tony didn't see Volkers again until 1968 when they met in that bar in Bangkok, though he had already done some work he knew was for Volkers' off-the-books operations.

An Agency facility near Rome would lift the fingerprints, Jones hoped, but it might take days to get a match, if one could be made. So Preston returned to Washington while Jones waited for results and tried to keep an eye on Antonio, but now, surreptitiously. For a day and a night Jones literally shivered as he lay hidden in the woods that surrounded Antonio's cottage. I should have brought a flannel-lined sleeping bag, he thought. And how the hell did he know I've never killed anybody? Lucky guess, I suppose.

Not that he ever wanted to kill anybody. We collect information, not kill people. At least, normally we aren't supposed to. Jones didn't even know of another agent who had ever even used his weapon, though like everybody else he'd heard of the supposed abuses; the stories of kidnapping and rendition and torture. The public tends to think we're all high-tech geniuses and that we kill without feeling, but for the most part it's paperwork, reading, and interpreting scads of information, trying to figure out which bit of data is vital and which is bullshit. Jones wondered if the extracurricular activities of the Agency still went on more than the average guy, himself included, realized. Maybe you have to be higher up the totem pole, like Swanson, or this guy Volkers, to really know what goes on.

Before he was assigned to Langley Jones spent maybe a lonely night in many different cities in parts of the world that a sane person wouldn't dare travel to. Most of the time the work was boring. He found he had plenty of leisure time with not much to do with that time. So he read mysteries until he tired of all the angst that filled the lives of the heroes.

It seemed like everyone, be he or she a private investigator, government agent, or policeman or detective, suffered from the stress and constant strife of dealing with demons from the past. Pick one or several:

(a) loss of a young child due to bizarre accident or illness; (b) bitter divorce due to our hero's infidelities or our hero's spouse's wayward behavior; (c) heavy drinking, exacerbated by the stress of dealing with the woes of humanity on an everyday basis; or (d) some or all of the above. And, do not forget, (e) dreams that caused one to toss and turn and kick and sweat a pint of fluid until trapped in the sheets and screaming in terror, our hero is wakened to escape the horrors of his/her dreams only to have to now deal with the agony of getting up and going to work and wondering which of his former wives or partners or criminals he'd let get away, would rise up to haunt his daylight hours.

Yes, Jones had been married, and he'd experienced the same issues and problems most human beings who manage to live a few decades have to confront. The marriage didn't last because he was away too much, and if he was home she was too involved in her work, which she had become obsessed with because he wasn't around much. It had been an amicable parting and fortunately there were no children, so the break hadn't been too difficult and it hadn't caused either one, as far as he knew, to sink into the misery of tortured dreams or addictions. They both just went on with their lives, occasionally having a lonely night and sometimes, at least for him, enjoying a good memory.

On the second day of his surveillance Jones began to fear that Antonio had slipped out somehow without Jones seeing him. Both front and back entrances were visible from the agent's hiding place, but at night, and with no moon, it was as dark as inside a cave, and it's possible the sly devil had slipped away.

With the dawn, Jones eased down the slope. No sound came from the cottage. Through a dirty window in the garage he spied a vehicle, a Mercedes of some years old. From here it was only a couple of miles to the village, not a walk that would have been impossible, where Antonio might have another car stashed, or could have arranged for a ride. Using his best imitation of a cat burglar Jones tip toed to the back door and tried the knob. The door was locked. He tried to pry up a window and found that it opened rather easily. A minute or so later he cursed his carelessness: clearly Antonio had gone and by now could be hours away. Away anywhere; in another European country or on his way to America. Great; Swanson won't be too happy with this.

Indeed, Antonio was hours and many miles away, sleeping aboard a New York bound jet, traveling under the guise of Tony Abbott, on a passport that had been expertly prepared with several stamped entries to aid the look of legality, helpful in this age of skittish security people. It took several hours for Jones to contact Swanson and to convince him to get local agents to search passenger lists on all flights out of the several airports within Antonio's reach for the past twenty-four hours. And several hours more before the name Tony Abbott struck Jones as a possibility.

"How many other Tonys did you come across?" asked Swanson.

"Fifteen, but only three to the States. This one interests me the most because the last name, 'Abbott', is just similar enough to other names he uses. Alphonse, Antonio, Antonini, I don't know, slim, I admit, but a place to start. And the other two were on flights that I don't think our guy could have made in time."

"Because Abbott starts with the letter 'A'? Kinda slim, Jonesy. But yeah, it is a place to start. I'll get the computers cranking on the Tony Abbotts of this world and see what turns up. Are you coming back now?

97

"Soon as we get something on the prints, or find we can't get something."

While the microchips processed, Alphonse/Antonio, now ensconced in the alias of Tony Abbott, having donned a mustache and dark glasses in one of the bathroom stalls at JFK airport, rented a car to take him to Grand Central Station where he got on a train for Philadelphia, after making a phone call. There, he rented another car and headed to Detroit. By the time he got there he was sure he would receive the information he had requested from an old pal he'd known in the New Jersey neighborhood. A pal who'd gone straight, got away from the familiar and negative lures of his boyhood, became a cop and then a private detective, a route that Tony still found amazing.

"Listen, Tony," his old pal explained. "Most of the guys we grew up with ended up dead, crippled, or spent the best years of their lives in jail. I didn't. I've got a house in the suburbs, a great wife and a couple of kids who don't get into too much trouble. I get free tickets to the policemen's dance and even know the mayor and the chief of police. What the hell you been doing? I thought you were dead long ago."

"Europe," Tony said, as if that one word explained it all. "Can you locate some guys for me? I knew them in, well, we worked together on some jobs once. Thought I'd like to get together with them while I'm in the country."

"Sure, I'll try. Come for dinner tonight, meet the family."

A family visit was not in Tony's schedule but his friend was so persistent Tony decided it would have to be a cost of doing business. Before he left that night Tony gave his pal the names of Bill Jenkins, Curtis Howard and Kit Walker, the old buddies he'd done some business with many years ago. The contact from his New Jersey neighborhood told Tony to call him in a day or so.

Eventually the computers found fingerprints that matched those on the mug. They belonged to one Tony Abazini, who served in the Army in 1969 and disappeared while stationed in Vietnam. At first he was thought to be AWOL but later was listed MIA, though presumed to be dead. Further investigation showed that Abazini just seemed to appear at the 11th Finance base near Bien Hoa one fine day, but disappeared only a few weeks later. Other data from his Army file regarding basic training or any other assignments was missing. To Syd Swanson's surprise the name caused a low level alert to arise in regards to the name Abazini, and a reference to contact the Defense Intelligence Agency if any information regarding this man was still an active default.

Shortly after that Syd Swanson met Walter Cushman for the first time.

>>NINE<<

"Major Fears"

The Defense Intelligence Agency, as the name suggests, advises on matters of military intelligence, such data invaluable to the Secretary of Defense and the Joint Chiefs of Staff. It wouldn't normally get involved in something as relatively minor as the possible re-appearance of a non-commissioned officer who went AWOL in Vietnam in 1969. The possibility of his being on the official list of MIAs might open someone's eyes, if only for the publicity of settling one of those damn nuisance cases.

But more so, because of heightened security in a world where the threat of terrorists had risen to levels previously unimagined, certain names raised additional flags.

Major Justin Fears received a secure message indicating that the name of one Tony Abazini had popped up in a CIA investigation, details not included. Abazini had been located in Italy but current whereabouts were unknown. The message added that Abazini was not considered dangerous and did not appear to be involved in any activities threatening United States security.

He had been waiting for this since the day before when a contact at the CIA, someone Fears did not– and likely would never know– had sent him that same information and a little more. This notice would now allow him to operate openly on the case.

The name rang a bell but was not something Fears or anyone ever spent anytime on. It was an issue way below the radar level on the intelligence services that dominated the time of he and his staff. Still, the case, as he read the file that had been stored away in a warehouse in Bethesda, Maryland, was interesting.

Several years ago Fears had done some staff work for the Select Senate Joint POW/MIA committee, this at a time of heightened interest in the Vietnam MIA cases due to supposed sightings of captured Americans in Cambodia and Laos. Nothing came of these supposed sightings and no such incidents had occurred in some years now. But while at that job he came across some obscure cases with unusual facets to them.

The case involving Tony Abazini was one of the strangest of the lot. Maybe because Fears had a little more financial background than the others he worked with, the fact that Abazini has disappeared so soon after the one and only time an Army truck full of cash had been robbed by highwaymen in Vietnam, stuck in Fears' memory. He had to thank some unknown clerk who happened to link that information together because there were no clues that Abazini had been involved in the robbery. Officially it was a Viet Cong attack, resulting in the death of the truck driver and loss of $4,155,099 in hard American cash. With the exception of a few thousand dollars the money was never recovered and certainly was not considered recoverable after three decades and more.

So why is the CIA interested in Tony Abazini? Where has this man been; how did he get out of Vietnam; who is he really, and what has he been doing? Is he responsible for the death of the truck driver and the robbery? Seems impossible that this guy could have pulled off such a caper—without a lot of help. Like maybe from, let's see now, the CIA? How about that for a wild-ass guess?

And maybe the money didn't just rot away in the jungle. Maybe it went somewhere, somewhere that Abazini knows. Me thinks I must pay a visit to my friends at Langley.

"I'm Major Fears," said the tall and lean soldier as he introduced himself to Swanson and Jones. His uniform was spotless, his shoes a mirror. His hair was cut short and showed a hint of white above the ears.

"Glad to meet you, major. I'm Syd Swanson, this is Ed Jones. Have a seat. Coffee?"

"Yes, thank you." Fears sat down talking as he did so. "Jones, you're the agent who met Abazini? Talked to him?"

Jones, sitting on the edge of Swanson's desk, nodded. "Alphonse Antonini, at least that's the name he uses where I found him, a little village called LeDione. Quiet place; you'd think it's too tame for anybody who could be much of a troublemaker."

"But you've got a match on the fingerprints, right? They match up to Abazini?"

Jones nodded. "Do you know of any other aliases he's used? Do they always begin with the letter 'A'?"

"The prints and the names," chimed in Swanson, ignoring the question; "Could be coincidence, but I doubt it."

"Major, if this guy is your Abazini, who went AWOL or died or whatever happened to him, why is the Army so interested after all these years? Another one of those MIAs to clear up, or do I smell a little more here. I mean, sending a major ..."

Fears sipped his coffee, thought for a moment. "Officially I work for the Defense Intelligence Agency. If you're afraid I'll try to take this matter away from you, you're somewhat correct. Am I going to have any trouble?"

"Whoa, there," said Swanson. "We get into enough cat fights with the FBI We don't need any with the DIA, too. But you've got to understand, major, we were into this first, and we already know there's a suspicion about one of our former agents."

"You mean Volkers? I know that."

Swanson and Jones exchanged glances. "Okay, you've impressed me. You've got friends in places higher than I do. Hell, I never heard of him before a few days ago. What is the DIA's interest? Or are you representing the Army?"

The soldier didn't directly answer the questions but said, "Gentlemen, in this day of multi-billion dollar budgets and weapons systems that cost several millions of dollars apiece, four more million dollars may not seem like much. While we haven't been spending any time on this matter, once your inquiry hit on Abazini's file, it came to my attention. Well, to my staff sergeant. It's an old case, but still open. An old AWOL wouldn't interest us that much, however, but the MIA possibility does, and more so, the four million dollars. When I read the file, there was quite an investigation at the time, especially since Abazini was never found."

When Fears paused, Jones asked: "So did they come up with anything at all?"

"A man thought to be one of yours was found floating in the river, two bullets in the head. We're not sure of his name, but surely you have old files that can confirm if an agent of yours went missing then and was never found. Two ARVN soldiers were found dead in the jungle, several miles from where the robbery took place, along with a bag of the money. The bag only contained a few thousand dollars. The rest of the money was never found. After awhile nobody looked much anymore, other than to keep Abazini as an open MIA. The consensus was he drowned or got shot and rotted in the jungle somewhere, along with the money."

"But somebody didn't let it go," Swanson suggested.

"Well, again, the MIA aspect, not to mention the money. And, ah, one other matter. The driver of the truck was shot and killed by the bandits. He was certified as killed in enemy action, got his name on the Wall and everything."

Swanson and Jones waited for the major to go. When they didn't say anything Fears told them of the Army's other concern.

"Plain, simple case of murder, gentlemen. If this truck robbery was a scheme involving any of our men, not an enemy attack, then the driver was murdered. If this Abazini is still alive, we'd sure like to know what he knows about the robbery. In fact, I'm planning on talking to the other people who were there, too."

Jones piped in, "We can probably save you some time there. The notes Volkers left us clears the other three, Howard, Walker and Jenkins."

"Just them? What about the driver?"

"Well, interestingly enough he doesn't say anything one way or the other. He specifically mentioned that the three men guarding the money were not involved. They just happened to be the three guys assigned to the job. He doesn't' say 'Yay' or 'Nay' about the driver."

"Anything you can show me?" asked the major.

Swanson shook his head but couldn't restrain the slight smile. "No can do, sorry."

"Need to know? I may have a need, Mr. Swanson."

"But that's not for me to decide, I'm sure you understand."

Fears nodded in acknowledgment. Swanson changed the subject.

"You suspect a CIA connection to the truck robbery, don't you, major," it was said as fact, not a question.

"Actually, Mr. Jones, I don't think anybody did back then. When I reviewed some of the old cases, like this one, the thought occurred to me, but I haven't had time to pursue it. Until now."

"Major, we'd love to work with you if it'll help both of us. We believe we have a vital stake in anything that may involve our people and operations our people were involved in—sanctioned or not. Mainly, we'd like to get …" Swanson stopped, afraid he'd said too much.

"Get what, the money? It's not yours. Belongs to the Army, if anybody."

Jones realized that Fears might not know about the Swiss bank accounts. That was what stopped Swanson. Why give up vital information for free?

"We'd like to find out if Antonio knows anything else about what operations Volkers may have run," Jones cut in.

"I thought you already talked to him."

"He wasn't going to give me anything unless we made it worth his while. And we don't want to promise him anything unless we think it is worth our while. So for now we are just keeping tabs on him. Maybe my talking to him will stir him up, go see some people. Who knows, maybe nothing will come of it."

Fears stood up, clearly not satisfied. "I don't buy it, I'm sorry. You must know more to have gone this far. I'm willing to trade information, but if I have to go over your head, I'll do that. Why don't you think about this; you can reach me at my office. Good day." And with that, Major Fears made his exit.

"Keeping tabs on him?"

"C'mon Syd, don't rub it in. This major's a cool fellow and he's on to us."

Swanson said, "Yes, and he's right about the money. I just didn't want to tell him we probably know where it is until he has something to give us in exchange."

"Such as?"

"Oh, he may have much more in his files about Antonio and Volkers and other agents that we might like to have."

"But how did he know so soon about the fingerprint ID?" asked Jones.

"Ah, I wondered about that. Upstairs just told me to talk to Fears and cooperate as much as I could without compromising ourselves."

"As much as you can, eh?"

"Gives us some leeway."

"Sounds to me like the people upstairs don't want us to cooperate too much, tell the truth."

"Then who leaked the info on the Abazini ID?"

Jones flailed his arms up in feigned disgust: "Interagency cooperation that you and I aren't privy to."

Swanson wasn't amused. "Maybe; stranger things have happened. But we still don't know how to get access to those accounts."

"And if we figure out how to get in, it'll be fun to see what's there and to watch the fight over who gets it!"

Actually, Swanson was wrong. The ambitious Major Fears had next to nothing on Antonio or Volkers. What he did have was the contact ensconced in the CIA who had given him the Abazini fingerprint identification. And he had a suspicion and a fierce desire to find out what happened to Tony Abazini and whether he had any involvement in the truck robbery and the murder. And, maybe more, to get the four million dollars. He too, knew that four million dollars banked and even if only earning plain interest, was now a lot more than four million dollars. Recovering that would be a gold star on his career resume.

>>TEN<<

"Old Buddies"

Antonio had long thought that he been used and screwed over those many years ago in the jungle. That wasn't necessarily true: Volkers had intended to pay Antonio, but the mercenary didn't know that. He hadn't carried a big grudge though, for sometimes those things happened in his business. Since Volkers had died Antonio knew of no one else he could go to for his money. He bided his time, went about other business, and as the years passed tended to forget about the money run operation.

Still, there was a lot of money unaccounted for. He'd assumed the CIA had benefited but the visit from Jones made him rethink things. Now Antonio realized there might still be millions to be had, enough so he'd never have to worry about money again. Even if he only got the money Volkers had promised, if it has been invested all these years it alone would be a small fortune. And if all the money from the robbery had been invested and never claimed by anybody, it would be a king's ransom by now. Jones wouldn't have come to see Antonio if the CIA was able to get to the money. So they must not know how and might not even know how much money there is. They probably were wondering if I've had access to it and have been dipping into it. Surely they have watched me long enough to know I haven't been near that bank in years.

So who would know? The driver was killed off to keep him quiet, but Antonio had had no instructions about the soldiers riding along, guarding the money. They, presumably, were not in on it, were not in for a share, and were no danger. But was that true? Did they know anything more? It was a place to start. His old pal had provided addresses and some information regarding the apparent financial situation of all three. It wasn't promising. Only Walker appeared to be well off, though not rich, and the other two did not show any indication of wealth. But was it possible they knew something but didn't know the significance of their knowledge? Like other people who were involved, or who was supposed to get the money. Or maybe they were paid a small amount, back in 1969, had spent it, thought nothing of it, and had long forgotten about the incident. But not likely. No one would forget that, not if reminded by someone who was there at the time.

So for something to do Antonio decided he'd start his search by visiting old Army comrades. He'd received the information he'd requested and found that Bill Jenkins lived in Gadsden Woods, a small town in central Michigan. He ran a hardware store and it was unlikely he'd have a stash of money hidden away. The dark glasses and mustache were gone now. They had probably not been necessary and Antonio was sure he gotten away without a tail and did not think it possible that anyone had trailed him here. Jenkins might not recognize me with my new nose, but let's see.

It took one stop to buy maps and one more to clarify directions before Tony could find Gadsden Woods. Once he found the village with its one main street, it was easy to find the hardware store that his information said was owned by Jenkins.

Antonio went into the store and wandered among the aisles of bolts and nails, pipe sockets and tools. It wasn't long before a man of about his own age, shorter, grayer, meek-looking, asked Antonio if he could help him find something. Antonio said he was traveling and his shaver needed new batteries. As the man was ringing up the sale, Antonio spoke up.

"It's funny, I'm sure I've never been in this town before, but you look familiar. Ever live in New York City?"

"No, never. Lived around here all my life. Rarely ever left the state. Well, except when I was in the service, hell of a long time ago that was. Here's your change, sir"

"Service, hey, that's it! Vietnam, '68 or '69, we were in the same unit. My name's Tony Abbott."

I don't remember the name but then it was a long time ago."

"Well, my name was Tony Abazini then. I changed it; too many misspellings."

"Okay, yeah I think I do remember."

Tony pointed at his face. "I had a nose job, too," he said, a sheepish smile forming. "It was a real ski lift."

Jenkins laughed. "Well, I wasn't going to say anything about that, but I think I do remember you."

"My nose anyway, right?"

They both laughed, shook hands. "Bill Jenkins; nice to see you again, Tony. So you're just passing through? I mean, where to? Up this way, if you're not a hunter there's not much reason to visit this little burg."

"Had some time on my hands. I'm going to Chicago to meet people on business, but I left early so I could take a few detours and see the country up here. It's beautiful."

"Sure is. Hey, some coffee?"

Tony agreed and in-between customers they reminisced about the Army.

"I don't remember that you were in our unit for long, were you, Tony?" "Tony shook his head, sipped the strong coffee. "No, I wasn't. Got transferred to Long Binh. They needed some help in the repair shop and I had some experience."

"From finance to mechanics? Versatile guy."

"Well, it was unusual, but a buddy of mine was able to make the transfer on a temporary basis. I only had a few months left in 'Nam, so that's how I finished up. What about you? Do anything after the service?"

Jenkins pointed out into the store. "This is it. My family owned this so I came back and worked here. Took some college classes on the G.I. bill but I never cared to move from here. Now I own it and on the weekends my grandkid works here."

"So you'll pass it on to him someday, eh?"

Jenkins shrugged. "Naw, he's smarter than me; so's his Dad. He's a lawyer in town, and the kid will become one too. Only he'll move to the big city, make some real dough. This is a nice life, even if you don't make any money. But I'm happy.

"So what do you do, Tony?"

"Oh, machinery broker, that sort of stuff."

Jenkins said nothing, his thoughts about the days in Vietnam starting to clarify, returning to him in vague wisps of events, the sequence and timing of events clouded by the passage of time.

"You know," he hesitated. "What you said about being a mechanic, and then now about machinery, it's got me thinking. I'm trying to remember now but it was you who got sick the day of that truck robbery, wasn't it?"

Tony hesitated in turn, his memory sure, but not wanting to act as if it was clear to him. He looked upward, as if trying to remember; then nodded.

"Yeah, that's right. I was sick for a couple of days, and then I got transferred. I heard about that robbery. Were you one of the guards?" he asked, as if he didn't know.

"Yeah, I was. The driver got killed; I got the crap scared out of me. Thought I was a goner for sure. Curtis, that was one of the other guys; did you know him? We've stayed in touch, sort of; I guess that truck fiasco kept us close."

"No, I didn't know him. Wasn't there another guy, too?"

"Yeah, there was. What was his name, like the comic strip character, Walker or something. I didn't stay in touch with him. Don't know why; Curtis and I just hit it off better. But what I remember, other than being scared, and seeing the dead driver, was how we were grilled in Saigon about the robbery."

"Really? Didn't know that," Tony said.

"Yeah, for awhile I was afraid they thought we were in on it somehow. You know, the driver gets killed, but we don't. Hell's bells, I didn't know what was goin' on. Neither did the others. They asked about you, too, that I remember."

"Me?" Tony didn't have to act surprised.

"Yeah, like how well did I know you; did I know you were sick; did I know you before I was in the Army, all kinds of questions. I'll have to call Curtis, tell him I saw you."

"Don't do that, maybe I'll drop in and surprise him myself."

"Yeah? I thought you said you hadn't known him well? Besides, he's in California."

"Oh, yeah, well, maybe not such a good idea."

"It gets hard to remember after so many years. You see, Tony, seems to me I recall that the three of us who were in the truck were asked about you again, weeks later. They said no one knew where you were. That seemed odd. But you say you were in Long Binh?"

"That's right, I was." Tony didn't like where this was going. He played the bad memory card back at Jenkins.

"You know, if I recall there was a day or two or maybe longer where there was some confusion. You see, I still wasn't feeling well. Must have had some bad jungle hooch," he laughed. "So when I was transferred to Long Binh first thing I did was report to the hospital there. Had some kind of intestinal thing. A day or so later two MPs come lookin' for me, said I was AWOL. It got straightened out, but maybe that's what you're thinking of."

"Could be, could be," Jenkins said, nodding as he stood up and set down his coffee cup. "Well, I've got to get to work. I see a few customers wandering around lost in here. If I don't help them soon they'll run out to Home Depot. Nice seeing you, Tony. If you're around tonight come by the Country Grill. My wife and I will be there, we can have dinner."

"Okay, maybe I'll join you."

As he was leaving Tony stopped and turned around.

"Say, did you ever hear what happened with the money? I mean, did the VC get away with it or what?"

"Darned if I know. I figured they did, that's why we got called back to Saigon for another grilling. In fact, a few weeks after I was home from 'Nam I got a visit by some Army brass. Can't recall his name, but he asked me pretty much the same questions. Had me worried; I was afraid they still thought I knew something about it. But, hey, if I got any money would I be running a hardware store in a town of eight thousand people in the middle of the Michigan woods?"

Tony waved, "I suppose not. See ya later."

Tony hadn't registered in at a motel yet. As far as he knew no one but Jenkins had seen him in this town. Best to keep it that way. Hope Jenkins doesn't call this Curtis Howard anytime soon. Can't let that happen. Sure enough the suits will come to talk to Jenkins soon, and then he'll tell them about me. And I don't want him contacting the other two guys before I can get to them.

Tony did not show up for dinner. He drove back several miles to a fast food diner located just off the main highway, a place that served many strangers and where no one would remember five minutes from now who'd been there on any particular day. He took a room in a motel next to the diner paying with cash and using a phony name. The next morning he was up and out before sunrise and drove back to Gadsden Woods.

The alarm system for the hardware store was easily overcome by Tony. Inside, he selected a crow bar in his gloved hand and wondered exactly what he would do if anyone other than Jenkins opened up the store. Promptly at seven he heard someone enter. Tony had re-wired the alarm and he heard Jenkins punch in his code. A few seconds later the hardware store owner stepped into the back storage room where Tony hid. Jenkins felt the pain of the strike for the tiniest split second before he crumpled to the concrete floor.

Tony carefully wiped the crowbar and put it back in the rack with the other ones. He pried open the cash register and took what cash was there, not for need, but for show. He walked briskly across the alley in back of the hardware store to where his car was parked, and by the time the first customer of the day was wondering where the heck was Bill, Tony was sixty miles away. At a rest stop he dumped his gloves and the rag he'd used to clean the crowbar into a trash bin and then continued on his way, keeping his speed only slightly over the limit.

In Langley, Syd Swanson received the latest in cyberspace electronic miracles about Tony Abbott– whoever he was– who had boarded a British Airways jet in Florence, was traced to a car rental that lasted only an hour, then to another car rental the next day, in Philadelphia.

"Probably took the train, paid with cash," said Kirstie, the young, very bright, pretty, and precocious computer geek who knew more about how computers worked and what they could do than most people in the office. To be sure, Swanson was not as technologically handicapped as he pretended to be. He had learned a lot about what these machines could do by asking questions even when he knew the answers; he often picked up shortcuts and tips on how to perform certain functions in more efficient ways. It was somewhat silly, a spy's habit, but Swanson liked to keep some of his knowledge to himself.

"This is pretty basic stuff, Mr. Swanson. Now that we've got a trace on him we should be able to find where he returns the rental car within minutes after he does so."

"And if he gets on a plane a few minutes later?"

"If he uses the same name or uses any of the credit cards he's used so far, we should be able to keep tabs. He might not be who you're looking for, you know. Doesn't seem to hide his credit card information from us."

"Could be he's too sure of himself. He made one mistake already, letting us get fingerprints, so he may be careless enough to let us keep on him. If he's the guy," he added, rolling his eyes to the ceiling.

"On the other hand, he could be smart, too. We have no idea right now which direction he headed out of Philly. We're running a check on the name, 'Tony Abbott', and you'll find several in every major city."

"Sure, sure. But, Kirstie, how likely is it that a legitimate, law-abiding American citizen named Tony Abbott got on a plane in Florence, flew to New York, took the train to Philadelphia, rented a car there, when all he's doing is returning from a business trip to his white picket fence home in Cabot Cove or Cleveland Heights? If he doesn't live near New York, why fly in there? Why not fly into Philly? If he doesn't live near Philly, why take the train there? And...this Antonio guy that Jones was watching disappears at the same time, with the Florence airport his most likely choice. It's curious, so keep at it. Let me know if he shows up again."

"Right, chief."

Back at her cubicle Kirstie tapped the Enter key on her laptop, clicked on her address list, then entered 'Majfears77@diaadmin.gov.sec.' She entitled the message as 'Abazini update', punched in her code that would encrypt the message, and began to type.

Tony returned his rental car to a small office in a suburb of Chicago, twenty miles from O'Hare airport. Instead of using the credit card with which he'd reserved the car, he used a different one, a card he hadn't yet used in the United States. He didn't think anyone was onto him yet, but one never knows in this business. Certainly by now Jones and his friends were looking for him, and certainly they would hear about Jenkins, though that could be a few days before they made a link. Time to start being a little more cautious, at least until I'm prepared for them to find me. Using an ATM card he hadn't used previously, Tony extracted several hundred dollars. With cash he purchased a ticket for San Francisco, using the Tony Abbott ID.

When the fingerprints showed up Major Fears re-opened the Abazini file. The major studied the old reports about the soldier and about the truck robbery, familiarizing himself with the names, history, and any recent updates. He immediately ordered his staff to obtain current information on Kit Walker, Bill Jenkins, and Curtis Howard. Not being one prone to accept coincidences, when he received the news that Bill Jenkins, veteran, who's Army ID matched the Jenkins from the money run caper, had recently died in a robbery, he made this case his priority. This gave him several more people at his disposal, one of which he dispatched to California to locate Curtis Howard and Kit Walker. A sharp lieutenant, probably being nosier than required, came up with the fact that Kit Walker had a cousin currently in the Army; a general, in fact, stationed in Hawaii. This *could* be a coincidence. Now he would find out how serious anybody was about finding the money, finding what happened to Tony Abazini, and finding out who killed the truck driver and the CIA agent in the Vietnamese jungle. Bucking this information upward, unfortunately, slowed the process. Fears sat on the case for several days, during which time Tony Abazini, now Abbott, flew to California, took a taxi to San Jose, rented a car with cash, and drove south towards the Los Angeles area.

Curtis Howard lived in a new development, a middle class area of the San Fernando Valley, not many miles from Kit Walker, unbeknown to both of them, not that they would have cared anyway. Like a lot of uneducated young men who'd spent a couple of the best years of their youth in the military, and maybe a year of that in the mud and grit of Vietnam, he did not know what to do when he returned home. He was not spat upon—such stories were urban legends, events no one could ever show to have actually happened anywhere—and he did not feel bad about himself, or bad about the war. Of course, he hadn't been a grunt who'd maybe seen his buddy's face blown off and then had to wipe the gristle of the explosion off his own face with the bloody sleeve of his uniform. He didn't want to think about 'Nam when he got home, just wanted to get on with his life. The easiest thing to do was to return to the supermarket he used to work at. They were eager to give him a job and that kept him busy and put a few bucks in his pocket.

The ensuing decades were similar to the life of millions of other people. He took some classes at the local college, met a girl, got married, had a couple of kids, went to Little League games and piano recitals, held barbeques in his backyard with friends, and tried to save money for the kids to go to college, and maybe a little for retirement— he should be so lucky to be able to retire before he keeled over. The Howard family had even been able to recently purchase a new home in a housing tract that was just beginning to develop.

The supermarket job became an assistant manager's job, then a manager's job. Another seven or eight years and he would retire, not wealthy, but comfy.

Tony did not want to attract attention to himself by idling inside the store, so he watched from across the street to see if he could spot Howard, if he could recognize him at all. A little after eight p.m. a man wearing a green jacket that identified him as a manager of the store strode out and got into a SUV of some sort. It was already dark but the man looked enough like what Tony thought Howard would look like to follow him, and sure enough the destination matched the address Tony had been given for Curtis Howard. The next morning Tony waited with coffee and a donut sitting in his car across from the market. Near nine o'clock Howard showed up. Tony followed him in, then took a cart and proceeded to shop while watching where Howard went. The manager stopped to talk to a few people, went into his office, and came out again only a few minutes later. Tony followed him and bumped into him with the shopping cart

"Sorry, Bud, wasn't watching."

"No problem, sir. Anything I can help you find?" asked Curtis Howard.

"Ah, yes. What aisle is the bread in?"

"Aisle 7; I can show you."

"That's okay, I'll find it." Tony glanced at the name badge on Howard's green jacket. It said, 'Curtis Howard, Store Manager'.

"Say, you look a bit familiar. Curtis Howard, right?"

Howard pointed to his badge, "Yes, that's right."

"11th Finance, Bien Hoa, 1969. My name's Tony. Remember?"

Howard didn't remember Tony, and only vaguely even as the customer pressed the conversation. But Tony was persuasive and charming and before long the two arranged to meet for lunch at the restaurant a block from the store. Tony said he'd return and meet him there at noon.

It wasn't difficult to turn the conversation to the time in Vietnam and specifically, the truck robbery. Howard confirmed the story Jenkins had told about the suspicions of the Army Intelligence officers and the grilling—he called it the same thing as Jenkins had—on two different occasions. Then he and Jenkins were both transferred. They didn't see each other again until after Vietnam, when Howard came across the address Jenkins had given him. The latter had come on a trip to California and after that they stayed in touch with occasional phone calls and Christmas cards.

"So you and Jenkins ever talk about the truck robbery?"

Howard shrugged. "We did when we first talked back about those days. But after awhile, no, not really. Nostalgia's not all it's cracked up to be, I say. We both got visits from the Army shortly after we were discharged. Guess they were still trying to find that money. I think they were still suspicious about us, but hell, I didn't know anything. I just assumed it was a VC attack. And neither of us kept in touch with the other guy who was with us."

"Yeah, Walker, I knew him pretty well," Tony lied.

"Oh, yeah? Where's he at, do you know?"

"Not far from here. I was going to stop in on him, but I didn't know you lived in this area. This is quite the coincidence. I've never run into someone that I hadn't seen in so many years. Looks like you've done alright for yourself."

The store manager nodded. "Yeah, no complaints."

"You said they questioned you about me, about the robbery? Why me, I wasn't there."

"Beats me. If they were suspicious about me, why not you? Didn't they question you?"

"Oh, yeah," Tony lied again. "I was sick then, got sent to the hospital in Long Binh. MPs came to see me, but I hadn't even heard about the truck thing until then."

The conversation was difficult to maintain for long. Howard did not recollect much about Tony, and even though they had a connection from having served in the same unit, he did not feel any real desire to talk of old times with someone he hardly knew then, nor remembered now. It did make Curtis think of Bill Jenkins and he promised himself he would call Bill soon.

Obviously Howard hadn't yet heard about Jenkins' demise, and he certainly didn't seem to have any information of value to Tony about the truck robbery. But he too would be visited soon by Jones or someone like Jones. And Tony did not want them to know he'd been here.

That evening when Curtis Howard left the store the sun was almost down, the sky was overcast, the traffic cluttered. Tony had cased the route and knew that once Howard was off the main streets he would drive along several blocks of open land until he reached the new development of suburban homes where the visibility at that time of night was not the best. What traffic there would be was anybody's guess, but he felt his plan would work.

Once Howard drove off Tony sped ahead in the car he'd stolen only minutes ago. This was the weakest part of the plan, the chance the car would be reported too soon. He had stolen it from a mall parking lot and the owner might spend a long time thinking they'd forgotten where they had parked before reporting it as stolen. He waited now on the shoulder of the road, engine humming, just a few blocks from Howard's home in an area a good hundred yards from any other house and with no street lights. To the left ran a culvert and on the right of the road, the side where Abbott waited, the dirt was torn up from construction vehicles, the ground rough and unfit for normal automobile travel. He'd memorized the look of the front of Howard's car and watched for it in his side mirror.

It was less than a minute later when Tony saw the headlights of a car coming up the road from behind him. He waited long enough to be sure it was Howard, then, lights still off, he suddenly pulled in front of the approaching car. Howard had no choice but to veer to the left and try desperately to stay on the road. But Tony kept pushing towards Howard's car until it slid down the embankment and overturned. Abbott's plan then was to hurry down to the wreck, check on Howard's status and, if he was still alive, finish him. If someone came along he could say he was hit by the on-coming car and had gone into the culvert to see about the driver. Then he could slip away in the dark. All this was fine except for the unexpected, a speedy car recklessly tearing up the road; probably some dumb-ass teenager. The driver of this third vehicle saw Abbott's car just in time to swerve to the right, but lost control and bounced along the hard dirt until his car got stuck in the ruts.

It was time to leave. Abbott slipped into the ditch, the darkness covering his movements, and jogged as quickly as he could away from the crash site. He could only hope that Howard had received fatal wounds. The other driver might also leave the site, but soon someone would call in the accident. The stolen car would put someone in deep shit until he or she could convince authorities they hadn't been driving it, but by then Abbott would be far away. Even though this area was away from the main stream of traffic, in fifteen minutes he would be in a highly populated area. It wouldn't be too difficult to steal another car, something that would get him away from immediate danger.

>>ELEVEN<<

"Breaking the Code"

"We must be going about this the wrong way," said Jones.

"How can you tell if there's a right way?" Preston Volkers replied, as he ran his hand back through his hair, not combing it, just expressing frustration.

The two men sat in a shopping mall, outside a Johnny Rocket's diner, the remains of lunch still on the table, with a copy of the notes Preston's uncle had left.

"The only thing I can figure is that he intended to leave me with the access codes to the account in Switzerland. And without the codes, them damn bankers, you just can't get to the money."

"If it came to 'national security' we probably could, but I don't think we're there yet."

"His illness took him very quickly, too fast to do whatever he was trying to finish up. I don't think he ever expected this, this poem, or clue, or whatever it is, to be needed. I think he was trying to make compensation for his misdeeds, if I can describe them as mere misdeeds."

"It's tough," Jones said. "He being your uncle and all..."

"Yeah, his misdeeds may have been some awful stuff for all we know. In a way, he's responsible for whoever got killed in the truck robbery scheme. That's more than a misdeed. Still, he was my uncle and was awfully good to me."

"He wouldn't be the first government worker who decided it was acceptable to break the rules, justifying that it was for the greater good. Doesn't make it right, but it happens often enough," Jones said.

"Getting back to this note… this poem, or ditty, that he left– don't the accounts require a number to gain access?"

Jones nodded. "Yes, that much we were able to establish. Eight numbers, or a combination of numbers and letters. That and identification as an officer of Columbia Consortium. But like I said, other than a deal at a level way higher than us, and with very specific evidence as to why we should be allowed into those accounts, this is all we have to work with for now."

In the spirit of cooperation not always in evidence between the various federal law enforcement and intelligence agencies, and private services, Preston Volkers was granted temporary clearance to assist Ed Jones and Syd Swanson. Jones was surprised been that easy to get, even if Preston had previously had a fairly high level clearance when he was with the Feebies.

Exactly what they were trying to do wasn't very clear. Access to the Swiss accounts, of course, because of the hunch that a bundle of money was there, information about the illegal operations Karl Volkers had been running in the 60s, and establishing the true identity of Antonio/Abazini, see where it might lead, that much, at least.

The notes Volkers had left for Preston, meant to be found many years ago, gave only general information about projects Volkers and others—unnamed others— had initiated, using funds that had been available for 'as needed' situations.

"As far as we can determine for that period of time," Syd Swanson had explained to Jones and Preston Volkers, "the only person who would have had access to such funds, *and* would have been running agents in Southeast Asia was Karl Volkers. He doesn't name any of the other people. He does indicate there were only two others who knew the ops were off the books. We think we can figure out who they are—were; one of our suspects is deceased. But if Volkers broke the link, these operations would have died at that time."

"Any real idea of what those operations were?" asked Ed Jones. "His notes make reference but since they were in the 60s, I don't know what to make of them."

"Need to know," Swanson answered. "That's what I was told when I bucked this up. Personally I think it's a waste of time for anybody to follow up on his notes. Except for this money run deal."

"And that is why, dare I asked," piped in Preston. "I mean, why a waste of time on the other projects? Ancient history?"

Swanson nodded. "Right. Even if we can track back from his notes to connect to whatever agents during the relevant time frame were doing what where, unless it involves a murder or, well, lots of money, what good does it do? It seems the principals are dead and the field people probably thought what they were doing was authorized. The concern is that someone who was young, new, and ambitious back then is still around and may either still be involved in such operations, or at least knows something about them."

"That's not our concern, is it?" asked Jones.

Swanson's look said more than his words did. "No way, not your concern anyway. And officially, not mine. But off the record, from what I can gather the one suspect who is still alive is near-ancient, but is considered a respected statesman and he still keeps his hand in; special

127

commissions, and so forth. It wouldn't look good for it to come out that he was involved in shady deals back then. Things happened in those days that some people aren't too proud of. So, we are only interested in Antonio and Swiss banks accounts. Just do what you can."

"Isn't there something else we should be interested in, Syd?" asked Ed Jones. Swanson waited.

"Remember, Major Fears said that a guy thought to be one of ours was found in the jungle, shot dead. If he was one of ours, and Antonio did it, don't we owe him?"

"Officially, I was told it would be best if we forget about that. But the consensus is that he was one of ours—I'm not supposed to mention his name, though I think Fears already knows it—and he was probably one of Volkers' field men."

"So since when do we let a contract hit man take down one of our people and forget about it, even if it is decades later?"

"Oh, the usual secrecy crap. Embarrass the Agency, that sort of thing. But unofficially *they* hope that in the course of our work, we'll somehow deal with Antonio. At least that was the impression I got."

"*They?*" said Jones. "That's funny. I thought to the public we were 'they'! Now it's getting to where there are 'theys' within the 'theys'!"

Swanson smiled but turned serious. "Well, I've got no specific orders regarding how to deal with Antonio after we get whatever information we can get out of him. You know how it goes; deniability. We do have someone looking for him, trying to pick up his trail. At this point it would be nice to find out where he is and what he's up to. Your talking to him roused him enough to come to the United States. But why? He can't think the money from that robbery is here, can he? I'm surprised there doesn't seem to be more interest in that aspect."

Preston, who had sat quietly through most of the discussion, chimed in. "I hate to sound cynical, since I'm also one of those 'they' that the public doesn't always trust to do the right thing; but, I think it comes down to what you said earlier, Syd— embarrassment. Volkers used Antonio on the money run, and likely other things, too. Best to let Antonio alone lest he reveal things that the Agency might not want brought to light. Especially if, as you suspect, the guy who led up the illegal operations is some famous, gray-haired, wise and well-loved old geezer."

"Listen, this isn't easy for me either. What if we do find out this wise old geezer was involved in dirty tricks? Do I decide if they were dirty enough to make a stink over? Were crimes committed?"

"Using government money for personal operations? Yeah, I'd say that was a crime, but realistically, one that probably happens more often than we know," chipped in Preston.

"Sure, I understand that. But let's stay on course. Let's find this Antonio and find out why he came to the States; and why is he making such an effort to slip our tail after his contact with Jones? And what the hell is he up to?"

The mall was getting crowded and people were looking longingly at their table, so Jones and Preston began to walk.

"You were saying, Ed, about looking at this the wrong way. Any ideas?"

"What I was thinking was that your uncle expected you to find this stuff long ago, right?"

Preston nodded.

"So this poem he left, it would probably relate to something that was contemporary to him."

Preston stopped walking. "How do you mean, Ed? I've had that same line of thought but haven't been able to put anything together."

Ed pulled out a sheet of paper. They had reached a small alcove with a table near a coffee stand. "Let's get some coffee and look at this."

"He says, 'One number is the small bear's.' If we assume the *one* he's referring to is the number for one of the accounts, then it's a number that somehow ties in to a small bear. Agree?"

Preston shrugged. "Sure, but in *his* mind. I don't know anything about a small bear. Or a big one either. Maybe it's something that was going on in his head as he was dying, like Kane's sled."

"Maybe, but based on him setting up these accounts and leaving you the notes, the investments and all, it seems he was cognizant of what he was doing. At least until his last day or two when you said he went into a coma."

"So let's assume he's giving us a hint as to the numbers. So one number is the small bear's. Another is the big man in town. What town? What big man?"

"I think we have to start with the assumption he meant Washington."

"So the big man in town would be the president, right?"

Ed didn't respond at first. "That's seems too obvious. Think about back then, Preston. What did your uncle do, I mean outside of work? Did he have any hobbies or activities he was involved in?"

"He was pretty much a workaholic the last few years. He talked a lot about how he felt hamstrung at work. How the Agency seemed to let too much get past. At times I wondered what he was doing. You know, what operations he got involved in, but he never talked about his work in detail."

"He wasn't supposed to. Besides, that's spilt milk. His colleagues didn't catch on to him so how could you have known?"

"Baseball," said Preston, belatedly responding to Ed's earlier question. "That was his one diversion. He'd go to the games, read the sports pages. He took me to a few games too"

"Was he a fan of any particular team?"

"No, not really. He went to the Senators' games because they were the local team. I don't think he rooted for anybody in particular."

"Let's hit the book store," said Ed, slurping down the last of his coffee.

"For?"

"Baseball books. I want to see who played for the Senators in the late 1960s."

In short order they found a Borders bookstore and went straight to the sports section. Ed Jones picked out a thick paperbound book that contained, in mighty fine print, the detailed records of every player in major league history. He flipped to a section that gave yearly records for each team.

"What are we looking for?"

Jones started to speak, but only an uncertain "ah" came out. He flipped the pages, and then said, "Numbers, I guess. I'm just trying to figure what kind of numbers he would choose for those accounts. Baseball is all numbers, but I'm not sure what I'm looking for."

"Wouldn't he just pick random numbers? That'd be the safest. He certainly didn't pick his birth date."

Jones nodded agreement, then asked, "What about his favorite player's birth dates?"

Preston thought about that but couldn't think of anybody that his uncle was a particular fan of. "I don't know if he had any favorites. Let's see, late 60s. Yaz was a big star then. So was Bob Gibson, Denny McLain."

"Hmmm. Yeah, Pete Rose, and look, Frank Howard of the Washington Senators led the American League in home runs in 1968."

"Howard?"

"Yeah, Howard was the name of one of the guys on the truck."

"The other two were Jenkins and Walker."

Jones went to the index, looked up Jenkins. "Ferguson Jenkins, he was a big star for awhile, with the Cubs."

"The Cubs? No shit!"

"Look at this; he won twenty games in 1967, again in '68, twenty-one in '69, twenty-two in '70, twenty-four in 1971, and twenty in 1972. Wow!"

"Okay, great," said Preston. "But are you thinking what I am? Their stats? Hey, what about Walker?"

Searching the index again Jones found only one Walker who was active in the late 60s, and he wasn't a star. "Maybe it's just a coincidence." Jones continued to browse while Preston picked up another record book and also searched.

"Well, even the scrubs generate statistics. If my uncle wanted to use some of these stats to set up his account numbers, then the name Walker would fit along with Howard and Jenkins, the three guys who were in the truck."

"But does it mean they were involved, or are they just names and numbers?"

"Beats me, you're the spy, you figure it out."

"Thanks pal. I'm going to buy this book," said Jones. "We can take more time with it later."

"Maybe better not go back to the office with it."

"Right, might be hard to explain."

About this time Tony Abbott was driving along Van Nuys Boulevard, maintaining a safe speed and obeying the traffic lights and signs like a driver in training. The car he was driving he'd stolen out of the parking lot near a bar, probably someone who'd stopped on the way home from work for a drink or two. Let's hope it's at least two, Abbott thought.

He only kept it for a few miles, parked it with the valet at a large hotel, called a cab, and directed the driver to Burbank airport. There he rented a car using a driver's license and credit card for an Anthony Abruzzi, one that he'd never used before in the United States. The credit card was legitimate and the bills would be forwarded to an accountant he used in Naples, who would see to it that charges were all paid promptly. He drove east towards the Pasadena area.

A few miles away a scared teenager was on his cell phone calling for help. His car was stuck in the muddy ruts of a construction site and when he got out to inspect the situation he could hear a faint moaning sound. He'd located the sound, coming from across the road where an overturned car, one of its wheels still spinning, lay in the culvert. Having called for help he edged his way down the slope towards the sounds which were becoming fainter every second.

Frightened as he was, both because of his close call in crashing the car, and because of the trouble he feared he was in, the teenager behaved heroically in freeing Curtis Howard from the vehicle and stopping the bleeding from a wound in Howard's arm. The kid wrapped his shirt tightly around Howard's wound and kept it there until the paramedics arrived.

"You did good, fellow," the teen heard someone say, though his thoughts were more on how badly damaged his own car was.

It was not a coincidence that an Army lieutenant visited the injured store manager in the hospital, but he was unable to get in to speak to Howard. Major Fears had instructed Lt. Davidson not to call Jenkins, Howard, and Walker, but to visit them personally to get a feel for their lifestyle and see how composed they were under questioning. The lieutenant had been waiting for Howard at the store manager's home, trying to assure Curtis' wife that his visit was merely routine, though how routine could questions be when they were about a man's military service of over thirty years ago?

As Howard's normal time of coming home passed Emily Howard insisted the lieutenant be more precise as to what he wanted to ask about.

"Curtis doesn't even talk about his time in the Army, except sometimes on the phone to his friend, what's his name, Bill Jenkins. What could you possibly need to know about, Lieutenant? Does it have to do with those MIAs? I doubt if Curtis would know anything about anybody missing in action."

The lieutenant stalled until a phone call brought a gasp from Emily Howard. "He's been hurt in a car crash. I've got to run to the hospital, Lieutenant. I'm sorry, your questions are going to have to wait."

"I'd like to go with you."

"What for? He's been hurt! I'll not have you questioning him in the hospital. Now excuse me."

Lt. Davidson persisted. "Mrs. Howard, please, just one minute. You need to know something I wasn't going to mention yet."

She paused at the door, just long enough for the lieutenant to grab her attention.

"Two days ago I was in Michigan to see Bill Jenkins. But I got there too late."

"What do you mean, too late?"

"I mean he was dead. He'd been killed in an apparent robbery attempt."

"Good Lord! Curtis doesn't know that. Is that why you're here? Never mind, let's go if you want to go, I can't wait here any longer."

Davidson drove as Emily Howard directed him. And he talked quickly as he drove. "Did you husband ever talk about the time the truck he was in got robbed, and a man killed?"

"Oh yes, he's talked about that a few times, but not in years."

"Bill Jenkins was there too," the lieutenant said. "Yes, I know. I met Bill Jenkins and his wife many years ago. They came out to California to do all the touristy stuff and they stayed with us for a week or so. Curtis and Bill had a good time talking and reminiscing. They did talk about the truck robbery, but not to any more extent than anything else."

"It's a complicated story, Mrs. Howard. A few weeks ago it came to our attention that a man named Abazini, who was in the same unit with your husband and Bill Jenkins, and who had gone AWOL, was apparently still alive."

Emily looked at the lieutenant blankly, like, so what?

"The problem is," he went on, "that the man who died in the truck robbery may have been set up to be murdered, and the money was never recovered. I can't tell you everything but there's a good chance the money ended up in Swiss bank accounts, and this Abazini, who now may be using the name of Abbott, is trying to get to it."

"What in the world does that have to do with Curtis? Does this person think my husband knows where the money went? That's crazy!"

"Yes, ma'am it does seem crazy. We know your husband and Jenkins don't know anything about the money, but

Abazini, or Abbott, seems to think they might know something. We think he killed Bill Jenkins."

With a shock the concept hit home. "Oh, dear. So you think maybe Curtis' car crash wasn't just an accident!"

The lieutenant shrugged, "It could have been an accident, but I doubt it. We have good reason to think Abbott headed this way after the Michigan incident. I was here to warn your husband, for one thing.

"I hope you weren't too late, Lieutenant."

"I truly hope he'll be okay, Mrs. Howard. I'm also hoping he can tell me if this man Abbott has been to see him. I doubt he would have tried to crash your husband without speaking to him first."

Preston Volkers and Ed Jones enjoyed their second less-than-healthy meal of the day as they perused the baseball record book, trying to puzzle out how Karl Volkers' silly poem fit in with the names of the men on the money run. The trouble was they kept finding interesting tidbits of baseball minutiae that distracted them.

"You see this: in 1968 the American League batting champion only hit .301!" And Bob Gibson had an earned run average of only 1.12!"

"Gibson was in the National League."

"I know, I was just saying."

"Let's stick to Howard and Jenkins and Walker, shall we?"

"Yeah, that's fine, but what year do we look at? The money run robbery happened in between the 1968 and 1969 seasons."

"Maybe it doesn't matter. Maybe it's just the names."

"Well, if we're looking for stats that your uncle used as account numbers where the hell do we start?"

Preston put down the book, took a sip of coffee and said, "I need something stronger", and then, before moving on that idea, added: "It must just be the names, not the statistics."

"Enlighten me, please."

"Okay, Frank Howard and Ferguson Jenkins were big-time stars, but there is no one named Walker who was a significant ball player during that time."

"Well, this guy Luke Walker started fifteen games for the Pirates in 1969."

"Yeah, but that was after my uncle set up the accounts; after he was dead, in fact. Let's look at his clue again. It says: 'One # is the small bear's'. So what's a small bear? A cub, right?"

"Now Jones saw the light. "Jenkins! A Cub, for God's sake, and one of the guy's names is Jenkins."

"And the 'big man in town' isn't the president, it's Frank Howard, who was a big man at the time, both physically and in his hitting for the Senators. And one of the other guys is named Howard."

"That fits, right," said Jones. "But the third guy was named Walker, so how do you get that out of, 'And the third is the phantom's'?"

"Let me get a drink and then I'll explain. It's after regular working hours anyway." They were at Preston's house; he went to his so-called liquor cabinet– one shelf of the bookcase– and poured drinks.

"You should have thought of this, you're older than me."

"As I said before, smart-ass, enlighten me."

"Actually it just came to me", said Preston. "There's this comic strip, I used to read it though now I think it's only available on-line; *The Phantom.*"

The bulb going off in Jones head could have lit the sky. "Oh, my, you're right. His name, this crazy guy who lived in the jungle and could never die, was Walker, wasn't it?"

"At least that's the name he uses in polite society. So that gives us the three names, Jenkins, Howard, and Walker."

Jones raised his hands in exasperation, spilling some of his drink. "Dammit! So what do we have? We knew those names!"

Before Preston could respond, and at the time he had no good answer, Jones began to put the pieces together. "You're right, it's got nothing to do with statistics. He's just telling us that the key is the names of the three guys who were on the money run, not the baseball players."

Preston nodded, getting it now too. "At the time it probably seemed clever. Their identification numbers, I bet. Army IDs! He probably never even connected it with baseball until he realized he was deathly ill and wouldn't have time to finish up what he was working on.

"I remember now." The memory was becoming clearer to Preston. "A few days before he died we went out to a ball game and to dinner. He was talkative; told me about his cancer, that much he did. He hinted at other things, but I guess he couldn't get them out. He said he had a few things to clean up and within the next month or so we'd go over his estate. It wasn't something I wanted do dwell on, death, and all that. But as it turned out he died before we could talk again."

"So without specifically saying so, he wanted to indicate that the names of the guys on the money run are somehow tied in to these accounts he set up?"

"I'm betting on it now. Obviously he'd set the accounts up several weeks before. He probably thought it was clever, using the ID numbers of the guys on the truck. Later, well, who knows what goes on in someone's mind when they are suddenly facing the end of their time. He tried to think of a way to clue me in and knowing baseball, the names were familiar to him, except for Walker. But he knew that comic strip, so to him it made sense."

"Do you think it's the names themselves that he used?" asked Jones.

"I doubt it. Didn't you say the accounts need eight numbers or letters? Jenkins only has seven, Howard six, and Walker also six. But an Army ID number, back then anyway, had eight numbers if I remember correctly."

"Sounds too easy now."

"Well", said Preston, "I'm sure you guys have access to their IDs, and if not I can probably get them from the Bureau. Then I'm going to Geneva with this. If you want to come along, call Swanson and let's get going."

"I think we'll need one of the officers; either that or phony up one of us. That's what Volkers' notes say; any officer of Columbia Consortium, identified by legal passport, and the account codes."

"So we need the cub, or the big man, or the phantom, is that it? Or do we need all three of them?"

"If I understand Volkers' notes, any one of the officers will work, if he has the access numbers for all the accounts. You know, we may need to suck up to the major to get the ID numbers and find out where these guys are. It was fine for me to go to Italy to look for Antonio, and going to Switzerland is no problem. But if we are going to be operating in the States, Swanson was specific that I keep a low profile."

"Yeah, I can see that. But I have some resources I can use to at least find out where they live. I'll get started right away."

In a few hours they had the same information that Major Fears already had about Jenkins and Howard.

"Wait a sec," said Preston. "Didn't my uncle's note say that I, too, would have access?"

"Yes, with proper identification. I'm not sure what that means, but it could mean you have to have a passport in the name of one of the officers, with your picture in it.

We might pull it off, but if we get caught the bank could rightfully shut down any access at all until they could be sure who has a legal right to the accounts."

"Looks like we need to get to Kit Walker before Abbott does. Let's get started."

>>TWELVE<<

"The Set Up"

The CIA has smart guys, and Army Intelligence has smart guys, too. It is called *intelligence,* isn't it? But Francisco Antonio Abazini/Tony Abazini/Tony Abbott/ Santini Bruzzi/Antonio/Alphonse Antonini didn't survive on the streets, in the jungle, and in the world of espionage, treachery, and deceit by being stupid. Of course he knew was being tailed. He'd picked that up a few days after he'd settled into his hotel in the west end of the San Gabriel Valley, only a few miles from the home of Kit Walker, and was positive he'd picked it up the first time the tail appeared.

Actually, he was somewhat disappointed with himself that he had been tracked so soon, or at all. He thought he'd taken precautions, but if they – whoever they are— probably those goons at the CIA, know about Jenkins and Howard then they must figure me for the deeds. It's the years; getting old makes one careless, or not care enough, anyway. What it proved to Abbott was that the missing money was still missing, and that nobody yet knew how to get at it. And apparently nobody was going to pull him in for questioning yet.

Abbott changed motels just to see if he was right about a tail; he was. That's okay; he may have been older but Abbott was confident of his ability to lose the clumsy oaf when he wished to, and let him be when Abbott didn't care if he was followed.

The fact that he was being followed, and certainly the man he'd spotted did not look like FBI or like local police, meant that whoever it was, he wants to give me some room. Either they want to see where I go or who I go to see. If they have tracked me here it must be via Jenkins and Howard. And that also means that despite what he'd done to those two, for now Abbott wasn't going to be pulled in, at least as long as the Feds could hold off any local gendarmes.

He checked the Los Angeles Times for any story about Curtis Howard. Finding none he went to the Pasadena library to check other local papers. Still no luck, so he drove a few miles into the San Fernando Valley and bought a paper there. He finally found it, a story about the manager at a supermarket having lost control of his car and crashing into a culvert. The man had survived largely due to the fortuitous actions of a teenager who had crashed trying to avoid the first accident.

Fortuitous, my ass; bad luck. Howard must have been able to talk, but if he'd squealed to the police about me, I don't think they'd be merely tailing me. Someone who wants to keep me on a long leash got to him. So they think I can find a way to get at the money, and if I do, I have to find a way to get to it without them knowing I know. And whether it was still four million dollars or many times that, if it was safely invested in securities via a Swiss bank account, it would be enough to keep him comfortable for the rest of his life. If I can figure out how to get my hands on it. If those fools would just let me have my fair share, we could work together.

Abbott spent several days just thinking. He hadn't formulated a definite plan before he came here but had just reacted to the visit by Jones. Now he wanted to slow down, think about things and maybe see what was happening around him. And he had to be careful with Walker because he was the only one left of the three. If he doesn't know anything, then what?

Abbott had known Kit Walker, at least slightly, for a few weeks in Vietnam. It seemed to make a difference in his thinking as he planned how to approach Walker, as opposed to the other two men, who he'd barely known.

Jenkins and Howard certainly didn't know anything useful, and maybe Walker doesn't either. Abbott's snooping had shown him that Walker lived in a much wealthier neighborhood than the other two men, that he didn't go to work in the mornings, and he and his wife both drove late model, expensive cars. He was probably retired or works from inside his home. Well off, but not exactly the life of someone who might have made off with several million, but he might have had just a small cut, who knows? It was times like this Abbott wished he had a trusted partner. He'd always preferred to work alone and had found that in this line of work those who trusted the least, lived the longest.

At worst, his new-found shadow was a pest, but not yet a problem. Abbott had already found that the tail didn't show up until well past sunrise. They must assume I'm a late riser. So for several days Abbott had risen while it was still dark and was gone before the dark Ford showed up in the parking lot. It amused Abbott but also made him wonder who was following him, as he was sure neither the CIA nor the FBI would be so inept. Sitting in a café drinking coffee Abbott grinned internally at the thought of the man arriving and sitting outside for hours, then feeling chagrined when he sees Abbott return, after thinking all day that his quarry had been inside.

When he located the Walker house he realized that it being in a tight niche in a cul de sac, there was no practical place for a stakeout. He would be easily noticed by the neighbors or by Walker himself.

In back of the Walkers' house was an empty field, scoured by hundreds of gopher holes, which served as the last slope of the mountain range that provided for gorgeous views from the Walker backyard patio. A small park set among a grove of oak trees separated the field from a water reservoir site. From the park, trails wound up into the mountains. Some of the trails meandered deep into the small canyons that sliced upside and across and made this range particularly rugged. It was not unheard of for people who lived within site of these trails to get themselves lost and in need of an experienced team of rescuers, including bloodhounds. A few careless hikers had lost their lives.

Abbott explored the area and found that from a couple different spots on one of the trails he could see the Walker house and the backyard. Sometimes he could stand here for a long while before another hiker passed. But rather than let himself get too conspicuous he searched further and located a setback up and above the main trail that provided a comfy hideaway. Sitting there, he was virtually invisible from any hikers on the trail below. By cutting off a few small branches from the bushes that surrounded this nook he was able to make a window in the leaves from which, with binoculars, he could see everyone who came in or went out of the Walker house. When he wanted to observe he either left his motel early, before his shadow arrived, or took great effort and care to dodge Inspector Clousseau, park his car a half-mile or so from Walker's house, then hike the rest of the way to his observation point. *Good thing I'm still in reasonably good shape, for an old fart,* he thought.

For the most part his spying proved uneventful and boring. He did this for a few hours for several days, just to see if he could spot any patterns to their life, or anybody interesting coming or going. Any longer became uncomfortable. But one day he stayed later, until it was near dark.

Abbott saw the Walkers go for a walk with the dog. So he waited two more evenings in the tree to see if this was a regular event. They were gone for forty-five to fifty minutes the three times he observed this. So the next time he saw them leave with the dog he hurried down the trail, dashed across the field, praying he didn't step into a gopher hole, and sidled up to the fence that separately the Walker backyard from the field and the trail that ran perpendicular to the row of houses that included the Walker's. He saw no one around and as it was nearly dark didn't expect to be surprised by any hikers at this time of night.

He miscalculated the problem of climbing over the fence. It was a chain link one with jagged ends, and while on the field side it was only about five feet high, because the ground sloped down so sharply the drop on the other side was about nine feet. And, it was difficult to brace himself for the jump down because of the jagged ends of the fence. Finally he felt balanced enough to leap; just as he did he felt his shirt snag on the fence and trying to reach back he sliced his arm on a broken link that jutted out.

"Shit!" he spat out as he fell to the ground, relieved that at least he hadn't sprained an ankle. He wrapped a handkerchief around the gash that was already showing a line of blood that appeared dark brown in the dim light. He was sure no snoopy neighbors had seen him because the trees and bushes all around the house made it nearly impossible for anyone to see into the yard, except from the way he had just come.

The back door was unlocked. He looked at his watch and realized it had taken him almost twenty minutes to get to the house.

He didn't steal anything and was careful to put anything he moved back to where it belonged. The house contained an office, so it was possible Walker did some work from home. There was a safe, but Abbott left it alone; he could probably crack it but did not have the time. There was nothing to indicate Walker was hiding any large amounts of wealth, but there could be jewelry in the safe and he could have a fortune in stocks. There wasn't going to be enough time to try to crack into the computer system either. He did see several postcards on the kitchen bulletin board from someone named Rick, sent from several different countries. Abbott thought he heard the family returning as he slipped out the back of the house and through the yard to the place behind the fence where he had first entered the yard. He now realized he could not possibly climb up from this side.

Searching the area, Abbott noticed a walkway on the far side of the garage. There was a gate, but it was unlocked. Trusting souls, these people. Careful not to drag his feet or step on anything that might make a noise, he edged up to the front of the garage. Trash bins crowded this end of the walkway but Abbott was thin enough to squeeze by without making a sound. Now, if someone came out the back door, he was caught; he'd have to simply run for it. But no one came out and he began to quietly and slowly step down the driveway. He heard the dog bark and the sound of the doggie door flip-flopping as the dog dashed outside, barking louder now. At this point Abbott dove into the bushes that separated the Walker house from the neighbor.

"What is it, Bret? A possum? Hope it's not a skunk."

Abbott lay in the bushes, not breathing. A half-minute passed and he heard the back door open again and the man and dog go back inside. His makeshift bandage had come off and his arm was bleeding steadily. He re-wrapped it with the soiled handkerchief. Then he boldly rose and walked down the driveway of the Walker's neighbor, looking every way and at every window, to see if anyone was eyeing him. He saw no one and walked down the street, swifter now, bitching under his breath at his clumsiness. It took Abbott another ten minutes to get to his car. He reached into the glove compartment and took out a flask of whisky. He poured some on his wound, and then took a long swig.

The next morning Abbott stayed in his motel all morning. Shortly before noon he drove to a sports bar for lunch and a beer. For several days he'd been going to this same place at about the same time of day. He made it easy for the dark Ford to follow him. The following morning he again rose very early but he returned to the same sports bar for lunch, and grinned inwardly when he saw the dark Ford there, waiting for him. Trained him quickly, I did.

Predictably the next morning the car was there early; maybe had been there all night. It was time to deal with the situation. He walked directly to the car, and watched as the man, in uniform, straightened up in his seat. Abbott pulled out a knife, unsheathed the blade and stuck it deep into one of the tires. The man jumped out of the car. Abbott noticed several chevrons on his sleeve. The soldier was younger than Abbott but his paunch showed he'd been a desk jockey a number of years. Probably hasn't done a pushup since the Reagan Administration.

"What do you think you're doing? This is a government car," said the sergeant.

Abbott didn't answer but simply kicked the man in the knee then punched him in the ample stomach as the man bent over with a yelp. He then pushed the man down to the ground and kicked him again in the ribs.

"Tell your boss, whoever he is, to get somebody competent to follow me!"

For good measure Abbott stuck the knife in another tire then calmly walked back to his room. He had his bag packed and he threw it into his car as the soldier sat up against his vehicle, breathing deeply. It would be interesting to see how long before a new person would pick up his trail. Abbott made it easy by going to the same bar for lunch, but he always managed to lose the man when he wanted to go back to his new motel.

For the next few days Abbott continued his surveillance from high above the hills overlooking the Walker house but changed his pattern so he wasn't always there at the same time of day. He also explored farther a field. He came across a dilapidated wooden bridge that at first looked too unsteady for him to set foot on. But it held and he ventured deeper into the woods until he was stymied by immense and thick brush and wild, tangled plants of all sorts. He was sure that through the thicket was the edge of the reservoir.

His daily hikes had made him accepted by other hikers and joggers but he varied the time of the day he went up the trails. With the binoculars his hideaway in the trees gave him a near- perfect view of the comings and goings of the cul de sac in which the Walkers lived. He wasn't sure what he was looking for. One Saturday he was in the hills earlier than normal; it was still dark when he started up the trail and he had to watch his footing carefully. He had decided he enjoyed the morning mountain air and he could espy the Walker house at a different time of day than he had done before.

Strangely, it appeared that someone else was watching the house. A car he hadn't notice in the neighborhood before was parked a few houses down and facing away from the Walker house. Through the binoculars Abbott saw Kit Walker come out to get the newspaper. He watched as Walker looked at the paper, waited for the dog, and went back in. As he did so a man got out of the car and walked towards the Walker house, punching buttons into his cell phone as he walked.

Abbott hurried back down the trail and while he was reluctant to break into the car in the broad daylight he felt it was a chance he needed to take. It was still early enough—and a Saturday—that there was a good chance no neighbors would be up and about yet.

Breaking into a car, even one with an alarm, was child's play for someone with the mercenary's varied skills. The rental form was for a Rick Walker. Abbott retraced his steps and returned to his own car, parked at the bottom of the cul de sac, closer than he usually parked. He waited until the man who must be Rick Walker returned then followed him to his motel.

What does this all mean? Who was the other Walker? Abbott would pay a visit to the motel later, when its occupant was gone. In the mean time he would return to his own motel, clean up, and then continue his habit of lunch at the sports bar he had been frequenting. He'd done this to set up a pattern, one that might be used later, depending on whether he wanted to meet Kit Walker alone or in a public place.

Just after noon that same day Abbott was not really too surprised when he saw Kit Walker and the other man enter the pub. They are here to meet me, so who is chasing whom, he wondered slyly. Well, let's go make their acquaintance.

It had been so obvious they were there to scope him out that Abbott could all but break out laughing. He almost wanted to say, hey, let's work a deal here. You want the money, I want the money, let's put together what we know and we can all get rich. Trouble is, Abbott had no idea of how to get the money—which he now suspected was locked up tight in Swiss bank accounts– and if they were too convinced of that, they might figure they had no use for him. Good old Karl Volkers did something with it, then he died, and come to think of it, do I even know his death was natural? Yet, the CIA agent Jones would not have come to see me unless they thought the money was still around. And maybe I know enough about Volkers that we could do some trading of info. He recalled a story from his mentor.

There was a time when Karl Volkers was a young and physically strong man. But at age thirty he was a few years older than many of the men thrown into combat. Never exactly lean, he was durable and in good condition. He'd had to be to handle the heavy machine gun he'd toted all across France and Belgium for a year starting in June of 1944. While most of the guys in the unit he started with had been wounded, killed, or transferred long before they reached Berlin, Volkers and Owen O'Shea had managed to stay together the entire time, fighting together, freezing in the snow together, patching up wounds, and being cold, hungry, and tired together most of that year.

They each were awarded a couple of bronze stars and a purple heart. And they could have had several of the latter if all their wounds were counted. Each collected several flesh wounds that one or the other had patched up without ever having reported to the medics. You couldn't keep running back to the rear lines every time you got a scratch when the fight was at the front.

Serendipity made them an acquaintance of a young captain who was looking for men for special kinds of work post-war. Undercover work to keep tabs on the country's enemies. Before Hitler died in his bunker and before Hiroshima was annihilated it was clear that a tension would exist between the victorious armies coming towards each other from the east and the west. And the world had, temporarily at least, had its fill of war. So it was going to take subterfuge, tact, and espionage to stay ahead of the game. The Office of Strategic Services was glad to get a Karl Volkers—even his name would help in post-war Europe. Some people had at first mistaken him for a captured German when the organization was in the recruiting stage. Owen stayed on briefly but one day he quietly disappeared.

The OSS was officially disbanded after the end of the war, but a small unit, the Strategic Services Unit, as part of the War Department, remained active, albeit little known. After a short time back home, Karl Volkers continued to learn the secrets of the men who trade in secrets. For a time he worked for an agency called the Office of Reports and Estimates.

Fittingly, Karl Volkers spent several years in Germany, learned the language well enough to cross over to the East, and survived several close scrapes on both sides of the Berlin Wall. And every time he or one of his cohorts survived an escapade that had left them appreciating their life in the West—or worse, when one of them did not return—they would gather and toast to each other, or to victory, or to just plain survival. They damned the Reds and when the evening hours got larger, and then began to get smaller as the new day began, and the bottles were near-empty, they bitched about how they were expected to perform miracles of espionage on the slimmest of budgets. There was never enough money for the equipment they needed, never enough money to pay people who would provide vital information. It wasn't long before most veteran field agents found there were ways to make the funds stretch, whether it was the time-honored tradition of salesmen in padding expenses, or the more serious form of selling desired Western goods on the black market, and writing reports explaining how the equipment had been lost during a hazardous escape or stolen by traitors. It was a dangerous game that became far too normal an activity.

Being a field agent in the line of fire is wearing, psychologically more than physically. Those who survived with their body and sanity intact eventually got their opportunity for promotion, which usually meant a desk job wearing a suit. Most of these men opted out of that when first offered the chance. It sounded too boring for men who had lived on the edge for so long, but the spy game was becoming one of more brains and less brawn.

In late 1947 the Central Intelligence Agency was formed for the purpose of evaluating and coordinating intelligence reports, in the interest of national security. The young captain who had been Volkers' boss and friend in the post-World War Two days in Germany saw this as an opportunity. He explained it this way to Karl.

"I want to be in on more important things than sneaking across the wall to find out how well next year's potato crop is expected to be, or sneaking out another one of those damn atom bomb scientists. And, I want some semblance of a personal life. And I'll keep you in mind, Karl, when you're ready for a change."

"You think a feisty redhead like yourself can settle down to an administrator's job?" "We'll see. Call me when you get ready to come back to the states, Karl."

"I'll do that, Walter."

It was less than a year later that Karl sat one chilly evening in a café in East Berlin. Despite the damp cold he sat at a small table outside, the better to move fast if the need arose, than to be trapped inside. One hand held the coffee cup and the other a newspaper, though he hadn't read much of it. Coming towards him on the sidewalk was a man dressed similar to Volkers; a heavy black coat with the collar up around the neck and a woolen cap pulled down over the tips of the ears. There was enough familiar about the man so that Volkers wasn't worried. The man sat down at the table.

"Hello, O'Shea, long time no see."

"Please, comrade, no names."

"I wondered what happened to you, but I heard you were in the East. Working against us?"

The man ordered coffee, shook his head. "Nah, for you, actually. There is a man who needs to stay here in Berlin."

"A scientist, by chance? There are a lot of them around, but mostly we and the Russkies are trying to get them *out* of Germany."

"This one's record is so bad that your people don't want to take him, but they don't want the other side to get him either. So I will try to see to that. Pays well, Karl, much better than your organization."

Volkers nodded agreement, picked up the cup and held it close to his mouth to let the steam warm his face before he took a sip. "You're probably right, but what's the future hold? What will you be doing ten years from now, twenty years?"

"Don't think I haven't thought of that. I've met a lot of people here and there since the war ended. I never dreamed so many people were in the business of stealing and trading secrets! And I still have connections in the neighborhood back in Jersey. I'm going back soon. This job and maybe another and I'll have enough money."

"Good luck, hope you survive long enough to get home."

"And you? Have you been back yet?"

"No, but soon, I think."

A man walked by, stopped to look at the menu posted on the side of the wall near the door, then walked on. Neither of the seated men looked at him.

"So what happened with Walter, the captain with the bad hair?"

Volkers couldn't help but laugh although the movement generated a chill. "Yeah, the redhead. He always worried that the hair made him conspicuous so he dyed it. But it was such cheap stuff that every time it rained a little it washed out the black dye. He's in Washington, running things now."

"Instead of running, eh? Not smart like us."

"Right," said Volkers. "Not smart like us, sitting here shivering and wondering if the next person who walks by will arrest us or stick a knife in our kidneys."

Volkers took a deep slug of the coffee and said, "I have to be going, old friend."

"Hope I didn't mess up anything for you," said O'Shea, pointing with his head in the direction that the passerby had gone.

Volkers wouldn't answer or make any committal to O'Shea's comment. He rose, said, "I would have let him know if there was a problem. He'll meet me around the corner. Wants to go west, young man, and build rockets for the capitalists."

"Maybe see you some time, comrade." Volkers left and O'Shea took a long look around before he too got up to go, pulled the collar of his coat closer around him and left, walking in the other direction.

The story O'Shea told Tony didn't mean much at the time. It wasn't until later, when Tony remembered the other story O'Shea had told him about meeting the redhead from the State Department.

"The point, being, Tony, is to remember these people, cultivate their friendship, or at least, be on friendly terms, don't let them know too much about you, and don't say too much to people you don't trust implicitly. Just listen and learn. People like those two can be useful when they need a job done and don't want to use their own people. They pay very well. I'd be surprised if we don't hear from them again some day."

"I didn't realize you had so many contacts in Europe, Mr. O'Shea."

O'Shea smiled, said: "Most people think I'm a petty crook in a New Jersey neighborhood running some gambling and extortion. That's fine; it gives me a home base. I still like the old neighborhood. But I made good contacts here after the war, working for the OSS and then on my own. Lots of money to be made if you're careful. I never stay in Europe after a job here. I return to Jersey and play my role as a big fish in a little pond. But you've been to my house Tony; how do you think I can afford all that? Stick with me and I'll keep you rich and busy."

And in a flash Tony put it all together; Walter, the red head. O'Shea had said he and Volkers had worked together for the OSS for a brief time. Then they apparently joined ranks again at the CIA. But Walter didn't stay with the CIA; he ran for office, won two terms in the lower house then one term as a senator. He could have been re-elected but had an opportunity to return to the Central Intelligence Agency at a time when the Agency was floundering and needed a tighter rein on reckless agents, and a more efficient use of its limited—supposedly limited—funds. After several years there serving in a manner satisfactory to almost everybody of both major political parties, he ran again for the Senate and was easily elected again. I'll bet all the money I didn't get in the truck robbery that it was he who was Volkers' boss for their secret operations. And what's he doing now, that old son-of-a-bitch. Must be over eighty years old now but Walter Cushman was wealthy, respected, still consulted by every president and often used as a goodwill ambassador. I wonder how much the CIA would pay to know that Cushman had been Karl

Volkers' protection? I wonder how much they'd pay to know about the file the captain gave to Volkers? Not to let it be known, but to keep it from being known! It had to be important: too important to keep, and too important to destroy. So what happened to it over all these years? Maybe it's a good thing I brought copies of those pictures with me; must have been good instincts.

Later he would prepare a package and have it mailed to Ed Jones. No, better yet, I'll mail it to Kit Walker, he decided. Might be interesting to see what that stirs up.

So now Tony waited to meet Kit Walker for lunch. What Tony Abbott had no way of knowing was that the team of Ed Jones and Preston Volkers were, at the same moment as he sat at the bar at 'Sports 'n More' in Glendale, California, on their way to meet with Kit Walker They needed him to come to Annemasse as one of the officers of Columbia Consortium. They had been able to obtain the Army service IDs for Walker, Howard, and Jenkins, and they felt sure these numbers, along with one of the officers as set up by Volkers over thirty years ago, would gain them access to the accounts set up by Karl Volkers. If they did, and were able to extract the funds, Abbott's efforts would be for naught.

>>THIRTEEN<<

"Rick"

Rick Walker's road to major general, with the possibility of another star, would seem unlikely to anyone who knew that at one time he went to a seminary to consider studying for the priesthood. It didn't take long to realize he was too young to give up the potential of his youth, and was not ready for the discipline the priesthood would require. Still, he ended up in an avocation that required great discipline and obedience. His career hit all the required stops along the way: combat service in Vietnam, the Rangers, and graduate school on the Army's dime. Along the way he managed to survive parachuting into Cambodia and a bout of malaria. Then it was back to school at the War College, a teaching assignment at West Point, service in Europe in a tank battalion, duty at NATO headquarters, and an exemplary performance as commander of an armored brigade in Desert Storm that all but assured his first star.

About ten years in he knew it was time to either decide to stay for the duration or get out. In a chance meeting, when both he and his cousin Kit Walker happened to be visiting the old hometown one Christmas season, they had a chance to discuss their lives since college. Other than a few hours in Saigon several years ago they had not seen each other, Kit having moved to the west coast, Rick bouncing around wherever the Army needed him.

"It seems the kids go to a new school every year. And Marilyn is constantly changing jobs."

"She's a nurse?" asked Kit.

Rick nodded. "Yeah, so she doesn't have a problem getting hired. Still, it gets tough. And you know, I'm a homeless person."

"Say again?"Yeah, I'm never in one place long enough to buy a home and settle down. If they kicked me out now, I don't know what I'd do."

"I don't think that's going to happen."

"What about you, Kit, what have you been doing?"

"I'm in a small accounting firm. Mostly I consult with companies who have had problems with taxes, or need help setting up basic accounting systems, or a whole variety of financial problems that they need some advice on. I tried going with one of the big firms, but it was too regimented, too cutthroat. This suits me better; I've got more control over my work, and more free time, too."

Rick's decision to stay with the military had proved sound as he moved along steadily up the ranks, even though the kids had to keep changing schools. Likewise, Kit's decision to stick with his accounting and auditing work, combined with sound –and some lucky— investments, had proved fortuitous in solidifying the financial future for he and his family of wife Jane and their son Chris.

General Rick Walker was close to retirement now. He didn't really think another star would be forthcoming and wasn't sure he wanted to strive for it anyway. He was tired and ready for a change. Of course, he had to admit being stationed in Hawaii was not bad duty. Having been recently on the east coast of the United States, it had taken him awhile to get used the starting times of the football games. He was more or less committed to another year working in Special Forces covering the Pacific and Asia, after which he would likely become a civilian. As he sat in his office staring out the window at the blue sky and the blue water, instead of studying the paperwork in front of him, he realized that yes, he was ready for more time contemplating blue skies and less time on reports and projects. And then the phone buzzed.

"Thanks for coming by Rick. I need a favor"

"Yes, sir. What can I do?"

"How about a quick trip to California?"

"Quick? General Lytle, I'm leaving with you on Monday for…"

"I know, I know. I mean there and back, real quick. I have an old friend at the Defense Intelligence Agency who would like some help with something. He specifically asked for you."

General Rick Walker scratched his chin and did a quick mental checklist of who this might be, and why. He did not come up with an answer.

Rick Walker was not a tall man, not short either; as average as you can get. He had a look that made people, upon first meeting him say to themselves, 'where have I seen him before?' Those who met him when he was in civilian garb usually figured it out: oh, yeah, a little chubbier and he'd look like Jack Nicklaus. Rick could only wish he could play golf like Jack Nicklaus.

"It's a little mysterious and a little complicated." General Lytle picked up a file that was in front of him on the desk and dropped it back down. "You can take this with you and read it on the plane. Here's the crux.

"Seems there's some old, I mean real old, business, involving an international mercenary, who, if you can believe this, once was in the Army and served in Vietnam in 1969. He's popped up due to some old business regarding the robbery of a truck full of money."

159

Walker's eyes widened, his mouth gaped just a bit. He started to speak.

"Remind you of something?"

"I have a cousin, in California– he was involved in something like that– he and I were in Vietnam at about the same time. He had been drafted. He told me a story about a truck full of money being robbed. Said that was probably the most danger he ever faced during the time he was in Nam."

"Good, you're halfway up to speed already," Lytle offered.

"So I'm to go see my cousin? Is that what this is?"

General Lytle leaned back in the old leather chair that creaked when he moved, and gathered his thoughts. "The way I'm told is this mercenary, name of Abazini… well, he has had several names as you'll find out when you read this;" he pointed at the file.

"He may be a soldier who was in the same company as your cousin at the time of this robbery. He wasn't at the scene of the robbery but he disappeared the same day; thought to have gone AWOL. But where the hell do you go AWOL in Vietnam?"

"Well," interrupted Rick Walker. "It's crazy, but lots of guys did. Most of them showed up in Saigon a few days later, drunk, busted, and scared to death."

"Yes, well, this one never reappeared. And his Army records were virtually non-existent. So it may come as no surprise to tell you that the CIA is also looking for him now."

"Hmmm. The plot thickens. But how is Kit, my cousin, involved? General, nobody thinks he's got any of that money do they? I mean, he's done okay for himself, but I can tell you he's no millionaire. And I know he wasn't involved in that robbery."

Waving him quiet, the general said, "Hold your horses. Nobody thinks that. But one man was killed during the robbery, and there's no statute on murder."

"Murder? Then this wasn't a death by enemy action?"

"Officially, yes. But there was always a question about it because of the daring of the scheme and because the money was never found, and because this man Abazini, or whatever he called himself, was never found. Another thing is that it appears a CIA agent was killed, too, at about the same time, although what his involvement was I'm not clear about."

"So what nerve was touched that brings this up now?"

"Again, rather complicated. The DIA and the Army think the CIA knows where the money is...in a Swiss bank, no less, and are trying to get the money. Also, they may be trying to get to this mercenary."

"To grill him or kill him, sir?"

"Yes, Rick, good thought. The answer to that I don't know. General Asher has a hotshot major working for him; apparently he is pretty good at digging around and following a faint trail. If this guy Abazini is their AWOL man—Abbott, as he calls himself now, that in itself is no big deal. But if he was involved in the robbery, and the death of the driver, than they are more interested. And... I don't think they've missed the point that all this money, if it's been invested all these decades, is lot more now than it was in 1969."

"With all due respect, sir, this sounds..." began General Walker.

"Yes, I agree, a little far-fetched. And it's really none of our business. But, Charley Asher asked me if I could con you into talking to your cousin, see if he can find out anything."

"I don't get it. How is Kit supposed out find out anything?"

"Seems that Major Fears, Asher's man over at DIA, has tracked down Abazini and has people watching him. They think Abazini is contacting the men who were at the site of the robbery. His actions indicate that he—Abbott,

I guess I should call him to avoid confusing ourselves, thinks these men may know something. In other words, he for some reason has decided after all this time the money is still up for grabs. The Army wants to know what Abbott finds out."

"And they want to use my cousin? Could it be dangerous?"

"Now you see why I want you to go."

"Yes sir. Maybe this is why you're the boss and I'm not. But I don't get it."

"Because, Rick, General Asher's bloodhound, Major Fears, will go see your cousin about this anyway, and the CIA probably will, too. I figure you can at least alert your cousin, maybe keep it safer for him."

"Could he be in danger from Abbott?"

The general only shrugged. "What they've asked is for your cousin to meet Abbott, sort of by accident. This Major Fears will catch up with you in California. You can call him before you leave and make whatever arrangements you need to. But I'd advise you not to pressure your cousin. He's only a civilian; he's got less reason to get involved in this we have. So I'll give you some leeway here. Our meeting in Bangkok isn't until Wednesday. If you need to stay longer to help your cousin, do so and just plan on meeting me when you can. Rick, Charley Asher and I are old friends, so I want to help him. But more important, once your cousin's name came up, I wanted you to know about this. So figure that you're doing this to help him, because to tell you the truth I'm concerned that some of these people, people in our same line of work, Rick, can get reckless with other people's lives."

The visit with General Lytle seemed like weeks ago, but it had been only a few hours. Now Rick was in California, and had already set up his cousin to meet with Abbott.

Sunday gave Rick and Kit a chance to both relax and work. Nine holes of golf with a beautiful mountain background, brunch with Jane at a Pasadena café, and then back to Kit's home to meet Major Fears and talk about the meeting with Tony Abbott, set for Monday.

"If you're nervous about wearing the bug you don't have to do it, Kit," said Rick.

This was not what Major Fears wanted to hear and his disgusted look said so. Kit was intimidated by Fears' grimace but Rick wasn't.

"I mean it. You're under no obligation."

Fears gambit was to remind the cousins that the death of a soldier, even if it happened over thirty years ago, was still unexplained, implying that maybe Kit Walker was still a suspect for the death of the money run truck driver. Actually, Fears had learned from Swanson that the notes left by Karl Volkers appeared to clear any of the soldiers who had accompanied the truck.

Again, Rick was not buying it. "Careful, major. This is a civilian, not someone you have any command over."

"Sorry, sir." Fears had a bad habit of forgetting when officers senior to him were around. This guy will never make colonel if I have anything to say about it, thought Rick Walker.

On the other hand, he is thorough and you've got to hand it to him for having tenacity and a clever mind. And it may be that he's honestly interested in clearing up a possible murder.

Kit would wear a bug; a listening device. The cumbersome sort with wires and a microphone that was difficult to conceal, not to mention uncomfortable to wear, was history. The cliché pen microphone was too obvious. This device was simply dropped in the pocket of Kit's shirt. It would pick up normal conversation and background noise and voices could be filtered out later.

A van would be parked in the lot along side the restaurant where Kit was meeting Tony Abbott. There was no reason to think Kit would be in any danger. Of course, Major Fears hadn't said anything about Bill Jenkins and Curtis Howard.

"Major, are you sure there isn't anything else Mr. Walker should know?"

"Such as, general?"

"The fact that Curtis Howard and Bill Jenkins have both been viciously attacked, and that Jenkins is dead. Did you not think maybe your general and my general share relevant information?"

For one of the few times in his career Fears was at a loss for words, but only momentarily.

"I, I apologize, general, Mr. Walker. Of course I knew this information, but I didn't think it was something I should mention as yet. After all, we have no proof that Abbott is the one responsible."

"And come to think of it," added Fears, on the offensive again. "Why do you think he seemed to so easily admit to you that he was Abazini, when he has to know that the Army was looking for him when he disappeared from your company after the truck robbery? How can we be sure this is the same guy?"

"Give me a break, major. Didn't your own people get an ID on him from Curtis Howard? I thought that was how you got on his trail in the first place."

Kit raised his arms as he cut in, "Hey, hey, hey! Wait a minute. I didn't start this. You guys, or... or somebody else did. I'm willing to help but you're pushing me now. I'll let you smart guys figure out why he would do that. Maybe he feels safe after this amount of time."

Rick interrupted, "If he's been some international hoodlum who had the wherewithal and the assistance to pull off this truck robbery, escape with the money, and escape from the Army while in the middle of a war in the jungle, then he's pretty resourceful. Not somebody to take lightly."

"Except somewhere along the line it appears he lost the money," Fears added.

"Anyway," said Kit, "I'll do this one meeting. I'll try to talk to him about 'Nam and about the money run and see where it goes. And after the meeting is over you guys need to promise he doesn't follow me."

"Well, Kit, seriously, if he wants to he already knows where you live. Hey, don't even worry about it. But just in case that's why I've arranged for all of us to stay at a place in Orange County, enough miles away from here to be safe, I'm sure. Some friends of mine are away traveling for several weeks and we are free to use their house."

"And we do have a man on him all the time," said Fears. "That's how we have been able to track his movements. He's not going to get away if we don't want him to, and he's not going to be any danger to you."

"Major," said Rick, "you seem to be in contact with the CIA people involved in this, but I get the impression you and they are not sharing all your information. Is that true?"

"I think it's more the other way around, sir. I mean, all I know is that Abbott is likely the same person as Abazini, the one who disappeared in Vietnam right after the truck robbery. We think he may have some information about it, and we think the man who was killed, the driver, may have been involved too. Except he certainly didn't expect to be shot. Most likely he was promised a certain amount of money to take a detour.

"Certainly I'm also interested in what happened with the money. And I think the CIA has some idea that the money is still recoverable, but they aren't sharing everything with me yet. Maybe a general might help with that, sir."

Rick nodded, thinking he needed to contact General Lytle real soon.

"Alright, alright," Kit interrupted. "Let's go over everything one more time before I change my mind. But I really don't think you can expect him to admit to attacking Jenkins and Howard, if that's what you expect."

Later, after Fears had left, Rick and Kit reviewed what had been discussed in the meeting, until it got personal.

"Ought to send him to Iraq," was Kit's suggestion.

"Yeah, he'll get his chance, I'm sure."

"How about you? Won't they need experienced generalship there?"

Rick laughed, almost a forced laughed that was as much a grimace. "Probably so, but I've been there, don't want to go back again. I've talked to a few people. There doesn't seem to be any plan other than to beat the crap out of the Iraqi Army and then, presto! Iraq becomes a peace-loving democracy. Bullshit. It's not going to happen. The history is there for anybody willing to look and listen. You can't just expect a country with no precedent of democracy to miraculously become one because we say they should. At least for the American Colonies there was some background regarding the rights of the governed, even if England was still ruled by a king."

They were sipping wine, munching on cheese and crackers. Kit waited for Rick to continue. "Besides, my planned retirement date has been approved, not that they couldn't change my plans. But I've got a three-star who wants to keep me close and has projects scheduled for me right up until the last hour of my last day.

"However, having said that, just between us and the walls…"

"Don't forget I'm still here, you guys," chimed in Jane as she entered the room. "Dinner's in the oven so I thought I'd join the boy's club, unless you've too many secrets to talk about."

"Join us, sweetie," said Kit, not caring any more whether Rick was concerned about what they talked about. Jane certainly had a right to know what Rick was going to be doing.

"Kit just asked me about Iraq. I will be going there, after my meetings in Bangkok. But it's a temporary deal; no more than two weeks—he said hopefully. But I shouldn't be saying anything so don't worry about it."

"I just hope it's only two weeks. So keep your head down and your helmet on, or your armor, or whatever it is you're supposed to wear."

"I will Jane, I assure you, I will."

They filled her in on the meeting with Fears, and Rick's plans to meet Abbott for lunch the next day.

"And if I object at this point?" Jane asked.

"Well, correct me if I'm wrong, Rick, but I think at this point it doesn't matter if I meet Abbott or not. And it doesn't matter that I went to see him the first time. It seems he is out to contact people involved in the truck robbery, and he's going to do it one way or the other."

"Contact? Let's see, he killed one guy, tried to kill the other; you call that contact? I should say so!"

"At least Jane doesn't beat around the bush," said Rick.

"He's not going to try to hurt me in the restaurant, Jane. And we are going somewhere Rick has set up for us, and as far as I'm concerned we aren't coming home until Abbott is either in jail or out of the country, and whatever is going on is done and over with."

"Well, dammit Rick, what *is* going on?" Jane said. "What does this guy want?"

"Best guess is that he was awakened by the CIA in their investigation. Abbott suspects the money from the truck robbery is still floating around so he's trying to find out who might know something about that. He probably realized that Jenkins and Howard didn't know anything but figured they would be contacted soon and confirm that Abbott had been to see them. So he had to eliminate them."

"Eliminate! They way you guys talk! He's a cold-blooded murderer and now he might be after Kit!"

"But Kit's the only one of those who were there who's currently functioning. And, to Abbott, you two may look to be financially much more well off than Jenkins and Howard. So he may still be wondering if you have some of the money."

"Hell, if I'd had four million dollars all these years, well, hell's bells, I don't know what I would have done with it, quite frankly."

"Rick, I'm sorry, but this is upsetting. Let's eat dinner."

At dinner the talk was light and fun, chatting about Rick's and Kit's adventures when they were kids. Playing ball, acorn fights in the woods, then golf when they'd outgrown kid's games. Eventually they again reached the time of their lives that this weekend had brought back to memory.

"You were at Walter Reed for awhile, weren't you Kit, before you went to 'Nam?"

"Yeah, boy, talk about the contradictions of life." He shook his head and for a few seconds stared straight out, lost in his thoughts."

"Specifically…" Rick hinted.

"Well, as an example, look at your work, Kit. You're a soldier. You've had to fight battles, kill people. But I know you're not a person who would enjoy killing people."

"Of course not. It's, well, I'm not eloquent enough to explain it any better than old Robert E. Lee did. You know what he is supposed to have said, don't you, Kit?"

"Wait," cut in Jane. "I think I remember; 'It is good that war is so awful, else we would come to love it so'. Or something similar."

The men were impressed. Jane couldn't restrain the developing smile. "I'm not a dummy, you guys."

"No, anything but, sweetheart. As I was saying about contradictions—the year or so I spent at Reed was one of the best times I ever had. I came to love Washington. My work was easy, five days a week, weekends off."

"Weekends off?" asked Rick. "Gimme a break!"

Kit laughed and raised a hand as in giving an oath. "I swear, I only spent one Saturday morning in all the months I was there doing extra duty. The key was to get your butt out of the barracks early on Saturdays before some pushy NCO came around to roust bodies for work crews on the hospital grounds. No matter how late I got in on Fridays I learned to rise early and clear out. Go to the mess hall or get in my car and take off for the day. There was no end of things to see in Washington, or as far as I could go on the weekend. There were concerts in Rock Creek Park, a weekend in New York City, the ocean; not to mention the Smithsonian."

"And the contradiction?"

"The contradiction is that there were such awful things to see I can't think of the good times in Washington without also remembering those horribly wounded guys at the hospital. You know what one of my jobs was?"

Rick shook his head. "You may have told me before but tell me again."

"I tracked all the incoming wounded, to see that the guy in the hospital fit with the info on his dog tag, and to see that his pay caught up with him. I'd see these guys all over the place; in the wards mostly, but the ones who were able to get out of bed I'd see in the mess hall or out taking a walk, learning to use a prosthetic. Some with no arms, or no legs, or one arm and one leg. I remember one guy who had one side of his face missing. Saw worst stuff there than I did in 'Nam."

"Not the greatest dinner conversation, but I understand what you mean," Rick said.

"C'mon guys. No more talk about war," Jane, the peacekeeper said. "If we are going away I need to pack some things. Just please promise me, both of you, to be careful tomorrow."

"Of course," the cousins said simultaneously. "Haven't we always been?" Rick added, with a wide-eyed smile.

As early evening darkened into night and timer lights brightened the windows up and down the neighborhood, Tony Abbott was enjoying his own type of domestic scene. He'd broken into many a house, motel, vehicle, and virtually anything that could be locked, more times than he could ever remember. So one more motel room was a piece of cake. But even as he was engaged in the deed he realized it was quite possible that this guy was CIA or Army or some intelligence agency, and it might be difficult to hide a break-in. So he would take as best care as he could, but not worry about it too much. After all, somebody is following him already anyway, so who cares if they know I'm aware of it?

There wasn't much to find. Naturally there was no wallet or other personal information. Very few clothes were in the drawers and closet; obviously a short stay was planned. However, among the clothes hung in the closet was a military uniform. It had stars to show this was a general, though Abbott could not recall the exact rank the stars designated. The nametag spelled 'Walker'. There was a leather folder in a drawer and it did contain one piece of paper with some interesting information. He may have been careless, or maybe didn't care, or more likely didn't expect anybody to break in here. A sheet of paper with the name, 'Maj. Gen. Richard Walker, Sp. Op. Ft. Shafter, Hawaii'.

So, *this Walker* is military, probably Army Intelligence. What the hell does the Sp. Op section do? So what do I make of this? Is it possible...yes, it is quite possible that the Army and the CIA are working together on this. Something happened to reopen interest in that old truck robbery...I can't imagine what...but both agencies want something; the money, surely, but it may be the CIA wants to find out if I knew anything about who was running extra-legal operations. The Army; hard to imagine what their interest is after all this time. But I think I need to push some buttons by Monday, right after lunch, whether I find out anything or not from Kit Walker. It is time to stop running around in circles.

>>FOURTEEN<<

"Lunch"

It was not a happy Jane Walker who left her home on Monday morning, along with the cocker spaniel, Bret, and two suitcases. It had been decided Jane she would go ahead, not wait for Rick, and meet her husband and the general later that afternoon.

Kit didn't like leaving Jane in the house alone while he was gone, and she suggested she go along with Rick. That idea was kiboshed because Rick wasn't sure what would happen after the lunch meeting. Major Fears was inclined to pick up Abbott and hold him. But Rick felt they would be pushing the edge of whatever authority they had. None of them technically had any legal authority to grab Abbott and hold him.

As had become his practice lately, Abbott had risen early for his hike up the path in the foothills overlooking the Walker house. By now he knew well the spots on the path from where he could see the Walker house. He stopped at one such place and feigned enjoying the scenery. A gray layer of smog was already evident, though not as noticeable as some days. As he watched he saw someone come out of the back door of the Walker house. He raised his binoculars and saw that it was the woman. She had a suitcase which she put into the trunk. Then went back into the house and got another piece of luggage. The dog followed her to the car.

So the woman is taking luggage and the dog. Which means she's not coming back anytime soon. I just might have time to follow her for awhile and see where she goes before I have to be back to meet Walker.

When she went back into the house Abbott began to jog down the trail. He'd been on these trails enough recently so that anybody who saw him would recognize him as an early morning exerciser. He needed to get to his car and to a place he could follow her before she took off, which appeared to be imminent.

Abbott pulled onto the cross street just as Jane was coming out of the cul de sac. She gave not a second thought to the other car and Abbott waited till she began her turn onto the next street before he slammed to a stop, turned around, and followed after her. He spied her about a block away and settled in for what should be any easy surveillance. At the same time he took precautions to see if anyone was following him, or any one else following her. He figured he could pursue her for up to two hours and still have time to get back for the lunch. Of course, if she went to the airport he'd have to forget about tracking her.

He had been in the area just long enough to know she wasn't headed for either the Los Angeles or the Burbank airports. When she turned south on the 57 Freeway he figured she was not going for a plane, and besides, she hadn't dropped off the mutt anywhere. Settling in he checked his gas gauge, figured he was okay for a couple hours. Once he passed her on the freeway and then let her pass him just to note if she showed any concern, but she seemed not to notice anybody else on the road.

That was true as Jane was deep in thought about what might happen today with Kit and his lunch meeting, and what might happen after. They had decided to stay at Rick's friend's house for a few days, and then they would fly to Hawaii. Bret would have to stay in a kennel while they were gone. It had been agreed, at least by Rick and Kit, to hell with Major Fears, that even if Abbott talked Kit into any further meetings Kit would simply agree, but would not show up. Rick or Fears or someone else would fulfill any future rendezvous with Abbott.

She turned off on La Paz Parkway and Abbott followed, letting one car get between them. Another five minutes and she began to slow, apparently looking for an address. Abbott stopped a hundred yards back and pulled over. He waited and watched as she pulled into the driveway of a house at the end of a street called Calle Costado. Good, Abbott thought, no neighbor on one side and quick access, in case I need to visit here later. He eased the car forward and drove by slowly without turning to look. As Abbott reached the corner he peeked over to check the address and to note that the woman was taking out the luggage. So this is where she will be, but what about her husband?

Abbott parked around the corner and waited. About twenty minutes later the woman came out again with the dog. They got in the car and she headed out. He followed again, staying far enough back to also see if someone else was following. She took several turns and eventually ended up at a dog kennel. That's good too, Abbott figured; no dog in case I need to go in. He again waited and followed her back to the house.

His errand over Abbott reversed course and headed back to Glendale. He stopped for gas then returned to his motel to freshen up, pack his clothes and gear, and check out.

"I need to leave a few days earlier than I had anticipated, I'm afraid. Some new business developed," he told the desk clerk.

"Certainly, sir. I hope you found your stay satisfactory."

"Yes, perfectly so. Listen; because I have to leave early I might get a call or even a visit by some colleagues. I left messages but just in case anyone asks for me may I leave a forwarding address?"

"Of course, sir. We'll see to it any callers get that information."

Abbott left a false address which should, in case he needed it, give him some extra time.

Being a Monday the pub was not as crowded as other days. Abbott made sure he got there early and selected a booth as far away from the bar as possible and closest to the exit. He spied a beat-up and rusty white van parked across the street and made a mental note to keep an eye on it. Oh, all these years of being so careful. Most of the time when he'd gone to extreme measures to assure his safety, it had turned out to be superfluous. But a time or two his extra care had saved his life. And there may have been more times he simply could not know if his caution had made a difference or not. It was not just habit, but a work ethic, and he was working. He knew where the Walker woman was, and he'd know where Kit Walker was when they met for lunch, but he couldn't be sure where the other Walker was, the general; maybe in that white van, for all I know, he mused.

As Kit neared the parking lot of the sports bar he spoke down towards his pocket.

"Ah, testing, anybody hear me?"

"We hear you. Don't look at your pocket, Kit."

"Oh. How'd you know…"

"Because it's an automatic action for someone who's never done this before. If Abbott sees you doing that it'll be a dead give-away. Just talk normally and we'll either pick it up or we won't. He's in there already so he may have picked out a table, and it might be in a noisy area. If so, that's just tough for us. Don't try to talk loudly or do anything unusual."

"Kit, this is Rick. Just wanted you to know I'm here too. I spoke to Jane. She's arrived safely at the house in Orange County; nothing to worry about."

"Thanks, Rick. Okay, I've reached the parking lot. I'll stop this chatter for now."

Kit admitted he wouldn't have minded if Abbott hadn't shown. Hearing that he was in the bar already actually calmed Kit. *Waiting would have been harder; I might have lost my nerve then.*

"I saw you drive up so I ordered beers for us; this okay?" Abbott said when they met.

"Sure, fine." *How did he know what kind of car I have?*

"So this is great, seeing you after all these years." Tony was now totally immersed in his persona as Tony Abbott, all-American, the European accent he could bring out at will now stored away for when he returned to his hide-away in Le Dione or some other village.

"Kind of odd," Kit suggested. "I've never kept in touch with the guys I knew in 'Nam. I think everybody just went their own way once they got out."

"Yeah, me too. A time best forgotten, eh?"

Beers and menus arrived. Kit took an inordinate amount of time to decide on food, because instead of reading the menu he found himself thinking of what to say once he had ordered. But as he'd been advised, best to let Abbott steer the conversation. When the waitress left he raised his mug and pronounced a toast, to Bien Hoa, and to not going back.

"Here, here," said Abbott, and Kit thought Tony's cheerfulness sounded phony.

"You mean you don't want to visit Vietnam again and see what it's like?" Abbott asked.

Kit shrugged, sipped the beer again. "Now that you mention it, it might be interesting to see. But I can't say it's high on my list of places I'm dying to visit."

"Can't imagine I'd recognize anything, anyway. I don't know if the airbase is even there anymore. Or the village for that matter."

"Well, if you go, Tony, say hello for me, but it won't bother me if I never get back there."

Kit realized he'd already forgotten about the bug in his pocket, then suddenly thought of it and wanted to peek into the pocket of his shirt to be sure it was there, but resisted by forcing himself to gaze around the bar. It wasn't too noisy so he figured the van must be getting good reception.

Abbott studied Kit, but the thought that he might be bugged Tony had dismissed as irrelevant. Even if the rusty, white van outside—which still sat where it had been when Tony arrived—was picking up the conversation, he couldn't imagine what someone expected to hear anything they didn't know already. To the contrary, it was Tony hoping to get info from Kit Walker.

"Oh, sorry, I was watching the TV," Kit said, as he realized that Abbott was speaking.

"I said, so you never connected with the other guys who were on the truck with you? You know, the time you got hijacked."

"No, I really didn't. And it wasn't a true highjacking; they didn't take our truck. We unloaded the boxes; come to think of it, I wonder why they did that instead of taking our truck. They just left it there."

"Well, I wasn't there so I can only guess, but maybe they figured it would be too noticeable.

"So the guy who got shot, did you know him well?"

Kit shook his head. "Hell, I didn't even know his real name! He was at Tan Son Nhut when I landed and drove me over to Bien Hoa. After that I didn't see him for several weeks. Then, out of the blue, he was back at the 11th. I rode with him over to Long Binh a few times, but we never got into much conversation. He said he was from Idaho, so people called him 'Tater', but the crazy thing was he didn't even like potatoes. So there you go."

"I just wondered why he got shot when nobody else did."

The food arrived and Kit remembered back to the questioning they had endured after the robbery. He'd put it out of his mind after all these years, though he did recall that one of the officers questioning them got rather pushy about the subject of Tater getting shot.

"At first, we were questioned separately. This one captain, for awhile I thought he suspected me of knowing something about the robbery. Christ, what did I know? Did I get anything out of it other than scared out of several years of my life! Jenkins and, what was his name… Howard, they said they got the same feeling. A little scary, but once it was over, the issue went away, at least for me. I can't say for the other guys."

Abbott said nothing, and Kit added, "I even went on one more run a few weeks later. Somewhere around that time Jenkins and Howard got transferred. I never saw either one of them again. No, I saw Howard in Long Binh a few weeks later, after I got sent over there. But that was it."

"So you never wondered if they had any part in it?" Tony asked.

Here it comes, Kit thought. Rick and Fears and the engineer in the van perked up.

Kit tried to act surprised and confused by Tony's question. "Any part? In what, the robbery?"

Tony smiled, laughed a forced chuckle. "Well, I just wondered. There was a hell of a lot of money, and they never found it, did they? And Jenkins and Howard, you said they got transferred. Maybe it was for more questioning. Or maybe someone higher up was in on it with them. Makes for an interesting scenario."

"Boy, you've got some imagination. I told you I saw Howard in Long Binh. He was doing fine. He said he'd heard from Jenkins, so it seems they were just going about their duties. Hell, beats me but I can't see how they could have been in on anything."

Abbott laughed again, "Yeah, well, it'd be interesting to see what they did after they got out. But that's so long ago."

"Tony, we had around four million bucks in that truck. I know, I counted it! It strains my imagination that any G.I. would have been stupid enough to get involved in a robbery in broad daylight, in Vietnam, and expect that anybody was going to actually pay them. For what? What did the robbers need us for? "

"Didn't you take a detour?" Abbott threw out the question casually, trying to look more interested in getting the waitress' attention so he could order another beer.

How did he know about the detour, Kit wondered. But it's a good question.

Did you know he was going to turn on that side road? Did you see the 'Detour' sign? Did you ask him why he was going that way?

No. No. And No, Kit had answered the captain's sharp questions.

Later, when he and Howard and Jenkins had had a chance to talk, they all said the same thing. No; after all, we were in back of the truck. We couldn't see where Tater was going, all we could do was sit there, bouncing around, and look out the back of the truck. We didn't see a 'Detour' sign when we walked back, either.

Kit was getting tired of this, had barely tasted his sandwich, and worst of all, he was bored with the whole thing. Kit said, more accusingly than he had intended, "What's this, this obsession with that old truck robbery, Tony; what the hell do you care for anyway?"

In the van Fears said, "Shit, don't push him!" while Rick smiled.

Actually, Tony liked it that Kit was getting edgy. It's the reaction he wanted.

"Obsession? Walker, do you have any idea what four million dollars, invested at maybe five, or even eight percent interest for over thirty years, is worth today?"

"Who gives a shit? The money's gone, man. Used to buy weapons, or drugs, or maybe buried in the mud of the jungle. It's history. And why are you so interested now after all these years? And why would you think it's been invested somewhere? Where, in Hanoi? You think the North Vietnamese robbed that truck so they could invest it in securities? Don't be crazy, Tony. Have a beer, forget the money."

"Hey, calm down, don't get mad. I have good reason to think it's still around because I was approached by, let's say, government people."

"You? You were approached. Why you?"

Abbott scrunched up his shoulders and a silly smirk spread across his face. "They must have some idea it's still around and are desperate to find it. How the hell do I know? I just thought that if they approached me, they did you. And maybe there's a reward in it."

"That makes no sense; what would either of us know about it?"

"Well, I don't know anything", Tony lied. "But I just figured, well, maybe you did, or knew something and forgot about it."

"Hey, I drive a nice car, I've got money in the bank, a 401K plan, a house worth more than I could afford to

181

buy now, but I haven't got a clue about any four million bucks. Sorry, Tony, and I don't want to get involved."

"So you can't help, old buddy?"

Old buddy? Kit was almost angry now, but he calmed himself. "Tony, we might have been acquaintances for a short time in 'Nam, but that's a long time ago. We haven't known each other since then and I was never friends with Jenkins and Howard, so I really know nothing about them. Why don't you go track them down; maybe they're actually Warren Buffett and Bill Gates in disguise."

"Hey, that's funny! Okay, well, forget it."

Kit remembered that Fears had wanted him to prod Abbott on any contact he may have had with Jenkins and Howard. "So, ah, you wondered about those other guys, Jenkins and Howard. Have you had any contact with them? Asked them what they remembered?"

Leary now, Abbott hesitated. "No, hell, I wouldn't know where to find them." He looked straight into Kit's eyes and knew that Kit saw the lie. And Kit could see in Abbott's eyes that the latter was aware Kit wasn't here to reminisce about fun, travel, and adventure in the Army.

After a minute of an uncomfortable silence Tony asked about Rick.

"So did you and your friend have a good visit?"

"You mean my cousin?" It dawned on Kit that he didn't remember having mentioned before that he and Rick were cousins.

"Oh, your cousin? I thought he was just a friend."

"Well, both. He's ah..." *do I say he's here, or does it matter?*

"It was just a short visit. He had to leave yesterday."

The remainder of their lunch was filled with small talk about jobs, travel, and families. Kit was eager to end this and never see Abbott again. Abbott was ready too, he was just thinking of how to handle the white van still parked outside. He was also thinking of the curiosity that Kit and this Rick–who is apparently in some military intelligence agency– are cousins. *Maybe this is who I need to deal with?*

Okay, Abbott thought. They've probably heard everything we've said, but so what? I still think this guy and the other Walker, the general, must know about the money, else why did they arrange for Walker to bump into me? So they think I can find the dough, I think they can, so is this a big fuckin' waste of my time? Well, I've come this far; there is one more thing I can try.

"This was great, Walker. Next time I'm in town I'll give you a ring," Abbott said abruptly.

"Sure, do that," Kit replied. *That's the last thing I want.*

They walked out together, both making an effort not to look at the white van. They are so conspicuous, so amateurish, Abbott thought. Fools!

The goodbyes and shaking of hands were obviously disingenuous, and Kit was glad it was over. Turning to walk towards his car Kit felt a tug on his arm. Tony was leaning towards him and Kit, startled, tried to pull away. But Tony leaned towards Kit and spoke directly into his ear in a whisper.

"And Walker, tell your friends in the van that the offer I made to Jones still holds. And a sample of what I can give him has already been sent."

Kit gaped but Abbott hurried away before Kit could respond. Kit stood there for a moment and watched Tony walk towards where his car was parked. Then he spoke for the microphone. "Did you hear that last part? Anybody?"

"What last part, Kit? We saw him speak to you in the parking lot but there was sound interference from a passing truck."

Kit got into his car and sat a moment.

"He said to tell the guys in the van that the deal he offered Jones still holds, and that he has sent a sample of what he has."

"Bastard's been onto us the whole time," a voice from the van said.

Kit stated to drive off. "That's it guys. Sorry if I wasn't much help. I'm heading back home to pick up the rest of our luggage and then I'm off to meet Jane."

"Okay, Kit. We'll see you there later," answered Rick.

"Let's follow Abbott anyway, even if he is on to us," Kit could hear Fears, in the van, command.

Abbott quickly fouled up the driver of the white van by exiting via the adjoining gas station instead of the restaurant parking lot. Then he made an illegal u-turn after doing a quick scan for any police vehicles. He floored it and in his rear view mirror could see the van caught at the traffic light. He thought he could see the driver slam his hand on the steering wheel.

But even as he put two blocks between them Abbott could see in his mirror that the van was not giving up. Free of the red light it was weaving in traffic, making it only too obvious that they were after Abbott.

Maybe I should let them catch me to see what they do. No, I can't expect they'd read me my rights and politely say they'd like to ask me some questions about a truck robbery thirty-some years ago in Vietnam. And oh, yes, a couple of dead people, too, if you don't mind, sir.

He'd studied a map of the area a little, and knew that a freeway ramp should be coming up soon. It was, but the ramp had one of those damn stupid lights to slow down the oncoming freeway traffic. I definitely do not have time for this crap. He sped through the light, causing one other driver to slam on his brakes, and tore onto the freeway. Almost recklessly he sped onto the first off ramp. A glance in his mirror revealed the van but he wasn't sure if the driver had seen Abbott's exit.

He was in luck; the light at the bottom of the ramp turned green and he took a sharp left. Two hundred yards away was an entrance to the freeway going the other direction. The light was red; Abbott slowed to a near stop, checked the traffic, then swerved around the car in front of him, and made a left against the red light onto the freeway ramp. He watched his mirror as much as he watched where he was going for the next few seconds and soon was sure he'd lost the van.

Now, back to the house he had trailed Walker's wife to. Abbott was sure that Kit Walker would not be going there immediately. He couldn't know for sure, but figured Walker would be meeting first with ...well, whoever the hell put him up to this.

Kit was unaware of what was happening once he left the parking lot. He headed home to tend to a few things before he drove down to meet Jane: check the sprinkler settings, bring in today's mail, and pack a few things he'd forgotten to put in the bags Jane had taken with her.

What Major Fears had not told either of the Walkers was that he had been in recent communication with Syd Swanson, and that the CIA was sending an agent, Ed Jones, along with an agent with some special credentials, a Preston Volkers, formerly of the FBI– to make it legal, since what the hell was the CIA doing operating in the States– to see Kit and would meet up with him at the Walker house when Kit returned there.

When Kit reached home, watching in his rear view mirror most of the time, fearful that somehow Abbott would be following him and there would be no one following Abbott, the black car sitting in front of his home looked for all the world like an omen of trouble.

"Shit, now what", Kit mumbled.

He parked in front, got out and waited for the two men in the car to come to him. They were not young, did not have that ambitious and careless look about them that Major Fears displayed. Both men showed signs of gray hair which to a senior citizen like Kit—depending

185

on what age you are considered 'senior', this made him relax a little, thinking for a split-second that these men will be reasonable and easy to talk to. But who are they and did Rick know they'd be here?

"Kit Walker?" the one in the dark suit asked.

"Yes...and you are?"

The other one in a dark suit offered his credentials. "I'm Preston Volkers, on special assignment for the Federal Bureau of Investigation." (Only a medium-size lie).

"And I am Ed Jones, an affiliate of Mr. Volkers." He didn't offer an ID, and Kit looked him square in the eye, smiled, and Ed Jones knew that this Walker fellow is pretty smart; he's got me pegged and that's just as well.

"I was expecting the CIA," Kit said, looking again at Jones.

"The Central Intelligence Agency doesn't normally operate within the United States, other than to maintain an administrative function," Jones said.

"Come on in, but I'm in a bit of a hurry."

As Kit led Jones and Volkers to the front door he punched numbers on his cell phone.

"Yes, Kit," answered Rick. "We lost him."

"Then you'll be hurrying down to where Jane is, right?"

"Can I ask who you are calling, sir?" interrupted Jones.

Kit answered instead into the phone. "Rick, I've got a Mr. Volkers of the FBI and his assistant (he again smiled at Jones), a Mr. Jones. They want to talk to me. Should I?"

"Put one of them on", said Rick. As he began to hand the phone to Ed Jones Kit heard Rick say, "Step on it, to the address I gave you in Orange County."

As Kit led them inside he stooped to pick up a package that had been delivered by UPS. Curious, he opened the padded brown envelope but as he did he was able to hear portions of the telephone conversation on Preston's end.

"We've met with Fears; he was supposed to inform you that we were on our way. Check with him."

Kit couldn't hear Rick's response. "You bet I will! In the mean time, let's cut to the chase here. Jones is CIA and shouldn't even be there. But we can let that pass. But I want Walker here—he knows the address—in an hour. You can follow and when you get here we'll have a pow wow. And between now and the next hour I'll be on the phone to General Lytle, just so he's kept up to date."

"That's fine with us, general. We aren't trying to pull anything tricky here, that's why Fears was informed. It's seems maybe you and he need to compare notes. Here's Mr. Walker, so please tell him what you want him to do."

"I'm supposed to go on a trip with my wife in a few days, guys, so I hope you're not going to mess with my plans, are you? I've decided playing James Bond isn't as much fun as I thought it would be. Let's get going...no address, just follow me. We'll talk about this when we're with General Walker."

Kit had said this after Jones and Preston explained that they wanted Kit Walker to go to Switzerland with them, because he was an officer of a company called Columbia Consortium, a company Kit had never heard of. And, they wanted him to help them gain access to accounts which contained, they believed, many millions of dollars of government money. And wouldn't he love to do the patriotic thing and lend a hand?

And why not Switzerland instead of Hawaii for a vacation? Kit vocalized the idea and it was explained, because we aren't staying any longer than we have to and we'd feel real bad if anything happened to you after we

187

left, so it's just you, not your wife; someone will watch over her.

"Unless you're ready to kidnap me at gun point, we go meet my wife and General Walker first. No other way."

"That's fine, Mr. Walker. Now please, don't forget your passport."

"By the way, look at this." Kit handed Jones the contents of the envelope he had opened. Inside the larger envelope was a smaller one on which was written, '*for Ed Jones.*' Kit had instantly rationalized that since the package was addressed to him, and these guys in his house were not exactly invited guests, he had every right to see what was in it.

The smaller envelope contained several pictures, each of two men who appeared to be having a conversation.

"What are these?" Jones asked to no one in particular.

"Let me see," said Preston.

"This must be what Abbott was talking about in the parking lot, when we were leaving," Kit suggested.

"They look old, and are all black and white. Recognize these guys?"

Kit shook his head, Preston said, "No".

"Any idea where they were taken," asked Kit.

"No. But wait, let me see these..." Preston said as he took the pictures from Jones and looked at them more carefully.

"This guy here, I think it's my Uncle Karl."

"Who?" said Kit.

"I think at this point it's best you don't get too involved in these pictures," Jones said to Kit.

As Jones drove, following Kit to where they would meet with the others, Preston continued to study the four pictures. "I'm sure this man is my uncle. I don't know who the other person is. It looks like the other guy has a package that he's giving to Uncle Karl. Except Uncle Karl doesn't take it from him until the third picture. Kind of grainy, but I'm pretty sure it's him."

"They look like they were taken with a telephoto lens, don't you think?"

Preston agreed. "But I have no idea where they're at. It looks like they are standing on a bridge…or maybe it's a highway overpass."

"The lab guys may be able to figure it out."

Abbott had avoided the tail of the white van from the restaurant, and sped as fast as he thought he could get away with, but he wasn't sure that going to visit Mrs. Walker was a workable option, at least not yet. It could well be that they have someone down there with her already. Then he remembered: those suitcases were too light. Was she packed for a long trip or was she only taking enough things down there for one day and then would return home? I might have to adjust my plans again, but I need to check this out very carefully.

He knew he'd never get to Orange County ahead of anybody if he stopped now, but decided it was time to turn in his rental car. He then called a cab, had the driver take him to another rental company, explaining he didn't like the other, and rented an entirely different type and color of car than what he'd been driving. This all cost him over an hour.

He drove unhurriedly on the freeway south to Orange County. When he eased his way onto the street where he'd followed Jane Walker earlier this morning he saw the white van parked a half block away. He pulled to the curb a hundred yards short of the van, waited a moment, then slowly made a u-turn, thinking that maybe he was getting too old for this.

>>FIFTEEN<<

"Jane"

Jane Walker was a teacher at heart. She had started at the kindergarten level, moved up to second and third grades, and then to the sixth grade level, hoping to have some influence before the taste for learning new things that most children had early on was lost for good. If she had any faults it was her independent streak and her stubbornness. She wanted to do things her way because she knew her way was better than others—not humble, but she was usually right. Her insistence on doings things her way would soon propel her into danger the likes of which she never imagined.

The trouble was, Jane enjoyed teaching history and geography, subjects most kids found to be boring. It's a difficult task to convince a twelve-year old that it's important to know what went on in the world before today; why what happened made the world the way it is now, what mistakes were made, how to learn from what went on before, and the differences in culture amongst the people of planet Earth.

Not only were many students bored by the study of history but a depressing number of them couldn't read the textbook well enough to understand what they were supposed to learn anyway. Jane found herself spending half of her time teaching reading before she could get to the required texts.

Eventually she started to write up vignettes about events in history that she thought the students might find palatable, and which she believed were important to convey to them. Another teacher who had drawing skills helped out by adding illustrations to give life to the pamphlets Jane wrote. Topics like, 'Why the American Colonies Rebelled,' and 'How Columbus' Voyages Changed the Course of History', were energized by the illustrations and Jane's text, admittedly somewhat 'dumbed-down' from standard history books.

The pamphlets, which she handed out gratis to her students, since she was still required to use the standard textbook, took on a comic book look to them, which drew sneers from some other teachers, but were more often than not praised for that approach.

"Reminds me of those comic books I used to read when I was a kid, where they took famous stories and put them into an illustrated format," reminisced a co-worker.

Eventually the toll of dealing with undisciplined students, bitchy parents, and asinine school board polices led Jane to quit her teaching job and concentrate on her desire to provide educational materials that could disguised as fun reading material. If comic books they be, then fine, if kids will read them and maybe learn a little about the world around them. It was giving in some to the world of flashing lights and staccato imagines that appealed to kids, but sometimes you have to adjust to what's going on around you, she reasoned. With her friend Cindy, a co-dropout from the teaching profession, they eventually developed a series of softbound booklets that they sold on-line and at some of the local art fairs. They didn't make a lot of money, but were having fun and felt they were accomplishing something.

With their son on his own and developing his own career and life style, with Kit recently retired, and with a decent amount of savings and considerable equity in their property, Jane was enjoying her life as much, if not more, than ever. Even this temporary move from her home as a precaution didn't upset her too much, because she felt confident that whatever the issue was that had brought Kit's cousin Rick into their lives would be settled safely and expeditiously. Then, they could go enjoy the sun and waters of the South Seas.

Kit had called from his car, Rick had called, then Kit called again from home, saying that he would have company following him. *Company? Already, I can see our trip falling apart!* Of course, they were making last minutes plans and weren't even sure yet exactly what accommodations were available. Cindy worked part time as a travel agent so she was trying to squeeze them in somewhere on one of those last minute deals. Meanwhile Rick was also trying to arrange accommodations at the guest quarters at his home base in Hawaii.

She wasn't about to excuse herself from the discussions between the men who invaded the house shortly after Rick and Kit called.

"Some of what we have to discuss is sensitive information, Mrs. Walker," Major Fears suggested.

"Fine with me," Jane said. "We'll all speak in hushed tones; would that be alright?"

Amid his laughter Kit said, "Okay, no need to get too sarcastic, sweetheart. I agree; if these gentlemen want any more involvement on our part, everything has to be out in the open. No other way, I'm afraid."

No one objected and Rick stepped in to take command. He wanted to assert a position of authority before anyone else tried to.

"I'm going to assume leadership because, first of all, someone needs to and I have the military rank here," he glanced briefly at Major Fears, whose scowl showed his unhappiness.

"Also, because it's the Walker's wish that I do so, and, because as far I can tell, Mr. Jones has no authority here at all, and I believe, Mr. Volkers, at this point there is no basis for the FBI to assert any authority over the Walkers."

Rick turned to face Preston Volkers, who nodded.

"Can't argue that, general. My concern is more personal than official. Besides, I'm *former* FBI."

"So, why don't we round up some refreshments and figure out exactly what the situation is."

Not because she thought she needed to, but just because she'd been in the house for a few hours and had a better notion where to find things, Jane offered to procure beverages, on the proviso that no discussion begin without her.

"The first thing I want to say is that I expect everyone here to reveal all and everything they know, and please, no national security issues. I can't possibly see where that is a factor here."

"Excuse me, General Walker," cut in Fears. "Is it not possible that Abazini is connected to terrorists groups in this country?"

"Do you have the slightest evidence of that, major?"

"No sir, I just thought…"

"Then it is not an issue. Before I summarize my own involvement I want to be assured, major, if the Army will be providing security while the Walkers are staying here, and also to keep an eye on their house in Madre Hills."

"Yes, we are. DIA, technically, but I have people on temp duty. Lieutenant Davidson will be arriving here soon, and of course Sergeant Rowlins, the driver outside in the van, can assist, too."

"Alright, if I say anything that anyone here understands differently, please speak up."

Rick thought a second, sat back in his chair, and began. "As I understand it, a question regarding a deposit box at a bank in Washington led Mr. Volkers—Preston– to contact the CIA"–he glanced at Jones–"and this led to the discovery of another box, in a Swiss bank, along with numbered accounts in the bank that have existed since 1969."

He looked around, and no one objected so he continued.

"The accounts were set up by Preston's uncle, Karl Volkers, in 1969. Correct?"

"Right," Preston confirmed.

"Karl Volkers' notes indicate he was involved in certain operations that were not sanctioned by the CIA, but that he and other agents ran off-the-books, so to speak." He cleared his throat, and then continued. "I think we all know by now that in the 60s, if not later and who knows now, there were definitely cases of renegade operations run by both the CIA and the Pentagon. Enough blame to go around."

Rick looked at Jones. "Now don't worry, I really don't need to know, and don't want to know unless it is relevant to the safety of anyone, what Volkers' notes say about illegal operations he was involved in. Except it appears that one of those operations involved the theft of money from an Army truck in Vietnam, in 1969. Which is why we are here today, pondering the peculiarities of human scheming." Rick grinned and everyone but the stolid Major Fears exhaled a slight laugh.

"My involvement came about because my boss has a friend who is your superior, Major Fears, and the major has a very competent staff who found out that I am related to Kit Walker, who was one of the soldiers who accompanied the truck that was robbed in Vietnam. Have I got that right, Major Fears?"

"Yes sir, I believe that is correct."

"I was told Major Fears would brief me once I got to California, but it seems the major has forgotten to brief me on all things relevant a time or two. Is that also correct, major?"

Fears nodded agreement. "I felt there were certain details that weren't relevant to be shared, general. My apologies."

Ed Jones spoke up. ""Major, forgive my curiosity, but I don't understand how you so quickly locked on to this guy, Antonio, or Alphonse as he called himself when I met him. Where did your info come from?"

Everyone stared at Fears now, and waited. The officer rubbed his hand across his mouth, saw the seriousness on Rick's face and realized it best not to screw with generals.

"General, Mr. Jones, all I can say is we have a source that sent us, me actually, information which as far as I know was generated by the CIA."

Jones sat up, interested but also slightly embarrassed to have it revealed that there could be such a leak.

Fears went on, "I can honestly say I do not know who this person is, and if I did, I do believe there would be a security issue. Sir, I feel that is something you'd have to take up with Generals Lytle and Asher. Respectfully, sir."

Rick nodded, and said, "Probably none of my business."

"Jones, maybe you and Preston can summarize how things developed from there until the point we are at now."

"Well, let's see. Preston and I went to Switzerland, got into the box with the key Preston had. We found money, more notes from his uncle, and found that the numbered accounts are in the names of the officers of a corporation set up by Karl Volkers. And any of these officers, along with the correct numbers, can access the accounts."

When Jones paused Jane popped in with a question.

"And what do you think these accounts contain, Mr. Jones? It must be something important to have you here wanting to take my husband back with you."

"Oh, yes, we think it's important. We think the money that was taken in the truck robbery may have ended up in one or more of those accounts."

"And if it's been there for what, thirty-three years or so now, would be how much?" Jane asked.

In Jones' mind he answered, *a fuckin' shitload.* He would have spoken aloud were it not for Jane's presence. Laughing as he spoke, Jones said, "If there was three or four million dollars stolen in that robbery, and if it's been invested for all these years, well, a whole ton of money."

"Depends what it was invested in," offered Kit.

Jones said, "Sure, but remember how high regular interest was in the 80s, and how well some stocks did in the 90s."

"If the source is the money run robbery, I believe this would all be United States Army money, even the gains," said Fears.

Deferring to General Walker, Jones looked at him. "I don't think anybody here will give you a big argument on that," the general said. "However, I'm sure there are legal issues that we aren't going to settle. I have already contacted General Lytle, and he in turn contacted General Asher, your boss, major, to set up an escrow account for anything that is retrieved in the Swiss bank by any of us."

That was when Kit began to laugh rather loudly.

"So I am stinkin' rich, aren't I?!"

Again, everyone but Fears thought that was funny and agreed the situation had its humor.

"We'll travel around the world, hey Jane?"

When the laughter had died down Jones continued. "If what we think is true, Mr. Walker is the only one of us who can access the accounts. And we think the numbers needed are the Army service numbers of the three men who rode in the truck that was robbed—Mr. Walker here, Curtis Howard, and Bill Jenkins."

"Speaking of which, what more do we know about those two men, major?"

"Lieutenant Davidson says Howard has regained consciousness and confirmed that the man he knew in Vietnam as Tony Abazini did come to see him. He can't say whether or not that was who ran him off the road. He's in no condition to go to Switzerland."

"And Jenkins is dead, correct?" asked Preston.

Major Fears nodded.

"Now this is the guy I want to hear more about," said Jane. This Abazini, Abbott, whatever his name is. Who is this guy really? Does anybody know for sure?"

"Jones? Do we get into a security issue here," asked Rick

"Not that I'm aware of, although I wouldn't want any of this conversation to leave this building. Best I can say is that this is a guy who has been a mercenary, a Jack-of-all-trades criminal since long before 1969. There are people like him, even today, who make a living as professional criminals. High-level, I guess you'd call it. Very sophisticated and ruthless. There probably isn't a government in the world who hasn't used people like him for certain operations."

"My tax money at work," said Jane.

"What can I say? Anyway, it appears he set up the money run robbery as a way for Karl Volkers to obtain cash for the operations he ran that were not officially sanctioned by the CIA. Antonio, as Volkers knew him to be, was supposed to get a cut, and we think Volkers left it in one of those accounts in Switzerland."

Preston Volkers added, "If we've got our timeline correct, my uncle died shortly after the robbery and didn't– maybe he forgot or didn't have the time– send

Antonio his cut. He had already set up the accounts, found out he was dying, and attempted to leave me the information. Of course I was only eighteen years old then, but I guess Uncle Karl didn't know anyone outside the Agency that he felt he could trust."

"So he did or didn't leave you the information?" asked Jane.

Preston shook his head. "Didn't. Tried to, but he got real sick very fast and went into a coma. He left me a key that I literally forgot about all these years. I had thrown it into a box with some of his things figuring that one day I'd find out what it was for. But I totally forgot about it. At the time, I probably had never seen a safe deposit key else I might have recognized it for what it was."

"Please explain to me how did Abbott, or Antonio, get into this? Are you saying he's been trying to get this money all these years?"

"Well, Mrs. Walker, I think you can blame us for that," said Jones. "After going through Karl Volkers notes we, me specifically, went to find him. He must be in his late 60s now, but looks younger. Lives in a small town in Italy. Acts like a European, but once he and I got talking I could see he's a fine actor. Fits in there like a native and here in the States like one, too.

"Our concern, or at least the concern of some people, is that he might have information about the operations Volkers ran back in the 60s."

"Ah. Which your people don't want to become public," suggested Jane, only slightly snidely.

Jones sighed. "Again, what can I say? You're hitting me where it hurts...oh, sorry. Sometimes I'm not even told why I'm doing what I'm doing. Anyway, my talking to him made him realize the money might still be around and he'd like to get his cut, or more. I'm sure it hasn't escaped him that his promised cut could be worth a lot more if it has been earning interest in a Swiss account."

"And he thinks that one of us knew something?" asked Kit. "Seems incredible."

"May seem incredible at first, but you do know something don't you?" Jones said, pointing at Kit.

"Me? What do I know?"

"You are an officer of Columbia Consortium! You can access the accounts, or at least one of them, with your Army service number!"

"But I never knew that! Hell, if I had, I would have gone to Switzerland a long time ago!" "The point is, you did have information, even if you didn't know it. So Antonio was right in his suspicion, albeit a pretty lucky guess on his part."

"So are you sure that this Antonio character is the same as the Abz I knew in Vietnam?" Kit asked.

Jones nodded and Fears broke in. "We're almost positive Abazini, Abbott, Antonio, and the man you saw in Italy, Mr. Jones, are all the same."

"And you want him for the murder of Tater, the driver?" asked Kit.

"Not sure we could prove that," the major said, "unless..." he looked at Ed Jones, "the CIA has information in the notes from Karl Volkers that would help us."

"I can tell you this. Volkers' notes tell us that Abazini was the man Volkers earlier knew as Antonio, a man who was already a seasoned criminal. Somehow Volkers got him into the 11th Finance Company for purposes of managing the truck robbery. Whatever resources he used for that he doesn't reveal so I doubt if we'll ever know. I think Major Fears can confirm that Abazini disappeared in Vietnam, according to official records, and was thought to have been killed in action, is that right, major?"

"He was listed as missing, but when his Army records appeared to be bogus he was taken off the official MIA rolls. Someone back then had enough suspicions to leave a trace in case his name showed up again, but it wasn't realistic for anyone to spend much time looking for him."

"So what do we do about him now? Any suggestions?" Rick asked.

"We're sure he didn't follow us here," said Jones.

"Or us," added Fears. "He ditched us and I think he may well have given up the game."

"Eh, I don't like it. Didn't you say, major, that your people had observed him going to that particular bar for several days in a row?"

"Yes, sir."

"And when Kit and I went there he acted as if he was expecting us. To me his action suggests he's been watching us as much as any of you have been watching him. I also understand there were many times over the past couple of weeks when your men were supposedly observing Abbott that he managed to get away for hours at a time."

"Which means what to you, Rick?" asked Jane, a little waver in her voice.

"It means I may have jumped to an assumption that Abbott won't find us at this house. So I want to be sure this house has security; I'll leave that to Major Fears. Especially if Kit is going to Switzerland."

Kit stood up, raised both hands in the air. "Okay, this is how it's going to have to be. At this point, I really don't care about the money. I know I'm not getting any of it anyway."

"We could be induced to provide for a small reward," Jones interjected.

"I don't think you have the authority over that money, Mr. Jones," Fears said.

"Easy. Let's not argue about such specifics right now. Go on Kit."

"Before anything else, what I'm wondering is why, if you guys figured out how to get at the accounts in the

Swiss bank, the meeting with Abbott today was necessary. Anyone?"

"I think the problem Kit, is that Ed and Preston didn't know about the meeting, and Major Fears and I didn't know what they had learned about gaining access to those accounts."

"This may sound like an excuse," said Ed Jones, "but because we don't have official duties within the borders, and because Preston's connections have no official interest, we didn't do a very good job of tracking Abbott. We tried to trace what we thought were his movements by linking to credit cards, car rentals and such, but the major's people did a better job."

"With the likelihood that Abbott killed Jenkins and has moved across state lines, we should have people on him very soon," Preston said.

"Alright, Rick. I'll go with Jones and Volkers to Switzerland and see if how many zillions of dollars there are in those accounts. I want Jane to go to Hawaii immediately and wait for me there. Can't she fly back with you, Rick?"

"I can make the arrangements but I have to catch a different flight. I can see that she gets put on the base, with instructions for you to catch up with her after Switzerland."

They all looked around at each other, then began to nod agreement. "Okay with me," said Jones. "And I think we can find a way to send you two on your island adventure once the work in Switzerland is done."

A sharp whistle brought the men to attention. Jane was waving her hand in the air. "Excuse me, folks; do I get a say in this?"

"What would you prefer, Jane?" asked Rick.

"I'd rather not go to Switzerland or Hawaii right now. I'll wait here tonight, as we planned, but I'd rather go back home."

What she didn't say was that she wasn't as all-trusting as Kit seemed to be. The idea of both of them being under the command of these people, in a foreign country or on an Army base, made her less than confident in what anybody said now. For all we know it'll be Switzerland, than somewhere else; who the hell knows what we aren't being told.

"I want Kit and I to each have cell phones that can call overseas, I want him to check with me, or vice versa, every day; more even, maybe two or three times a day. I want somebody's word that Kit won't be unguarded, and that it'll be strictly to the bank, and back."

"I've got phones already," cut in Rick.

Preston chuckled. "Mrs. Walker…"

"Jane is fine"

"Jane, I could use someone like you in my business. Looking for a change of careers?"

"Thanks, I accept that as a compliment, but no thanks. And Rick, I really would like your assurance on this."

"I'll talk to General Lytle and ask him to speak to General Asher to see if they can secure a few more people for security."

"What if we get there, to Switzerland, and I show my identification, give them these numbers, and someone says, 'No, sir, I'm sorry, we cannot allow you access'," suggested Kit.

Jones answered. "Then it may mean we were wrong about how the numbers code works, or there may be something we don't know about that voids what Volkers set up, just because of the length of time that's passed. I think it'll be a dead end for us. Probably something that'll get bumped up to a higher level."

"And Abbott? Does he just get away?" Jane inquired.

"Well, up till now it seems we've given him a lot of slack," said Preston. "Now that we know he's nearby we'll get some people on his case. I don't think there is anyway he can fly out of the country unless he's got yet another alias totally different from what we know. Of course, fact is, we don't know for certain that there are any crimes we can charge him with. But I do want to keep him away from Annemasse until we finish up there. Afterwards, I don't think there's anything he can do."

"Ah, our intelligence services aren't completely inept, Mrs. Walker," Major Fears said. "On our way here in the van I spoke to General Asher and he will be trying to arrange for local cooperation to bring Abbott in, if for nothing else than questioning on the murder of Jenkins in Michigan."

In a moment of silence, Kit spoke up: "So who all goes and when are we leaving?"

"Don't seem so eager, dear," teased Jane.

"Hey, hon, I just want to get this over with so we can head to the islands."

>>SIXTEEN<<

"Gambit"

In his motel Tony Abbott was trimming his hair and setting a mustache in place; just a little change of appearance. He knew that others in his line of work thought it silly to make minor changes in one's appearance. But Abbott knew his penchant for such mundane antics had on more than one occasion helped him escape from a sticky situation. Changing the color of his contact lenses was another touch.

At this point Abbott was unsure what he should do and seriously considered forgetting the whole thing and returning to his village of LeDione. Unfortunately, now even that idyllic hideaway would never be the same. He would send orders to have the cottage sold and his possessions put into storage until he returned. He'd have to find a new home and a new identity. Before that, one more gambit.

Abbott was correct that Kit Walker knew something about how to get at the money, but had been unaware as to the fact that he had such information. The impression Abbott got from the lunch meeting was that there are people who are pulling Walker's strings because they need the information he has, and they need to keep me, Abbott, out of the way. They must know I don't know how to get at the money, otherwise I'd be doing that—would have done it—instead of running around chasing after the people who were in that Army truck.

I'm wondering, he thought as he brushed the mustache, if they didn't chase me with more diligence because they just want to keep me out of the way. Walker didn't seem to press me too much for anything other than to tell me I'm wasting my time worrying about the money. But Jones wouldn't have come to Italy to see me, this General Walker wouldn't be here, and Kit Walker wouldn't have worn a wire, or microphone, if they didn't think I knew something that could help their cause.

Walker's wife packed and moved to that other house. So something is up. Or did she? Tonight I need to survey the landscape and act soon or the game will be over. Now, some sleep, and then I'll put a little pressure on the other side.

While Tony Abbott napped, Ed Jones, Preston Volkers, and Major Fears made their arrangements regarding transportation to Switzerland, security for the house Jane Walker would be staying at, and cell phones for the Walkers. Rick was not surprised to find that airline reservations were ready and waiting for the 6:35 p.m. flight out of LAX. The passengers would arrive in Geneva the next day at a about the same time.

Jane had compromised a bit and agreed she would stay here tonight, well-guarded, and tomorrow fly to Hawaii, where Rick would arrange for her to stay at Ft. Shafter until Kit met her, which would be as soon as Kit had completed his role in Switzerland. Unfortunately Jane sometimes changed her mind without telling other people who might have an interest in her affairs.

Kit was still uneasy about Jane staying at the house alone, except for whatever guards would be in the neighborhood, but Jane had finally convinced him.

"I'm not as trusting as you are Kit. I don't think it's a good idea for the CIA or the FBI or worse, that other jerk, to have both of us under their thumb, especially outside the country."

"What do you thinks going to happen? Look, if Rick wasn't involved I'd probably agree. But he's not going to let anything happen to us."

"Yes, but he's not going to Switzerland with you. He's off to Thailand or Pago Pago or somewhere or other. What help is he going to be if we end up in Guantanamo or God knows where?"

"Guantanamo! Don't be ridiculous!"

"Well, I don't care. I want to be here, in the United States, and I want to be able to reach Rick if I need to, if I can't reach you."

"You think if these people were going to do anything to us they can't block our cell phone calls if they wanted to? Or that they need to have us together to get our cooperation? What if they arrest me there and you here?"

"Now *you're* getting ridiculous!"

Just then Rick knocked on the bedroom door. "It's me, Rick. Can I talk to both of you?"

"Yeah, come on in." When Rick entered Jane said, "We were just arguing over whom to trust in all this. Who do you think we should trust, Rick?" The question was thrown out with more than a hint of sarcasm.

"Ha! Nobody, didn't you ever learn that? Don't you watch television?"

"You're encouraging."

"Seriously, I don't think there's anything to worry about. Having said that, I've taken some steps of my own. Here's my cell phone number for both of you to use. Until you are safely together in Honolulu I want both of you to call me at least twice a day starting from midnight tonight."

"At midnight?" asked Jane. "Are you sure?"

Rick nodded. "If you go to bed before then, call and let me know that you are okay. Then again in the morning, before you leave for Hawaii. Kit, you call me when you get to Geneva and again when you've been to the bank."

"You seem more worried than I am, Rick. So should I be more worried and share the gray hairs with you?"

"Actually I thought you'd like to know I'd done this; an extra layer of safety. If I don't hear from you, I'll call you, and if I can't reach you, I'll call in the cavalry."

To Rick's raised eyebrows, Rick said: "Never mind; hopefully that won't be necessary."

"And the others don't know about this arrangement?" Kit asked.

Rick shook his head. "If they notice you on the phone they may ask, but you don't need to tell them anything if you don't want to. Hey, it's not that I don't trust *them;* I've just learned to take little extra precautions in my job, that's all. It's the people I don't know that I'm concerned about."

"Like Tony Abbott?"

"He's still loose out there," Rick reminded them. "Though I don't think he could know where we are now. What gnaws at me is that Fears' man lost Abbott so often. Abbott may be an aging criminal, but he appears to be rather competent at his chosen profession. Nobody seems to know what Abbott's up to, but it can't be anything good, and I don't want to underestimate him any more than I have already."

Rick paused a bit, then added: "I'm not one hundred percent positive but I think someone was in my motel room. Something was moved, just enough to worry me. That's why I wanted to get you away from your house. I figure Abbott knows where you live and has probably been spying on you. He's followed me and it appears he's pretty sharp at picking up any tails on him."

"This is beginning to suck, big time, Rick."

"Yeah, Kit, I agree. I'm sorry about this, but as General Lytle told me earlier, you were going to get pulled into this anyway, so I'm still glad I came. I just wish I didn't have to leave soon. Now, you need to be aware that I've arranged for someone to stay at your house tonight in case Abbott shows up there. He's a PI we've used in certain domestic situations; guy by the name of Banning, not that you need to know, so forget what I said. I'm getting careless. If Abbott does show up we are going to try to hold him as long as we can, on some pretext or the other, whatever we can come up with."

"You're not involving the local police yet, are you?" Jane asked.

Rick shook his head. "Don't want to do that if we can avoid it. Too difficult to explain"

"Back to these", Rick said, pointing at the cell phones, "This way the three of us can keep track of each other. I'll feel better, even if you don't. Now I admit I might not always be able to answer. These are the best phones I could get you on short notice—I picked them up yesterday—but I'll be flying across the Pacific and with weather and whatnot, who knows if all the calls will get through. Generally the voice mail will work so you can leave a message even if I don't answer. Always tell me the time and where you are. I'll make sure I check for messages every few hours.

"And when this is over I want you to take out the batteries and smash these phones and toss the scrap into the trash."

"By the way Rick, the next time I say, 'let me know if you need help on a secret mission in some exotic land', tell me to mind my own business!"

"I will, cuz, I will."

Tony Abbott slept until well past sunset, then leisurely showered and dressed. He ate a substantial dinner in a quiet little restaurant in a strip mall. Not to his usual taste

209

but he wasn't in the mood for anything too fancy or loud. Besides, he was no longer confident that he wasn't being hunted for in connection with the Jenkins murder. It's just a question of whether the Feds want to give the local police the information they probably have.

He then purchased a few items at a market and returned to his motel. He sat for awhile flipping the channels on the television, not getting too involved in any one program. He changed clothes, putting on dark slacks and a dark shirt.

Shortly after midnight he left his room, closing the door softly behind him. He walked the long way around so that no one in the main entrance area would see him. He'd parked his car far from his room in a dark spot of the lot. In a few minutes he was rolling along Calle Costado Street. This is where he needed to be careful. A slowly moving car or a man sitting in a car this late would be notable to any cruising police, or anyone hired to guard the Walker woman.

He stopped the car a block away and around the corner. He checked for signs to be sure he could park here at this time of night, then just sat for a while, listening. He saw the headlights of a car approach and slumped down on the seat. The car passed and kept going; it was not police and didn't look like any feds, just a couple coming home from an evening out. After he hadn't seen anyone or any cars for fifteen minutes he exited the car after first shutting off the overhead light.

He walked towards the house of his interest at a slow but regular pace on the side of the street that was the darkest. When he got within a half block of the house he found a home with a square of bushes lining the front yard. He stepped behind the bushes, bent down and scanned the area. He was in complete darkness but the street lights allowed him to view clearly to the end of the block. There was a car sitting across the street from the end house and it looked like there was a person in the front seat. So there is at least one, Abbott thought.

He reversed his path and went all the way back, turned the corner and walked past his car and to the next street, the one parallel to Calle Costado. He saw headlights approaching and ducked behind a tree. It was a police car. Good, maybe there won't be another one soon. He noted the time. When the car had left he continued his walk but looked back often, thinking that a smart cop might return quickly just in case there was a prowler who, having seen the patrol car pass, felt it was now safe. But the patrol car did not return.

When Abbott got to the corner he crossed the street and looked for a vantage point to observe the house. He was in luck; he noticed that the house just across the adjoining street was dark and there were several newspapers piled up at the door. There was also a long driveway that was in total darkness where it ended at the garage. The light at the garage had burned out and the people forgot to stop their paper. Abbott could stand at the corner of the garage next to a tree and again espy the house and be confident he couldn't be seen.

If he stepped through the backyard and around the side he could also see the car parked across the street. The person there looked to be awake and alert. He returned to the corner by the garage and watched the house. There were two dim lights, one that flickered. The first was probably a night light, he figured, the other is a television. Unless the Walker woman has insomnia, there is a guard in the house. But who all is there, both Walkers, the cousin, anyone else? There could be as little as one guard and the Walker woman, or maybe as many as six or seven people.

There were no other vehicles near the house so this made him think the number of people in the house was less rather than more. He needed to risk checking the garage. To do this he needed to go back through the yard of this house, and while staying in the shadows, cross the street to the back gate of his target house. Fortunately for him there was little moonlight and tomorrow there would be less.

He waited at the back gate for a full five minutes listening and watching. He began to open the gate so slowly it was imperceptible. Little by little he pushed harder but the gate must have been well oiled for there was no squeak at all. Still, he took a full minute to push it open. The garage door had windows and on his tiptoes he could just see in. He squinted to look in and saw one car. He could just barely make out the car and was sure it was the one Jane Walker had driven in. More evidence that there aren't many people here.

Where would the Walker men and Jones have gone? Is it possible the money is here and not in Europe, or are they on their way to Switzerland leaving me playing midnight prowler. I am definitely getting too old for this.

I'll need to check some more tomorrow before I decide what to do, he reasoned. Possibly it'll be too late, but I hate to bust in there tonight without having an inkling of how many people are in there.

By the following morning Kit Walker was sleeping at an altitude of thirty-five thousand feet, on his way to Geneva, via London, along with Ed Jones, Preston Volkers, and Major Justin Fears. Rick Walker was in the air on his way to Bangkok, just a bit uneasy. Both Jane and Kit had contacted him at midnight and everything was A-OK.

Tony Abbott had awakened before six, grabbed coffee and a couple of donuts and was parked in the shade of an oak tree nearly a block down Calle Costado from Jane Walker's location. The dark blue car that had been there the a few hours ago hadn't moved, but there was no one in it now. Once I'm back home, money or no money, I will need to get some decent food in me. This crap I've been eating will kill me if a bullet doesn't first.

They have not got their best people on this, Abbott thought. On the other hand, if this is the best they have, it makes it easier for me. The concept barely had time to coalesce when he again had to adjust his plans. He hadn't yet finished his second donut, when he saw Jane Walker exit the house. She walked around to the garage and lifted the garage door, not opening it with a remote. Abbott couldn't see her from his vantage point but if he could have he would have thought that the woman was trying to be very quiet, as if not wanting to awaken anyone else in the house.

She soon appeared in her car and drove off. Abbott eased his car forward watching for any other vehicle that might be following the woman. He saw none and picked up speed.

Once again Tony Abbott found himself trailing after Mrs. Walker. Based on her route Abbott surmised they were returning to Walker's home in Madre Hills. They were cruising along at around seventy, quite a bit slower than the prevailing traffic. Once Abbott felt confident of the destination he moved over to the fast lane, passed the woman, and then sped on ahead, pushing the speed limit as much as he dared. And since when the traffic does flow on southern California freeways cars going only seventy, like Jane's was, are rare, Abbott was able to push it to eighty without much fear of hearing a siren.

As he sped ahead Abbott thought back over everything that had occurred the past few days and tried to make sense of it. Some assumptions had to be made, and whatever event transpired to start the ball rolling, whatever that ball was, he still couldn't imagine.

The CIA comes to see me, this Ed Jones, playing it coy but obviously interested in the money that was taken from the truck in Vietnam. I never got my share, found out a few months later that Karl Volkers had died, and I figured it was either an honest screw-up, or someone in Volkers' own company had double-crossed him, and thus, me too. But I truly thought the money was long gone. So now I'm thinking Volkers had put it somewhere that either wasn't easy to get to, and/or that no one else knew where it was, until recently.

A damn good guess then is that it was either dumped into safe deposit boxes, or was deposited into investment accounts. The latter makes more sense just because of the physical bulk of four million dollars in cash. And why put it where it doesn't work for you?

So Volkers croaks, maybe a natural death—I did hear it was cancer, but took that with a grain of salt. Who knows; maybe the news of a sudden and natural was true, and the poor sucker died before he could disburse the money or even arrange for others to handle it. And I was never again contacted by the CIA for any work, meaning that with Volkers gone no one else there knew of me, or was running the kind of operations that needed my talents.

I've never heard back from Jones—of course, I have been evading him, so maybe it's not his fault. So they aren't ready to deal me in; why? Another good guess is they don't want to bring up any old news that might taste sour to them. Stories of black operations, rogue agents, murders and other nasty business.

It makes sense now that the other guys who were involved in the money run never knew anything. If Jenkins or Howard had known something about the money, my showing up should have startled them. But it didn't do anything of the sort. Walker though—seems to have a lot of action going on around him. It could well be that the CIA thinks those three amigos have relevant information, but they themselves don't know they have this knowledge. Or maybe it's Army intelligence or some other one of those many spy groups the US government has that bump into each other; else what's the deal with this other Walker, this general? And he being related to Kit Walker is either some mighty fine coincidence or maybe it's part of what opened up this can of worms in the first place.

He noticed his speed had crept up to near ninety, which might be pushing his luck if a highway patrolman with a full pad of tickets to issue should happen by. So Abbott slowed to eighty and set the cruise control.

His reverie continued. So I visit Jenkins and Howard and they don't seem to know anything. I try to get rid of them so they don't tell anyone I've been to see them, but I know I've been tracked here because I've spotted a tail. But loosely; I think because of my offer to Jones they want to keep me around for awhile.

Kit Walker is obviously different, and that might be because of his relative, the general. I'm not sure what they hoped to hear from me when I met with Walker, but it may have been just a shot in the dark, to see if I would slip up and give them something they need to know. Of course, like I told Jones, anything I know comes at a price—except I did throw in copies of those pictures at no charge.

Now it seems everyone is gone. So for my third pretty good guess I'll say they have gone to Switzerland to get the money, which will shut me out of any kind of a deal. I think if Jones had just agreed to give me what Volkers had promised, plus maybe some interest, I would have been happy. But no, they've got to be greedy. However, by now Jones has got the pictures so they know I do have something to trade. Or, if they piss me off enough, I may just put them to use for free, just for the hell of it. Come to think of it, Jones may not know what those pictures represent, but I'll bet someone in their organization can figure it out. He laughed inwardly as he thought, they could always ask to old redhead.

So my one remaining hope, I think, is to pressure Walker's wife. They must have felt I had vanished so they left her. Still, they did move her to that other house. I wonder is she's being a little rebellious now by taking off on her own.

The thought made him look in his rear view mirror, but he was sure by now he was far enough ahead that she wouldn't be too close behind him. If the woman is going somewhere other than her home, I will lose her and then, I think I really will call it a day. Then I have to decide on the best way to get out of the country because something tells me that any identity I have used recently will light up the switchboards if I try to get on an airplane. Maybe I'll drive up to Canada, or better, down to Mexico; that's a shorter drive.

He was nearing the transition to the 210 Freeway and had to pay attention to his directions. He probably wouldn't have too much time once he got to the Walker neighborhood.

Unbeknownst to Jones, Fears and Preston, Rick had hired a guard– a retired Navy Seal– to spend the night inside Kit and Jane's Madre Hills house. The guard stayed awake and alert, without the TV or a radio on, without even a light to read by. He was a pro and he did the job he was hired to do. Nothing happened during the night; no odd noises, no one coming to the house.

In the morning he checked all the doors and windows to look for evidence of an attempted break-in and found none. He checked around the long fence that lined three sides of the yard, and found nothing amiss. In one way he slipped up, though it didn't seem like anything consequential at the time. Rick had wanted him to stay until eight in the morning, figuring that by then Abbott would have either shown up or not. But everything seemed copasetic, and he was hungry, so the guard cut short his assigned time by a few minutes. If he'd stuck around until eight he would have been there when Abbott showed up, and probably still there too, when Jane arrived.

Back at the Orange County house Sergeant Rowlins awoke and walked into the kitchen hoping to find some coffee. He saw a note on the table and his heart fluttered. He read it and exclaimed, "Goddamn it all to hell! The general will have my stripes!"

The note read: 'Sergeant: I remembered some things I need from the house. I will go there and then I have some shopping to do before I drive to the airport. I'll park my car there. Thanks for your help. Jane'

Ten minutes before Jane arrived, Tony Abbott had driven by, saw a couple neighbors outside, made a quick u-turn and left. At the entrance to the cul de sac he turned onto the cross street and parked. He got out and began the one block walk to the Walker house.

One of the many things Abbott had learned in his years of criminal activity was that the most dishonest person could get away with murder—literally—if they just acted like they knew what they were doing and avoided looking guilty. So he was confident he could stride up to the Walker house, go around back, and break in without it causing any alarm. The wild card is always a possibility and if he should run smack into a neighbor who knew he didn't belong there, then he'd have to go to Plan B, whatever the hell Plan B was.

So he walked deliberately up the sidewalk, looking straight ahead although he swept the area with his peripheral vision as best he could. The driveway for the

Walker house ran along the side a long way back to a garage that was a good one hundred feet from the front curb. As security against burglars it was nearly ideal, but then few people would be so bold as to simply walk up the driveway and open the gate, acting all the time as if they belonged there.

He knew from his first visit that there was no alarm system, and he'd seen the dog taken to a kennel. As usual, Abbott did not carry a gun; too much chance for trouble there. None of the immediate neighbors were out; a few houses down a man was sweeping the sidewalk and a lady was topping flowers. Abbott walked to the wrought iron gate and flicked the lever; it was not locked so he wouldn't have to risk climbing over. That would be pushing his veneer of confidence. For all the so-called intelligent people around these last few days, they seemed to have been careless about arranging security at the house.

Abbott wouldn't have thought that had he known of the guard who had only minutes ago vacated the premises. And had the guard still been there Abbott would have had a fight on his hands to get away. Better for him had that been the case.

It took mere seconds for Abbott to get into the house. Now he was quiet as a mouse as he stepped lightly from room to room, assuring himself there was no one there. Now to wait, but I must plan quickly.

>>SEVENTEEN<<

"Walter Cushman"

At age eighty-three the red hair Walter Cushman used to have was mostly gone, and what remained was gray and white, or silver, as he preferred. He appeared to be and felt reasonably healthy for his age, well aware that people in their ninth decade of life often went to sleep one night and didn't bother to wake up. No particular reason, just the heart saying, 'that's it, I can't pump anymore'. Hell, if a person's life can be condensed into one year, it must be at least Christmas Eve for me by how, he'd been joking for almost three years.

He'd led an extremely active life, most of it in some form of governmental service, and at this stage he did not need any more money nor did he desire any more power. In fact, he was glad not to have the power he used to wield. But he did relish and revere his fame.

So as he sat in his den in his Georgetown home, the twilight bringing a warmth to the room where he was enjoying the one and only cigar he allowed himself each day, and one of several Scotch and sodas he allowed himself, Walter Cushman reflected on events he'd thought he'd never have to ponder again.

A recipient of several medals for his actions in World War Two, Cushman had worked in a variety of intelligence service jobs before settling in with the young CIA. After being coaxed into running for Congress by acquaintances who provided the financial backing, and winning two terms, he moved on to the Senate where his prior intelligence experience gave him an ideal perspective. He was consulted frequently, usually on the quiet, by people he still knew at the Agency.

When the chance to return to the CIA came up he passed on a slam-dunk re-election to the Senate to return to the world of intelligence, intrigue, and secrets– work that gave him a high more satisfying than any vice he'd ever experienced.

Relaxing in his den now, Cushman wondered at the irony of him taking on the task of cleaning up some of the less savory activities that had been going on, many in South East Asia, and many he not only knew about, but had been involved in himself. Some of these operations had been revealed and been well documented; though fortunately in most cases the names of operatives had been kept out of the information the public was able to access. Of course we royally fouled up in the Middle East, Cushman recollected. Ousting Mossadeagh was one of the biggest mistakes we ever made. The repercussions from that ripple through every thing that happens in the Middle East a half- century later.

Although the CIA's mandate was to stay out of intelligence operations within the borders of the United States, Cushman knew there were a few cases where the arrogance of people who thought they knew better conflicted with the laws they were expected to uphold. He himself had been guilty of such thinking and was well acquainted with at least one of those operations.

It was funny, he thought, how the higher up in authority he went the more serious he took his duties and obligations. He actually had run a clean ship, which, of course, is what his reputation was for. His integrity kept him in the stream of information that flowed to the highest levels of government. Both parties swore he was one of theirs, and it amused him that a lot of people would be surprised if they knew how he had voted for various people and issues over the years. But if the skeletons in his closet ever came out, he feared he'd permanently lose the reputation he now held so dear. At the same, though it wasn't an excuse, he knew that for people who had toiled in similar lines of work, their closet was probably no cleaner.

Even now, officially retired for several years, he not only claimed the ear of presidents and congressmen, cabinet officials and ambassadors, and possessed what was likely the thickest 'black book' of privileged phone numbers and e-mail addresses of anyone in the country, he was constantly sought out by those who wished his advice and/or help, usually as it related to international situations. Moreover, Cushman's contacts over the years had enabled him to set up his own network of information gathering that often kept him ahead of those who would later seek him out on issues he was already more briefed on than they were.

His next tumbler contained more Scotch and less soda as he remembered back to Karl Volkers, who had died, yeah, about 1969, wasn't it? Karl, who worked with me, for me, and sometimes I think, against me; but then I will never know for sure. Karl, who ran a series of operations that arrogant intelligence people thought were needed to do the job they felt needed doing. Yes, arrogant people like Karl and me.

Walter remembered how shocked he was to hear of Karl's sudden passing, and rued the fact that almost in the same instant his concern for Karl dissipated into worry about what Karl may have left laying around that could have nailed him, Cushman, and a few others. But Karl appeared to have cleaned things up well, and what threads he left hanging I was able to cut off later.

So why, now, after all these years, decades even, do I have this gnawing in my stomach? Why are my sources telling me that the Agency has sent someone to see an aging mercenary named Antonio, and why is the Army or the DIA looking for a man named—now what the hell was his name?

Cushman never directly worked with Antonio, had never met him but certainly had known of him. And though the people Karl used were never specifically revealed to Walter, well, sometimes you did know, if only because there are only so many people you can use in certain places and for certain objectives. Finding people to do the things you need to get done, but can't do yourself– or won't do– isn't easy.

Now this money truck thing I don't recall at all. What does give me an itch I can't scratch is that damn old file I gave Karl. Damn it and cram it, I should have destroyed it myself. Stupidly I thought it was something that might be needed. But I was, quite frankly, afraid to hold on to it. I bucked it to Karl and that was chicken of me. I figured he would burn it, but then why should I have assumed he would? When he died his house and office were searched as well as could be, and I even had people go in again a year later, when the house was vacant for awhile.

What bothered Walter Cushman now, because he was a man who did not like coincidences, was that the information coming to him said that Karl's nephew, Preston Volkers, who used to work for the FBI, still lived in Karl's old house. And more bothersome, Preston had gone with the CIA agent, Jones, to Switzerland to a bank there. He may even have gone to meet with this Antonio fellow, who, if Major Fears is right, was somehow involved in this money truck robbery.

The truck incident, whatever the hell that was all about, he dismissed; I have no interest in that unless it somehow rips open a scab covering one of Karl's operations. I don't think I could ever be connected to it. But the file, God, my name and picture were in it. Did Karl put it in this bank in Switzerland?

Like a lot of people of his generation Walter could take computers or he could leave them. Still, they were a marvel and he sometimes contemplated how wonderful it would have been to have had cell phones when he was in the field, or a laptop that could connect to a satellite miles above. He still was worried about security but he had the best equipment money could buy and he had to trust it.

So he went to his computer, the one hidden behind the liquor cabinet, the last place anyone would look for it, he hoped. In a few seconds he was at the site he wanted and typed the message.

'SS...need to know what's in Switz...top priority...check upstairs if u r concerned...the others must not get what's there...no excuses...drop all other concerns... reply w/ understanding...C'

As far as the recipient of the message knew, the box in Switzerland had been opened when Jones and Preston had first visited the bank. They found some cash and a notebook left by Karl Volkers. Is that what Cushman wants?

Cushman waited patiently and sipped his drink. In a few minutes a reply popped up.

'Understood. They r on their way... I can get quick transport & meet them. Will retain what is found. SS'

Cushman left the computer screen on and went to the phone. If it's not there, in that safe deposit box in Switzerland, Karl either destroyed it, in which case I have

223

nothing to worry about, or it's still in the house. If so, it must be very well hidden. I wonder how much Volkers' nephew would want for the house?

Among the habits the old agent had acquired over the years was to not take anything for granted, and, as a codicil, don't leave any loose ends. When the phone was answered no one spoke and Cushman started talking without identifying himself.

"A man named 'Antonio'...goes way back...find out who he is...get back to me soon." He hung up without the other person ever speaking.

While her husband was gallivanting around the world, as she called it, playing at espionage, Meg Volkers had decided it was time to do some long-delayed re-decorating. The carpet in the family room was over ten years old, she had been aching for new window shutters, and that ancient carpet in the room Preston's uncle had used as a bedroom when he last lived here, had to go. Preston had told Meg he'd let her decide when to start the projects so now that he was gone for a few days it was as good a time as any.

In Uncle Karl's old room she remembered there was wood underneath the carpet. She wondered whether she should have new carpet installed or have the wood re-finished. We'll have to see how the wood looks and what Preston thinks about it.

While she pondered her decorating ideas, a few miles away Walter Cushman sat quietly and waited. Patience was a spy's virtue, even if at his age he hated it when anything took too long; there not being much time left on his personal clock. Walter read the newspaper and sipped his drink. It was fully dark by the time his phone rang.

"Yes?"

The voice on the other end spoke slowly and clearly. "He apparently is retired. Did jobs for the Agency in the sixties and seventies. But an agent contacted him recently in Italy and now he appears to have come to this country."

"Where?"

"I'm tracking him. What do you want me to do if I find him?"

"You know the answer to that. Send your best technician." Cushman abruptly hung up.

>>EIGHTEEN<<

"Kidnapped"

When Tony Abbott heard a car come up the driveway he carefully peeked out and recognized the car he'd been following. The woman got out and came towards the back door. Like a cat Abbott dashed to the room that was designed for use as a den or library, and hid behind the sofa.

When she came into the house she heard him call, "Mr. Banning, are you still here? Mr. Banning?"

Abbott heard her walk down the hallway calling for Mr. Banning, whoever the hell he was. She then went back towards the kitchen and he could hear her say, talking to herself, "Eight o'clock, time to call Rick."

Abbott waited as she punched buttons on her cell phone. He raised his head up from behind the sofa so he could hear better. This time Rick did not answer but his message came on. He had told Jane and Kit that might happen and that he would be sure to check as often as possible so they should be sure to leave a message whenever they called. When cell phones work the way we want them to, they are wonderful. When they cut out and give us static, they suck.

"Hi, Rick. I guess you can't come to the phone right now so I'm giving you my eight o'clock check in. I'll be leaving for the airport soon. I decided to come back to the house for some things and I have some shopping to do so I got up early and left a note for the Sergeant. So don't be mad at him. I'm fine and I'll call you again at four this afternoon. Well, I'll probably be in the air then so I may call a little earlier, or if I can't, don't worry. I'm going to call Kit now. Bye."

Abbott had heard enough to know that the Walkers had arranged to keep in contact on a regular basis. She said eight o'clock check in and that she'd call again at four, so she must be expected to call at regular intervals; probably eight or twelve hour cycles.

Abbott waited, not daring to move his legs, while he heard the woman punch numbers on her cell phone again. He heard her take a few steps and he ducked down behind the couch. Then he heard the sound of water and it sounded like she was getting a drink while she waited. It took over a minute before he heard her speak.

"Kit, sweetheart, how are you?

"Oh, you're still flying.

"Yes, I called him but only got his machine.

"Well, that could be it. He got us the best phones in the world but they are still capricious; sunspots or whatever. He was so insistent we keep in touch I'm sure he wouldn't have gone to sleep if he was expecting one of us to call.

"No, I left the house; I'm back at home…

"It's fine, the guard is gone and everything is peachy. I just wanted to get some things I forgot. I'm going to leave soon and do some shopping and then I'll drive to the airport and park the car there.

"Okay, okay, I'll be fine. I'll see you in Hawaii then when you get there. So…

"What time do you arrive in Geneva? I wrote it down, but…

"So what about your trip to the bank, when do you do that?

"Well, get some sleep tonight and be rested otherwise you'll get to Hawaii and do nothing but sleep for the first two days.

"No, I'm perfectly safe now. Yes, dear

"Okay, I love you too."

Abbott then heard her walk down the hallway and enter the bathroom. When Jane came out she would have wet her pants had she not just been to the bathroom when a strong arm wrapped itself around her mouth while another grabbed her left arm and twisted it behind her. She tried to scream but the hand over her mouth stifled any sound she attempted.

"Stop struggling, Mrs. Walker, it'll only make me angry if you continue to fight me."

Jane stopped moving for a second then suddenly kicked backwards with her foot, but it only struck air. The man laughed.

"I'm not an amateur at this, Mrs. Walker. Now I mean it, stop it or I'll break your arm and then you'll have something to scream about!"

What a stupid time for Jane to remember when her mother would yell at her and her brother when they were playing a little too recklessly, 'If you break a leg don't come running to me!'

This time she did totally relax and Abbott lessened his grip but still held his hand over her mouth.

"Now here's the thing Mrs. Walker. I have a partner in Switzerland. He needs to hear from me at certain times or else he has orders to kill your husband." The lies came easily from a man who was used to lying.

"And if he has to do that, then there is no reason for me to keep you alive either, is there?"

Jane wasn't sure she could believe the man, but his comments had a scary logic to them. And there was too much to risk—her life and Kit's—if he was telling the truth.

When he lifted his hand off her mouth a little more, Jane said, "Okay, I won't scream, I won't fight you."

"That's a good girl. Now do you know who I am?"

Jane knew, but she slowly turned around first to look at the man. He didn't look like a bad person, except for the hint of a sneer on his mouth and a gleam in his eye that, in view of his behavior so far, gave him a dangerousness mien.

"I suppose you're the man my husband met for lunch."

"That's good. I hoped I wouldn't hear any silly answer from you. So we can get straight to business."

Still holding her arm he led her to the room he had hid in. The only window in this room faced the backyard and there was a patio overhang immediately behind the room. So it was near impossible for anyone to see into the room unless they were standing right at the window.

"Like I said, my partner is in Switzerland, in Annemasse, and he needs to hear from me soon as to what your husband's fate is. Do you believe me on this?"

All the while Jane was spinning in her mind various scenarios by which she could escape the house and simply run out into the street and scream for help. She really doubted there was anyone waiting in Annemasse for Kit; but what if there was?

"I'm not sure if I believe you or not," she answered.

Abbott smiled. "An honest answer. But you can't take the chance that I'm lying, can you?"

No answer was needed from Jane so she gave none.

"I need to call my partner by nine tonight, Geneva time, to tell him what to do. That's noon our time, in case you haven't figured out the time differences yet. Oh, and I heard your call to the general, your husband's cousin. So don't think you can fool me into thinking he'll come charging in to save you at any minute. I know he's not available."

Jane shuddered slightly at this and more so, at Abbott's wicked grin. She couldn't know that Abbott had no idea where Rick was—how far away, actually—but again, what chances could she take when Kit's and her lives may be hanging on a thread as thin as floss.

"So…shall we call your husband now?"

She could only hope that when she called Kit was with the other people and somehow, someone could get a message to Rick so he would, as he had said, bring in the cavalry.

"He'll still be on the plane. He isn't scheduled to land until 6:25 in Geneva. What can you expect him to do?"

Abbott thought a moment, digesting this and wondering if she were stalling. He guessed no, she wouldn't likely come up with a precise time of arrival so quickly if she were lying. She would have said 6:30, or 7:00 maybe, not 6:25.

"So we'll wait. Make some coffee…and I'm right close by so don't try to run out of the house, or scream, or grab anything. Remember, if I don't contact my partner in Geneva, your husband dies."

Again Jane sensed he was lying but knew she could not afford to not believe him, for now.

"One other thing first. I heard you mention the sergeant in your phone call. He's at the house in Orange County, isn't he?"

Jane's gasp told Abbott that she was stunned to realize Abbott knew about the supposed safe house.

"Let's call him to make sure he doesn't do anything silly like coming up hear to rescue the fair damsel. Call him and tell him you are on your way to the airport and that everything's just fine. Shall we do that, now, Mrs. Walker?"

As Jane worked the numbers on her phone Abbott wrenched her arm a bit to remind her he was right there and said in a near whisper, soft but threatening: "No funny stuff—remember, your husband's life is on the line, lady."

Sergeant Rawlins answered on the first ring.

Sergeant, it's Jane Walker," Jane spoke quietly, trying not to let her fear show to Abbott, but hoping it might to Rawlins. "I'm...I'm sorry I snuck out on you. I..."

"You shouldn't have done that, ma'am," Rawlins interrupted. "Are you okay?"

She hesitated long enough for Abbott to twist her arm a bit more and put his ear to the phone, his breath so close to Jane's face she thought she might faint.

"Yes, I'm fine Sergeant. I'm on my way to the airport. I'll be okay. And thank you."

"You have my cell phone number?"

"Ah, yes, I do. I'll call you if I need you."

"Yes ma'am, please do that."

Jane shut off her phone, Abbott released his grip and she gasped for breath and dashed to the sink to get another drink of water, her sudden movement causing Abbott to reach out and grab her by the hair.

"Don't do that!"

"I wasn't trying to get away. I just need some water."

"Remember, you get away or anything happens to me, and I don't call my friend in Geneva, and your husband dies!"

By noon Abbott was getting impatient. "He ought to be at his hotel by now. Let's call. But first, remember this: do not tell him where we are or I'll call my partner to take your husband out; and then I'll take you out. Understand?"

Jane nodded.

"Tell me you understand!"

"I, I understand."

"Good. If he asks you tell him you were blindfolded and taken somewhere."

It took less than a minute to connect but it felt much longer. Finally Kit answered. As is often the case when these blasted cell phones do work well, it seems that the farther apart the two people are, the clearer is the reception. Kit sounded like he was in the next room.

"Jane...why are you calling again? Is something wrong?"

Before she could say anything Abbott grabbed the phone.

"Hello, Walker. We meet again, though distance makes us even fonder, hey?"

"What the hell? Abbott? Where are you calling from? Put my wife on!"

"Are you alone, Walker?"

"Yes, yes, goddammit, put my wife on!"

"Be careful what you say...just tell him you're okay and that he needs to do what I tell him", Abbott said before handing the phone to Jane.

"Ah, Kit...I'm okay, really I am; he hasn't hurt me."

"Are you at the house? What's he doing there? What does he want?"

"I'm not sure ...he took me somewhere," Jane answered. "He wants to talk to you and he said he has someone there who will kill you if you don't do what he says. Believe him, Kit, it's not worth the risk."

Abbott then grabbed the phone from her, took it in his right hand while holding firmly to Jane's arm with his left hand, tight enough to make her squirm.

"You got that, Walker? Now listen to me carefully and no one will get hurt and we'll both get out of this a little richer. How does that sound?"

"I'm not interested in getting richer, I just want you to let my wife go."

"I will once you go to the bank and get the money, which is what you are there for, isn't it?"

Kit made no response.

"I'm not sure how this all came together, I'll admit that, and I'm not even sure who all the players are in this game. However, I have a powerful hunch that they wouldn't have taken you to Geneva unless you had the key, or the information, to get that money, however much there is." When Kit still didn't respond, Abbott insisted; "Isn't that right, Walker?"

"Yes, but they just need my identification. Afterwards there's nothing I can do about the money. Hell, I've got people from three different government agencies with me."

"And I've got someone there too, Walker, watching you specifically..."

"I don't think I believe you Abbott. You don't know what's going on here..."

"Shut up, Walker! You're there and I've got your wife here, remember? You do want to see her when you get back from Geneva, don't you? And you do want to get back from Geneva alive, don't you? Well?"

"Yeah, yeah, okay. But I still don't see what I can do to get any money to you."

"Just listen to me then. I've got some experience with those banks. You're going to the branch bank in Annemasse, aren't you?"

Abbott's statement caused Kit to wonder if maybe Abbott did know more about what was going on than Kit gave him credit for. Actually, it was a guess by Abbott, albeit a good one because he knew from past experience that was the bank the CIA had used.

"Yes, that's right."

"What time? Don't shit me now."

"Noon, at least that's what they told me."

"Good, very good, because the bank should be open by nine, so you can be there then and make the withdrawals."

"I don't know if I can," Kit protested. Preston and Ed had explained to Kit how the system worked, at least from what they understood. Kit would need to show identification of who he was, which should match with the bank's record of him as a corporate officer of Columbia Consortium. Using the code of his old Army identification number would grant him access to the money in one of the Columbia Consortium accounts. The plan was to transfer the money to an escrow account in New York City.

"I told you not to give me any bullshit. They wouldn't have taken you there unless they needed you, so they must need you as an identifier to get into those accounts."

"But I'll also need an identifying account number," Kit interrupted. He wanted to see how much else Abbott knew, or could conjure up, and he was stalling for time as he tried to think what to say to Abbott while at the same time think about what was the best thing to do for Jane. Get in touch with Rick? Call the local police in California? Tell Jones and Fears? What would be the best way to help Jane?

There was a pause; Abbott was thinking about this, wondering how much more he could bluff. Probably a lot, as long as he had Walker's wife. The longer he didn't respond, the more Kit thought that Abbott wasn't sure about the extent of Kit's abilities to access the money on his own. Then in a surprise, it was Jane was on the phone again.

"Kit, he says you either have the numbers needed or you can get them, and if you don't, we'll never see each other again. Kit, you've got to find a way. I'm sorry, I should never have come back here."

Abbott grabbed the phone from her. "Yeah, yeah, she's sorry and all that crap. I would have grabbed her from the other house if she hadn't come back here, so I'd have her anyway, so don't think either of you can get away or hide from me."

Hearing that Abbott knew they had gone to the other house was deflating.

"Okay, Abbott, but listen, honestly, I only have access to one account. The people I'm with believe that Volkers set the accounts up using the Army IDs of the three men who were in the truck; me, Curtis Howard, and Bill Jenkins. I still remember my ID, but I don't know the others and if I ask for them certainly they'll get suspicious. And even then, we won't know till we try if these are the access numbers."

Again there was a long pause while Abbott chewed on this information. It sounded logical, he admitted to himself. And anyway, even if he only got the money from one account, that should be several million.

"All right, Walker, I'll buy that, for now, anyway. Now listen carefully...write this down because I don't want you to make any mistakes."

Kit waited and then wrote down Abbott's instructions. Kit was so nervous he had to print slowly so that he could read his own scrawl. Abbott gave directions for transferring the money to a bank in Florence, and he also gave Walker the account number and the access number for the transfer. He sternly reminded him that once he made the transfer to be sure he thoroughly destroyed the paper on which he wrote those numbers. It wouldn't matter anyway, because as soon as Abbott confirmed that the money was there, he would instantly transfer the funds from there to a different bank, where the accountant he used would invest the money in several different funds, sell those funds a few days later, each time putting the proceeds in different accounts in different banks, until the trail was too complicated for other than the most intense scrutiny.

Kit was to leave the hotel early and get to the bank when it opened at nine and make the transfer. Abbott said that once he confirmed the money had been sent to his account he would let Jane go.

As he wrote the instructions Kit heard a noise over the phone that he thought he should recognize; something familiar but in his nervousness it didn't register.

"What if the account I have access to doesn't have anything in it, or not much?" asked Kit.

"Just hope there's enough to satisfy me, Walker, just hope so."

At the time the conversation between Abbott and Kit Walker was ending, Rick Walker was sleeping fitfully on a Boeing 747 en route to Bangkok via a planned stopover in Tokyo. The plane was being buffeted by winds and rain and only a very tired person could expect to sleep at all.

Rick had checked his messages and the last one from Jane was filled with static, but it sounded like she was okay. Damn phones; I should have set us up with laptops. Settle down—that wouldn't necessarily have been any better. I'm probably worrying too much, yet, it may time to put Spiedel on ready call. Rick had been able to contact his aide who was already in Bangkok, but calls going the other way, and messages coming to him, were garbled by the storm or whatever other impish little ions fly around in the atmosphere and play havoc with electronics. I'll call later, he thought, as his eyelids drooped and he slipped back to sleep.

>>NINETEEN<<

"Annemasse"

Going through airport security with Ed Jones and Major Fears was a lot easier for the civilians Preston Volkers and Kit Walker than it would have been without the presence of those agents. Kit briefly wondered about the power of certain credentials; how good is security at spotting phony ones? Well, hell, we know not so good, don't we?

Anyway the group was on the plane and airborne and Kit felt like he was riding the runaway train ride in Frontier Land at Disneyland; or worse. Things were happening too fast, and now that Rick wasn't here he felt uneasy. He'd just recently met these other people, though they had deferred to Rick, so that was comforting. But Rick was on his way to who knows where; Bangkok, he says, then Iraq. What help will he be if I need him? And Jane, will she be okay? I should have insisted we stay together, but too late now. I'll see her in Hawaii soon.

The flight was long, stopping at London when it was mid-afternoon local time. Kit had finally been able to sleep, though he'd been awakened a little after midnight, his time, by the beeping of his cell phone.

"Sorry to wake you, cuz; just checking in with you," said Rick Walker.

"Oh, yeah, well, I was just dozing. Sorry, I missed the check-in time." "That's okay, I might not be available always either, but let's try to keep in contact until this is over. I talked to Jane; everything's fine with her. I told her I would call you and she sends love and kisses and an 'Aloha'.

"I still have my watch on California time so I'll call her in the morning and I'll check in with you once we get to Geneva."

"By the way, I haven't let been able to arrange for any extra security yet. But I think Jones and Fears are competent people, even if the major is a bit obnoxious. Now go back to sleep," Rick said, abruptly ending the call.

While they waited in London for their connection the four men went over the plan. Kit was concerned that he was wasting his time doing this because why would the bank let him have access to these accounts after all these years?

Ed Jones offered an explanation that was as much hopeful as it was positive.

"The way we understand it you are one of the people that Karl Volkers listed as an officer. You merely have to show identification that the bank finds acceptable, and you have to have the access numbers. It doesn't matter how many years have passed, the bank is going to figure anybody who has those two things either is legitimate, or was given the information by someone who wanted them to have it. With these long-running accounts that isn't unusual. The bank merely needs to take due care, as they say, to confirm your identification.

"Between your passport and, if they want, other identification, such as your California Driver's License, they shouldn't have any problem accepting you. But then, you need the account numbers. Those we have; the Army IDs of you and Bill Jenkins and Curtis Howard. Volkers used those–we think–figuring they were as secure a set of numbers as he could come up with. And it was a very good idea. Nobody would've ever have figured it out without some serious decoding abilities. The three guys who rode in the truck knew nothing about what was going down, so using their IDs was quite savvy of Volkers."

"There should be three accounts," said Preston. "We don't know how much is in any of them because we don't know how my uncle split up the money, or what he had it invested in. It could be many millions."

They had met later in the hotel bar shortly after checking in. Kit had decided he wanted to call Jane again, just to check on her so he excused himself to go back to his room. It was then that he got the call from Abbott.

In the normal lifetime of an ordinary person who is just trying to provide a good life for himself and his family, a situation like this never comes along. Only in the movies or spy thrillers. Kit tried first to calm down; he extended his hand straight out and it was still shaking.

Trying to think rationally was difficult because even if one concentrates on doing so, one can't be sure he is being rational. Kit's first thought was to tell the others. But they might insist that Kit stay until the bank opens. What was more important to them, Jane or the money? Sure, Jones would call someone and they'd assure Kit that the situation would be handled. But it's my wife, not theirs.

Calling the police in California seemed even less plausible. I can just imagine…and then, why not? It's a small town, would it hurt to call and say that I'm out of the country and I'm worried about my wife…I couldn't get through on the phone so could someone drive by and check on her? Yeah, but what if Abbott panics, uses Jane as a hostage or a shield!

He would call Rick. Kit tried several times but all he got was a pre-recorded message that the number he was trying to reach had been disconnected. Shit! Jane said she'd had problems calling too, so for all of Rick's concern about keeping in touch, it doesn't do any good now that I need him.

The unexpected– that might be his best offense. Kit called the front desk and asked for flight information. He found that he could get a flight out at 6:20 in the morning that would arrive in Los Angeles at 1:40 in the afternoon, Pacific Coast time. Trouble is, Abbott's expecting the money to be transferred in the morning. Even if I stall him, Jones and the others will be looking for me and they certainly have the resources to head me off, either at the airport or at the house. And again, the possibility of prodding Abbott into doing something… something Kit didn't want to think about.

And then the noise he'd heard while he was writing Abbott's instructions came back to him; hit him like the clanging of Big Ben. It was the grandfather clock, ringing out the quarter-hour! It's a noise that a person gets used to and often doesn't consciously hear unless it interrupts something else. So they were at the house! He must have threatened Jane to not to let me know. The most unexpected hiding place! But would he stay there? He's got to consider that I might not agree to his terms and instead will call for help.

Calmer now, Kit got on the phone. Fortunately for him, English is widely spoken in Switzerland and he had no problems making his arrangements. Kit returned to the bar, met the others and they all went to the dining room for a light meal. Kit wasn't very talkative and paid little attention to the conversation. He excused himself again after a few bites and said he needed a good night's sleep and would see them in the morning. When he returned to his room he left a wake up call for four a.m.

When the call woke him, Kit called the desk and ordered a taxi. If the spy movies he'd seen and the books he'd read were true, Jones or Fears or one of their apes would be waiting for him in the hall, or downstairs, or at the airport. Or maybe when he opened his door a bucket of water would fall on his head, awakening the others whose rooms were near by.

His concerns seemed silly, as there was no one watching for him and at this time of the morning not many people around at all, except for a few hotel staff, none of whom paid him the slightest bit of attention. Obviously the others are confident that there is no reason for me to not be here come morning, ready and eager to go to the bank and get this over with.

When Kit had thought about his plan he felt sure that when his absence was noticed Jones would check with the airlines, or have one of his agents do it, however these spies worked, and they would quickly find he was flying to Los Angeles. Long before he arrived they could surely contact agents who would be waiting for him. So he had to have a fall back plan.

The note he left in an envelope addressed: 'Ed, Preston, Major Fears', said:

'Received a call last night from Abbott...he has my wife, but I don't know where he's taken her...I doubt if it's anyplace we could locate easily but I need to get back anyway...he wants me to transfer money to his account...but I can't sit around for ten hours or more doing nothing while she is in danger...and I won't let you keep me here waiting for the bank to open...I'm on my way back...not sure what I will do but please don't send people charging in recklessly while Jane may be in danger...if you try to stop me I will consider our agreement broken, in other words, screw you and your money. I will try to get a hold of Rick in the mean time... Kit'

Kit wrote that he didn't know where Abbott had taken Jane because one, he wasn't certain Abbott would stay at the house, and two, he didn't want Jones or Fears calling in a whole squadron of sharpshooters. Not that at this moment do I have the foggiest damn idea of what I'll do when I get back to California, he admitted to himself.

By the time the others were waiting for Kit to meet them in the lobby of the hotel he was hours on his way. Ed and Preston were genuinely concerned about Kit; the possibility that Abbott or an ally had followed them here and kidnapped Kit occurred to them with a shudder. Major Fears, in his cynical fashion, suggested Kit Walker was at the bank already, trying to get the money for himself.

"With all due respect, major, that would be ridiculous for him to do. He couldn't possibly get away with anything and he knows it. C'mon, let's check his room."

Jones had kept an extra keycard for each of the rooms so they didn't have to bother anyone with explaining why they needed into Kit's room. Instantly they saw that bed was made as if unslept in, and there was nothing in the room that looked like Kit's belongings. Preston noticed the paper on the desk and they all eagerly read it together.

"Good God! That dumb sonuvabitch will get him and his wife killed."

"Goddammit!"

"So what do we do now?"

"No matter what his note says we need to get someone over there to intercept Walker."

"Like who?"

"Kidnapping is something the Bureau would get involved in," suggested Preston.

"Let's check flights first; maybe he hasn't even left the airport yet."

"I know the schedule," said Jones. "He would have gotten out hours ago." He checked his watch. "The flight would have to go via London, but it would have left there already."

"Does it stop in New York?" asked Fears.

"No, straight through to L.A. Should get there about ten-thirty tonight our time, which will be one-thirty in the afternoon there."

"It's about two in the morning in Los Angeles right now," said Preston. "I doubt if I could get a hold of anybody I know at this time, but maybe in a few hours. If we just call the local office they'll charge in, the whole SWAT-type scenario."

"He won't be there anyway. Walker's note said he doesn't know where he took her."

"So where's he going to look?"

"Jones shrugged, "Shit, I don't know. What would you do, either of you, in his place? Well, I'd be on the first plane I could get if it was my wife. I'd have to do something."

"Wouldn't it have been smarter to just do like Abbott says, and hope that he lets his wife go?" Fears said.

"Hope? The guy's a known killer and Walker can't be sure he can get any money transferred. Balls, man, we don't know ourselves for sure that we have the right code. I don't blame him for not wanting to sit around here."

At the same time the trio in Kit's room was trying to decide what to do next, Rick Walker was frantically calling Kit Walker. Kit had called Rick earlier but again had not been able to get through. But Rick had been able to retrieve messages. Gradually, as it neared four in the afternoon in Bangkok, whatever interference had been plaguing the atmosphere began to clear up and he was able to call out and receive incoming calls.

Sitting next to someone in the plane it was difficult for Kit to hold a conversation on the topic of his wife having been kidnapped. He told Rick to hold on while he went to a restroom.

"Okay, I can talk now."

"Do you have any idea where Abbott took Jane?"

"For all I know they could still be at the house, but I doubt he would stay there. I'm just hoping I can find something there that might give me a hint."

"When does he expect the money to be transferred?"

"Well, probably pretty soon. I expect he'll be calling me."

"And what will you tell him?"

"I'll try to stall for awhile. I'll tell him something about how because the accounts haven't been accessed in so many years they need to check my identification extra special. That they need to confirm with the State Department or something."

"Might buy you some time. But eventually he'll expect results, and you may be sitting in your house not knowing where Jane is and wishing maybe you'd stayed in Geneva."

Kit shook his head as he spoke. "No, I won't think that. I think more than anything this guy wants the money. And he's beginning to realize he needs me to get it for him, if anyone can. Of course, I still don't know for sure that I can get access to the money. Then I'd have wasted all that time waiting there."

"Sorry about all this, Kit."

"Hey, it's like you said before. Jones was going to come asking for my help anyway, and Abbott was going to find me sooner or later. I just wish you weren't so far away now."

"I'll try to contact Fears and insist that they agree to pay a...let's say a 'finder's fee' to Abbott; basically, ransom for Jane."

"That's an idea, although I doubt they'd come up with the cash very soon. And how would I convince Abbott to believe they'd deal that way with him?"

"I don't see why he and Jones couldn't work something out. We just need to find Abbott. I may be able to get away once I fill in General Lytle, but I'm not likely to get there soon enough to help. However, there are …resources I can round up…the cavalry… someone could be there to meet you at the house."

"Wait on that, Rick, please. If by chance he's still there, I don't want anything to get him riled up."

"You don't think your showing up there won't get him riled?"

"I have a better chance to make a deal. I have to use the power I have now and start to make things happen my way."

"Explain," said Rick, in his sharp military manner.

"Okay, the way I figure it is, I'm the one who can get at those accounts. It's my identification the bank wants. And sure, the government has its ways but I think if the CIA or the DIA or whoever else wanted to sidestep me they could have found a way. But now, I know enough that I can cause trouble if anything happens to Jane. And, Abbott needs me too. I'll try to promise him money if he lets Jane go, and I'll insist Jones and Fears agree to that."

"I don't think they're going to forget about what he did to Jenkins and Howard."

"I would hope not. But I don't think that issue needs to come up at this time."

"How about this," Rick offered. "I can get someone, a very well trained technician, to meet you at the airport. I'll tell him to do whatever you ask him to do. A little backup for you."

Kit digested this for a moment, then agreed. "Technician? That's swell, but I need to be sure he'll take my lead, okay?"

"You got it. Give me your flight number"

"Oh, a message is coming. It must be Abbott. I'll call him and call you back, Rick." Kit rattled off the British Airways flight number then cut off Rick without waiting for a reply. He checked the message.

"Where the hell are you Walker? You better not be screwin' around. I better get a call back from you in about sixty seconds."

Kit instantly punched up the call back number as he wondered if anybody in the plane was thinking what was taking that passenger in the head so long to do his business.

It had to be a little past two a.m. in Madre Hills, Kit figured. Abbott answered almost the instant Kit heard the first ring.

"What's going on, Walker? You at the bank?"

"Yes," Kit lied easily. "But it's taking a little time. Ah, something about the age of the accounts, my identification, ah, I need to talk to some high mucky-muck. May take a while yet. Let me talk to my wife."

Abbott wasn't pleased. "First of all, you can talk to her once the money's been transferred. Second…"

Like an old fashioned flashbulb going off the idea that had been developing in Kit's mind took shape.

"You wait, Abbott. You don't let me talk to Jane, I don't get any money for you. So here's the new plan. I'll transfer the money, however much is in the account once I get access to it, to an account that'll I'll establish in your name, but which will require you to personally identify yourself before you can access it. Then I'll come home, get my wife and you can go get your money. You don't like my idea, you don't get shit. You hurt my wife, I'll track you down and cut your balls off."

It was a risk, but Kit figured no worse than trying to stall Abbott for all the hours it'd be before he landed in Los Angeles. To anyone else it might seem foolish to dare anger Abbott, but from the two conversations he'd had with Abbott at the sports bar, Kit felt there was just the slightest hint of camaraderie between them. Killer or not, the two had served, albeit a short time together, in a war zone, and maybe a little nostalgia would be enough to temper the type of behavior Abbott had displayed in dealing with Jenkins and Howard, who he hadn't known well at all. Besides, Abbott needed Kit if he wanted any of the money.

"You're taking a big chance Walker. I make the plans, not you."

"No, not any more. The CIA found you once and they can find you again. Unless I make a deal with them about you."

"What kind of deal?"

"They can't get the money without me either. And Jones and the others are probably on their way here now, looking for me. But I can make a deal with them to let you have the money in this one account, and let you go, or I won't co-operate with them."

Abbott chewed on this, not happy and not sure how far to trust Walker. Abbott had always tried to be practical, bend with the wind, and take the route of least resistance. Walker too, seemed like a practical guy and he wants his wife back safely. Good thing he doesn't realize that I don't intend to hurt her.

"I want at least five million," he said.

"I'll try to get them to agree to five," said Kit. He knew he would have said yes to any amount at that point.

"When will I know?"

"I'll call you as soon as I have it arranged, but it might be a few hours." Kit said. "Now can I talk to my wife?"

"No, she's not hurt, Walker, but she's not here where I am."

"Which is?"

"Don't be stupid. Now she's fine, and if you do like you said, she'll stay fine. Just don't keep me waiting too long." He clicked off.

"God help me, I hope I know what I'm doing," Kit said to himself, but aloud. As he exited the restroom there was a long line. "Ah, had to make some calls," he said sheepishly, holding up the phone for all to see.

"The toilet's not for making phone calls!" an irate lady scolded him.

Kit returned to his seat and took the first good breath he'd had since he got on the phone. His throat was bone dry but he noticed that the nervousness that had made his body almost shake with fear as he was speaking to Abbott had dissipated. He wanted a drink but didn't want anything to muddle his thinking, not even one glass of wine. What I need is water and sleep, so I'll be rested for later. Already he was thinking about when he would have to call Abbott back, and trying to devise what he would say to stall him a bit longer. How long can I feed bullshit? How long will Jane be safe? Is she still safe?

>>TWENTY<<

"Into the Night"

Abbott had lied about Jane not being there. She had fallen asleep, on the sofa in the den with a length of cord tied around one wrist at one end and around a lamp at the other end. Her feet were also tied together. She was thankful he hadn't made the ties too tight. She wasn't gagged but the man had assured her several times that he wasn't joking that he would kill her and order her husband killed if she screamed or did anything else to attract attention. She still had doubts about him having a comrade in Geneva watching Kit but knew she couldn't dare to not believe that possibility.

It was shortly after three a.m. when she was awakened by her captor. Abbott untied her feet and said, "C'mon, it's time to move you." She couldn't reply because now he applied a gag. He led her out the back door and to the garage. The sky was clear with only a sliver of the moon and a handful of distant stars visible against the blackness. It was about as dark as the night gets in a suburb of a large city. With the mountains to the north and stretching for miles both east and west, much of the light from cities and residential communities was blocked.

Abbott helped Jane into the front seat of her car then moved into the driver's seat. Jane began to get terrified; was he taking her somewhere to kill her? Should she make a frantic effort to escape? Abbott noticed her slight move towards the door and he braked and reached over to press down the lock button.

"Don't try it, Mrs. Walker. I'm not going to hurt you if you co-operate. I'm taking you somewhere else for awhile but I don't want to hurt you. I talked to your husband; we have a deal going and as long as he lives up to it, you'll be fine. So stay put."

He actually spoke in a soft manner that could almost make one think he was on your side, except for the fact that Jane knew he was a dangerous killer who likely was not exactly concerned with anyone else's safety other than as to how it affected his chance to achieve what he wanted.

Once he got the car rolling he reached over and held her arm. "Just stay still," he reminded her again.

The drive was a short one. It took them around to a street that dead-ended near the wilderness park that flanked the houses at the foothills of the mountains. Abbott had spent enough time surveying the area so he knew exactly where he was going. The only problem would be the possible bad luck of a patrol car that might find a vehicle in this area at three o'clock in the morning a little suspicious. But it was a chance Abbott needed to take and in this small town it wasn't likely he'd be seen.

He guided the car as deep as he could into an alley that jutted off the street and parked at a fenced area that prevented vehicles from going any farther. The gate was locked, as was another one that led into the wilderness park trails. However, he knew there was a small opening at one end of the gate that provided just enough space for a person to squeeze through. People passed this way daily on their hikes. From here, one could then walk on the edge of the field to an opening in the brush that eventually merged with one of the trails that led deep into the mountains.

If the parked car was spotted by an observant policeman the worse that could happen, Abbott figured, was the car would be ticketed, and it was the Walker's car so what did he care? But his hope was that once he had the woman settled in he would have time to come back and move the car.

From the trunk he retrieved a bag of items he had packed while Jane was sleeping. He gave her the bag to carry and they started to walk into the near pitch-blackness. At this point Jane, who had also hiked many of the local trails, had an idea of where they were going so she was already thinking of how she would make an escape. But every time her mind went that direction she again wondered if the man was serious that he had someone watching Kit, and would have him killed if she did try to escape. To let her know he didn't completely trust her to behave, Abbott took the cord that was still tied to one wrist and tied the other end to his belt.

Once they had found the path through the brush and connected with a trail Abbott pulled out a flashlight and pointed it towards the ground. In this darkness it was too treacherous to walk blindly and there was scant chance of anyone being able to see the light.

They walked for several minutes until they came to the rickety wooden bridge Abbott had found in his earlier explorations. The bridge crossed a creek that usually contained only a trickle of water but could spew out a steady flow during a storm. The path across led to a pasture-like setting, a circle of land surrounded by oaks and other trees– not that much of anything was visible other than the few feet in front of them lit by Abbott's flashlight.

From here the footing became tentative, almost dangerous. Jane knew that the direction they were going led to the reservoir, a hug pit, for lack of a better word, which held the excess water that ran down during the winter rains, which, depending on the year, at times could be like a monsoon. At least once in the years she and Kit had lived here two people had been overcome by raging waters and washed down into this reservoir to be buried under tons of mud. It took two weeks of twenty-fours a day digging and hauling to find the bodies.

Her mind reeled at the thought that she was being led to her grave and she gave a tug. The sudden action startled Abbott and pulled the cord off his belt and for a moment Jane was loose. But that rebound was enough to knock her off her feet. She tumbled down the slope into the blackness.

"Hey!" Abbott yelled as he scrambled after her. The beam of the flashlight found her as she slipped a few more yards down the slope and crashed into a thicket, only a few feet from the drop-off into the pit.

"Dumb bitch! You crazy, or what!"

He dragged her to her feet as she spat dirt and leaves out of her mouth.

"You fall into that pit and you might not be found for weeks, you fool!" Abbott said, but this time quieter, though there certainly wasn't anyone within hearing distance. Still, at night, a voice can carry a long way and an insomniac even a couple miles away might wonder why voices were coming from the direction of the woods.

Abbott grabbed the cord and held it tightly, but without him seeing Jane was able to pull off one of the buttons from her blouse and drop it on the ground, a useless attempt at leaving a trail.

"I'll get the bag later. Now come on, and be careful."

Jane, her mouth still gagged, tried to say, 'where are we going', but it came out as a mumble. Her captor knew what she was trying to say. "I know a place here, but you need to follow my steps carefully, or the next time I'll let you fall into that pit and I'll kick rocks over you for good measure. You got that?"

Jane nodded and gingerly followed Abbott as he, almost gallantly, aimed the light on the ground in front of her while he himself took small, careful steps, as if maneuvering in a minefield. They reached the thick bushes that had stopped Jane's tumble.

"Now hold on to the cord with both hands and make sure you have a firm foothold."

Jane mumbled, again trying to ask where they were going.

The brush began to scratch her and she raised her hands to protect her face. Now there was no light at all as Abbott had turned off the flashlight. After a full minute of being led through the maze of the thicket, her face dirtied and bloodied from the snapping branches, her hair a tangled mess, they suddenly burst into an open area. At least, Jane felt it was open from the breeze of air, even though she could not see a thing.

Jane felt a tug on the cord and she was pulled backward, then turned and prodded with a hand on her back to step into a wall of black darker than any she had been through this night. She hesitated but Abbott pushed her harder.

"There's a cave. Go on, it's okay. I've been here before and there are no snakes," he said, reading her mind.

A few feet forward and she literally could not see her hands even has she brushed dirt off her nose. Then there was light as Abbott pointed the flashlight at her. The sudden glare startled her and she turned around; as Abbott moved the light in a circular motion she could see the walls of a cave she never knew existed. The man pointed the light farther into the darkness and again prodded her to move.

While the shape of the cave seemed to be an oval only a few feet deep from what Jane had first seen when Abbott flashed the light, she know realized that one branch tunneled much deeper. The ground was hard and a little damp but the footing was actually firmer here than it had been outside coming down the slope. They moved about twenty feet into the cavern.

"Stop," the man said. She did and once again began to believe she would die here and wouldn't be found until the coyotes had left nothing of her but a pile of shattered bones. Then a brighter light came on and the flashlight went off. Around her she could see a blanket on the ground, a pillow, a sleeping bag and several boxes.

Abbott reached to her face and Jane pulled away.

"Stay still; I'm going to take off this gag."

When he had removed the gag Jane gasped and thought this is what it must feel to a newborn taking its first breath outside its mother's body.

When she looked around she realized Abbott had set this cave up as a place to keep her; for how long she couldn't guess. There were bottles of water and some old rusty cans that she surmised were to be used for personal hygiene. Now it dawned on her that the bags she had been carrying contained items of food. A camper's lantern provided adequate but muted light.

What made this cave ideal for Abbott's use wasn't just the isolation of it. He was sure no one had been here in years. He'd almost fallen into the pit himself when he decided to force his way through the thicket. But the cave had been used in the past, probably as a storage site for some long abandoned mine. There were bits of metal and old tools and best of all thick iron rings bolted to the inside wall of the cave. They might have been used to secure ore cars.

Abbott had no compunction about killing a person, but it wasn't in his best interest to do in the woman, or even to hurt her too much. In fact, as he'd known for some time, he was bluffing about nearly everything. If he could scare Walker into transferring money for him, so much the better. He was shrewd enough and adept at changing his identity and could do so again easily, and obviously would need to. The mere fact that Jones had found him was a clear indication he'd become blasé in the past few years.

But if Walker called his bluff, or for some reason truly could not get to the money, Abbott figured he would walk away—or run, more likely—and not take revenge on anyone. Killing this woman would likely inflame passions that would hunt him down no matter where he went. I may be old and slow, but I'm not stupid.

So he merely wanted to secure the woman as long as it would take to determine whether or not Walker had kept up his end. He tied both her wrists with cord then attached the other ends to two of the rings. The ties were loose enough not to cut into her but the knots were virtually impossible to untie with fingernails even if Jane could reach the cord. And the knots on the rings were even tighter. He also took her shoes away.

"It won't do you any good to try to get loose because I won't be far and I'll see you if you try to get out of here. And I've explored the cave enough to know there's only the one way in and out. I need to be more in the open to where my cell phone will work better. Once I know the money has been transferred to my account, I'll let you go…well; I'll leave directions for your husband. In the mean time, get some sleep. I'll be back when it's light to see that you get some food."

Abbott went to the entrance of the cave and sat. After a few minutes he stepped back inside to check on his captive; she appeared to be asleep. He went out again and retraced his steps to retrieve the bag they'd dropped. He carried it with him to the wooden bridge and set it down where he could find it again. Then he hiked back to where he'd parked the car. Without putting the headlights on he eased the car out of the alley and onto the side street. He then put the headlights on lest he be stopped by a patrol car and drove back to the Walker home. He knew it'd be more convenient to have a car closer but he didn't want to leave anything around that might cause a cop or neighbor to get a little too inquisitive.

He then returned to where he had parked his rented car and drove it into the main section of town and parked it in city lot that allowed twenty-four overnight parking. The hike back was uphill and began to tire him. He stopped to catch his breath a few times, and kept to the shadows and darker areas. Whenever he saw the lights of a car approach he ducked behind a tree or bushes, but in this sleepy village there wasn't much traffic at this time of night.

It took him a half hour to reach the gate and stepping carefully in the dark it took another half hour to reach the cave. Jane was still asleep. He moved to the entrance of the hole and sat down, weary. He set his phone down next to him and soon dozed off.

It was now about four in the morning in the Los Angeles area, still very dark, especially behind the thick brush that hid the cave in which Abbott slept at the entrance and Jane deeper inside. It was about one in the afternoon in Geneva where Jones, Fears and Preston Volkers were picking over the remains of a lunch and the beers they had used to wash it down and pass the time. For the most part, the buck had been passed to Jones' boss Syd Swanson, who, as it happens, was on his way to meet them.

When Jones had called Swanson, expecting to awaken him at his home, he was surprised to hear is boss's wife answer. She knew better than to say much, but recognizing Jones' voice she, in her sleepy state, told Jones that she thought Syd was off to meet him in Geneva.

"Are you sure, Betty?"

"No, I'm sorry, you know I shouldn't say, even to you, Ed. I just thought, well, he said he'd be gone a few days and I'd overheard him on the phone saying something about Geneva. I just thought you knew."

"Well, I'm here; he knows where to find me. I'll just wait. I won't say you said anything, Betty, but if he calls home tell him I called. And sorry I woke you."

"Thanks, Ed. Good night."

"I still say we should go to the bank," suggested Major Fears. "Preston, as Karl Volkers' heir, might be able to gain access."

Jones shook his head. "No; we talked to the bank officials when Preston and I were here before. Our State Department would have to get involved, for one thing. For another, I figure we have one chance at those accounts. If we go in there and appear to be taking wild shots, they'll freeze up the accounts and force us to go to higher authorities. You don't want that, do you major?"

Fears chewed on what Jones had said. He felt that eventually, any money in those accounts would go to the Army. And he, Fears, should get credit for it. Likely as not the process would be held up in legal entanglements for months, if not years. By which time no one will remember who had found the Army's money. No, he'd have a better chance if Kit Walker could get them into the Swiss accounts, even if we have to transfer the money to an escrow account. At least General Asher would know what Fears' contribution had been. The major calculated that retrieving the money, and, if he could nail Abbott for the murder of the truck driver, would be a coup for his career.

"So why do you think Swanson is coming here?" asked Preston.

"First of all I don't know that he is. He wife blurted it out that she thought he was. If he shows up we need

259

to act a little surprised. I don't want to get his wife in trouble."

"What's the big deal?"

"He may wonder what else she tells people. Syd won't be happy; he can be strict at times. If Syd doesn't call soon I'll try him at the office when it opens, just to check if by chance he is there. Maybe I can find out something. Otherwise, I don't know what else we can do except wait."

He turned to Fears. "Major, I'm sure you want to stay, but I don't want to hold up all your plans."

"I think I should be here to see if we can access the accounts."

Jones swirled the remains of his beer. "Suit yourself, but I don't see us getting in there anytime soon."

"I'll have to wait until I can contact General Asher."

"Yeah, I suppose that's true. Well, there's plenty of time, but what I will do when it's morning in Los Angeles is call and arrange to have someone meet Walker when he arrives. I don't want us to lose track of him."

Kit Walker had probably read too many spy novels. There were those old Ian Fleming books and that wonderful Len Deighton series. He starting thinking too much like a secret agent. So he analyzed the situation and reasoned that Jones would expect Kit to take the earliest flight out of Geneva, and the one that would get him to Los Angeles the soonest. That would have been the British Airways flight at 6:20 in the morning.

But the CIA agent hadn't memorized the entire list of possible routes to the city of angels. A half hour *after* the British Airways flight was an Aer Lingus flight that went through Dublin and arrived in Los Angeles forty minutes after the earlier flight. Kit calculated that anybody Jones sent to meet Kit would be watching the British Airways flight and might spend a lot of time eyeing the people sift through their luggage, trying to spot Walker.

With a little luck, the Aer Lingus flight would land him before the agent could regroup and start thinking of other flights that had originated in Geneva. Kit only had a carry-on bag so he wouldn't need to stop for luggage. He envisioned himself acting nonchalantly as he strode off the plane unhurriedly; maybe pause at a newspaper rack or a coffee stand, while he knew inside his heart would be beating fast.

But no, I'll relax, I'll be ready. Maybe it's foolish to want to avoid help, but at this point these well-meaning buddies of mine have got me—and more, Jane—in a mess. Maybe it's time I need to think about getting us out of it myself.

When Kit had arrived at the airport he checked the board. He was dismayed that his flight was leaving ten minutes late. But he got a piece of luck when just before boarding he noticed that the British Airways flight was listed as departing twenty-five minutes later than scheduled.

It wasn't until much later that Kit realized he'd given Rick the wrong flight number. Originally he was going to take the British Airways flight, and had that number in his mind. When he had to abruptly finish his conversation with Rick he'd given him the BA flight number, not meaning to purposely mislead his cousin. On reflection he realized that was what he wanted to do and he wasn't going to correct the mistake. Not that he didn't trust Rick, but he rationalized that no matter what Rick's instructions were to whomever he contacted, higher powers might decide that Kit not be allowed to move around at his own discretion.

Kit delayed calling Abbott again for as long as he dared. As the plane soared over the Rocky Mountains, now less than two hours from landing in Los Angeles, where it was now around noon, he began to get nervous again, thinking about what he needed to say to Abbott and whether he could stall him any longer. He waited until the plane was only a few minutes from LAX, just before the announcement came for all passengers to take their seats, then he entered the restroom to make his call.

>>TWENTY-ONE<<

"Desperate Measures"

By the time Ed Jones was able to contact Syd Swanson by phone the latter was already in Geneva en route to the hotel where Jones and the others were staying. He had left a guarded message on Swanson's cell phone saying, '*KW flying back on his own...please advise next step.*'

Swanson seemed unusually unconcerned that Kit Walker had skipped out. He was more concerned about the safe deposit box that Preston Volkers had access to. It was late afternoon but still enough time to get to Annemasse.

"Syd, I told you before, Preston and I looked through everything in the box. You have copies of all of it."

"I have to get the original notebook, Ed. Just go along with me on this."

"That's fine, we can do that. Preston can get it for you. The money is still there too."

Syd turned to Preston. "Do you mind if we take the money?"

"You're actually asking my permission?" Preston feigned astonishment.

"Being polite. But if the rest of it also matches the serial numbers of the money lost in that truck robbery, then it's not yours anyway."

"Easy come, easy go."

"What about Walker, Syd? Shouldn't we get people onto him?"

"How do we do that without revealing that we are butting in where we don't belong?"

"For Christ's sake Syd, Walker's note says that Abbott has taken his wife! She's in danger and you're worried about protocol?"

Syd didn't answer for a moment, as if preparing a reply.

"It's being taken care of, Ed. Don't worry about it."

Jones in turn didn't say anything at first, confused by his boss's apparent lack of concern and his statement that rang hollow, as if he didn't believe what he was saying.

"And are we going to bring Walker back here to access the accounts?"

Swanson nodded, "In due time."

"There's these, too. I suppose I should buck them up to you." Ed handed a large orange envelope to Syd. In it were the pictures that had been delivered to Walker's house. "These are from our friend Antonio, or Tony Abbott, if you prefer."

Syd was confused as he scanned the obviously old, black and white photos. "Are we supposed to know what these are?" He asked, not expecting an answer. Jones gave him none other than a shrug.

Preston chimed in after a few seconds. "This man," he pointed, "looks like my uncle, Karl Volkers. I have no idea who the other one his."

Sys studied the photos for a minute or so, then put them back into the envelope. These will go to Cushman, I suppose, he thought; "I'll pass these on to the lab," is what he said. "They or the archive boys may be able to identify who and where and maybe what."

"Another one of my uncle's operations, you think?" asked Preston.

"Chances are I'll never find out myself once I pass these on. And if I do, fat chance I'd be allowed to tell you, Preston. But thanks for all your help with this."

Ed's wide-eyed snap look at Preston told the latter that Syd's abrupt attitude was not the norm.

In the thicket outside the cave Abbott waited impatiently. He wanted to call Walker but decided he'd wait a little while longer. It was past noon already; he'd slept until ten and when he awoke had a moment of panic that the woman had escaped. He'd turned on his flashlight and stepped into the cave. She was there, awake, but helpless to do anything. She seemed to have had only recently awakened too.

"Can you untie me? I need to pee and I'd like to clean up." She spoke it as a command, not wanting to ask for something that she should have been able to do normally and easily in the comfort of her own home.

Abbott released her bonds from the rings. "Don't get reckless now," he warned. "I'll be right at the entrance; take ten minutes then I'll return and fix us some food."

Jane did what she needed to do as quickly as possible then began to explore deeper into the cave, reaching out with her hands and stepping forward only an inch at a time. After a minute of this one foot didn't find the ground. She bent down slowly and reached out with her hands: empty space. She felt around her and found a pebble which she tossed into the darkness. It took several seconds before she heard a faint splashing sound. Just then she heard the man call out.

"I'm coming back in; make yourself decent."

She rushed back to where she'd been held captive and made like she was brushing her hair. Abbott reached in the bag and brought out a comb and a pack of packaged hand and face wipes.

"You think of everything, don't you?" Jane said

265

Abbott didn't answer but also pulled out nutrition bars and packages of juice. A faint beeping caught his attention. It was his cell phone, which he'd left lying at the entrance of the cave.

"That better be your husband," he said as he tossed the food at Jane.

Kit had become nervous again, his hand so sweaty he could barely keep a grip on the cell phone.

"Okay, Abbott. We've got a deal. There's about three and a half million in the account I can access." He hadn't thought much about what amount he would tell Abbott; a number just rolled off his tongue.

"How long is it going to take?"

"Ah, a few more hours. They…"

"What's taking so long? Dammit, Walker don't…"

"Easy, man. We're dealing with a lot of red tape. You know how the freakin' government works. These guys are fine with it but they have to get approval."

"They try to get approval from higher up and the whole deal might collapse! You can access the money yourself, can't you? So do it! You have to put it in my name, and my name only."

"What name, Tony Abbott?"

"No, you fool! Put it in the name of Francisco Antonio Abazini. And here's the passport number." Abbott reeled off the numbers from memory.

"And listen, Walker, that name and the number you don't give to anyone, you understand? I find out you double-crossed me and I can still come back and get at you. You know I can. And your wife, you understand me?"

"I got you. But one thing first…my wife, I want to speak to her."

"You're pushing me, Walker."

This time he was willing to beg, if that's what it took. "Listen, please let me talk to her. Give me break, Abbott. I'll transfer the money anyway but let me hear her voice."

Kit waited for several seconds while the phone was quiet. He listened intently for background sounds but the only thing he thought he heard was the chirping of a bird.

Finally Abbott spoke again. "Wait a second."

Again the wait, then Jane was on the phone. "Kit? Are you okay?" "Jane, thank God! Are *you* okay? Can you talk?"

"No, she can't talk," interrupted Abbott. "Just say hello and goodbye."

"I'm fine Kit. Just do as he says, please? I love you, sweetheart."

"I love you too. I'll see you soon. Abbott, you there?"

"Yeah, I'm here."

"When will you release my wife?"

"As soon as I confirm that the money's in my account. So get going."

"You know that still may take a couple hours before everything is finalized and you can get confirmation."

"Then you'd better move on it, Walker. I'm getting tired of this and I'm sure you are too."

"Should I call you again when it's all taken care of?"

Again there was silence. "No. I'll call the bank in two hours. Make sure it's all done by then." He punched off before Kit could reply.

By the time his plane was landing in Los Angeles Kit began to believe that he might have some good luck. The British Airways plane that should have landed forty minutes ahead of the Aer Lingus flight had been delayed further and was landing at virtually the same time as Kit's plane.

Now we'll see if anyone intercepts me. Now we'll see what steps Jones and Rick and who knows who have taken. Kit's heart was pounding as he tried to act nonchalant and be patient as he waited to make his way up the aisle to exit the plane. He felt sweaty and worried and was sure his anxiety was spelled out on his forehead in big red letters.

As he entered the terminal he forced himself to look straight ahead though it was impossible for his eyes not to wander left and right looking to see if someone was coming to intercept him.

There were people looking for him. But as Kit had hoped, they were first checking the British Airways flight that been the earliest from Geneva that Kit would have had a chance to leave on. Even intelligence agencies can't always get instant results on information requests and it wasn't until ten minutes after the BA flight had landed that the agent Swanson had sent to find Kit received the news: Walker was on an Aer Lingus flight.

As Swanson's man arrived at the arrival gate for the Aer Lingus flight—having been delayed by the red tape of arranging with security for him to get into that area—everyone was off the plane and a stream of people was scurrying towards the baggage carousels. At about the same time this man, and the other, operating separately, began to walk faster, not daring to break into a trot lest they worry some skittish security card and end up closing down the entire airport, though maybe that would be a way to keep Walker here, wouldn't it? They both moved with a purpose, cutting in and out of the throng of arriving passengers, hoping their quarry had checked luggage. Besides the CIA man there was the one arranged for by Rick; the cavalry, as he had put it. He was military, but in civilian clothes. He truly did have instructions from Rick to follow Kit's lead…but to a point. At all costs the man was advised to make the safety of the Walkers his priority.

Oddly though, the man had received nearly instantaneous instructions from two sources regarding the same situation. And so he had two priorities to deal with. This was not unheard of, but it could be difficult to satisfy two masters, especially when lives were at stake.

Kit had proceeded to the car rental counter at a pace as fast as he thought he could maintain without drawing attention to himself. He was out of the airport before the two men looking for him had even reached the baggage claim area. His prayers for light traffic must have been answered because Kit was miles away before his seekers gave up looking for him at the airport. The CIA agent was in a quandary: he was supposed to contact Swanson and only Swanson but when he'd tried to call he'd only received voice mail. He left a message, not realizing that the man he was calling was on another continent, and decided to get a cup of coffee while he waited for instructions from either Swanson, or the other agent Swanson said would contact him.

The other man had instructions to proceed to the Walker home if he didn't connect at the airport, and to call Rick Walker on the way there. At least his second source would not bother contacting him again, nor expect any contact from the man; he expected results and did not care to hear of anything else. Don't enter the house until we've had a chance to speak, General Walker had ordered, unless you think there is imminent danger.

In Annemasse Syd Swanson and Ed Jones sat in a booth poring over the notebook that Karl Volkers had left there so many years ago. They'd needed Preston to get the box for them but then Syd insisted that Preston not accompany him and Jones into the booth.

"There could be national security implications here," said Swanson.

Even Ed Jones rolled his eyeballs. "Syd, he's already read the entire friggin' book."

"Ed, I have orders that you don't need to know about. And this was put here by a former CIA agent. And nephew or not, Preston is not a member of the CIA."

"It's okay. I don't need to see it again," said Preston.

Major Fears was not so acquiescent but it did him no good.

"Major, you can complain all you want but for now I have no way of knowing whether the Army or the DIA or anyone else has any right to see what's here. So file your complaint with someone if you want, but stay out of my way."

He was not used to being spoken to this way, but Swanson was not swayed by mention of the names of several generals that Fears thought would intimidate Swanson. The major was shunted aside to sit and wait with Preston.

"Believe me, major. I've seen what's in the box. There's some cash of course, we told you that. The notebook does appear to relate to CIA activities and you are not likely to be allowed to read it."

"You did, didn't you, when you were here the first time?"

Preston nodded. "True, but we didn't know what we were getting into then. I'm not even sure we know now."

Inside the booth, Ed asked Syd what he was looking for in addition to what he'd already read from the copies Ed had made earlier.

"I really did give you everything, Syd."

"I don't doubt it, Ed. And you're right, this is a waste of time. I'm not sure myself what I'm supposed to be looking for. I'll just take this with me. You count up this money. I'll be back with a satchel or something to carry it in."

Abbott had re-tied Jane to the bonds that were then tied to the iron rings in the walls of the cave, and gagged her. He told her he'd be just outside but that wasn't true. He was actually going back to move his car so it would be closer to where he could get at it when he was ready to go. The woman wouldn't be told when he was leaving the area. Once he verified that the money had been transferred he would began to drive south. Maybe by the time he reached San Diego he'd call Walker and give him his wife's location.

He was beginning to feel crowded and anxious at how long this was taking. Sooner or later somebody would track his movements. They'd done it already and though he'd been able to spot the activity and avoid it when he wanted to, he had an itch that said danger was near. In Abbott's kind of work that itch often expressed itself when a job was taking longer than he felt it should. It usually meant things weren't going smoothly enough and it was time to depart. On more than one occasion responding to this itch had saved his life, even if it meant not completing a job on time, or at all.

And no one was paying him for this job—this was money owed him from before. No one seemed to be reacting the way he expected. Even this amateur, Walker, he seems to know how much he can push me. Damn, it's because I knew him in 'Nam, that's all. If I'd never met the guy before I wouldn't let him push me. But then, if I'd never met him I probably wouldn't be here in the first place.

Despite Abbott's taking care not to hurt her much, and to see that she had food and a comfortable place to rest, Jane was not one to sit and assume her kidnapper would release her soon, and safely. Every waking moment Jane was thinking how to get free. But dare she, even if the chance presented itself, unless she already knows that Kit is safe? And she'd been awake more than Abbott realized. She'd heard him as he broke through the thicket, this at the time he went to move his car, though she had no idea what he was doing or where he had gone.

In the darkness Jane felt around with her feet and with her hands as much as she could, but due to the way she was tied her range was limited. At the edge of her reach she felt something hard and sharp. She tried to dig at it with her fingers but all she accomplished was to cut herself and grind dirt under her nails. Her work paid off as a rock the size of an egg came loose, and the hole it left gave her some leverage to dig deeper. Now she felt something metallic. She also heard Abbott returning so Jane lay back and closed her eyes.

Kit found himself looking in the rear view mirror so often he had to remind himself to watch what was in front of him. After a half hour he eased up, almost sure no one was following him. He kept his speed at around 75 mph, faster than many cars but not the fastest. Instead of going into downtown Los Angeles he decided to go farther on the 105, all the way to the 605. It was a bit roundabout, but if someone was tailing him it might give Kit another chance to spot them. And, sometimes this route was faster even if longer, what with the potential for traffic foul-ups when going right through the heart of downtown Los Angeles.

And always his mind came back to, *what am I going to do?* He didn't think Abbott had stayed at his house, but didn't think he would have been able to move Jane very far without risking being spotted. Of course if he did something like tuck her in the trunk, who would notice anything awry? Still, the house was the place to start.

As he reached the cul de sac he looked around at the cars. They all looked like the neighbor cars he knew. He pulled over to the curb about a hundred yards down from his house. He thought of calling Rick; he thought of calling Abbott again; maybe he could hear something that would give a clue. But no, by now Abbott is expecting the transfer of money to have been made. I don't think I can stall him on the phone anymore.

Kit began to walk towards his house. He stopped in front of his neighbor and noticed that no cars were out. This neighbor always left his car out; if it wasn't in the driveway he wasn't home. Kit walked down the driveway at a normal pace, looking to anyone who might notice him as if he was simply going around back to see if his neighbor was home. Nothing unusual there.

Like he did it everyday, Kit opened the gate and walked into the yard.

"Bob," he called out, but not too loudly. No one answered. Because of the bushes on the side that abutted his own house, Kit knew he could not be seen here from anyone in his backyard. But he could peek through the bushes and spy into his own yard.

After five minutes of silently prying through the foliage he pulled himself up on the block wall, spread the bushes, and knowing he risked a sprained ankle or worse, leapt over the wall into his yard, scratching both arms on the bushes as he tumbled down. He quickly got up and spread himself tightly against the wall, waiting.

Another five minutes passed before he dared to move. Now he crept towards the back door, watching through the window for any movement. It dawned on him he should have a weapon. On top of the barbeque was a wrench he had been using to tighten a bolt. It was a king size wrench, one that felt solid in his hand. He wondered if he'd be able to use it on a person.

He decided to check the garage first. Jane's car was there. So she <u>had</u> come back here! This is where Abbott grabbed her. But are they still inside? If so, I cannot believe he hasn't come after me already, unless he's waiting to attack when I come in.

Kit's heart nearly stopped when he heard a beep and felt a vibration. It was his goddamn cell phone! The beep was loud enough to wake the dead, but fortunately being in the garage it wasn't likely anyone in the house could have heard the beeping. It was Rick.

"Jesus, Rick, you scared me!"

"You didn't meet my man at the airport. He's worried about you, Kit."

"Uh, yeah, well I gave you the wrong flight number. Not on purpose, Rick, but then I never did call back to correct it. I figured whoever you sent wouldn't let me come back to the house."

"He's sitting outside your house right now."

"What? Where, you mean, here, at my house?"

"Yes, he just called me. He said he sees a rented car parked and thinks it might be you. Are you okay? And where exactly are you?"

"I'm in the garage. I don't think anybody is in the house, but I'm not sure."

"Kit, listen to me. I can understand you might not be ready to trust anybody, but the man I sent is good. Work with him. I'll give you his number so you two can talk. He's an expert, Kit."

"An expert what?"

The contact momentarily broke off and Kit feared they would lose the connection. Then he heard Rick say, "He's an expert at what he does, Kit. Talk to him."

"Alright, I will. Give me his number."

This is nuts, Kit thought. Rick calls me from Bangkok to give me the phone number of a guy who's a hundred yards away!

"This is Commander Spiedel," Kit's call was answered.

"Ah, you're from General Walker, right?" Kit asked.

"Yes sir. And you are Mr. Kit Walker?"

"That's right. I'm in my garage. The general said you are in front of my house."

"I'm parked nearby. I don't think anyone is in the house. I'd like to go the front door, with your permission."

"Go ahead, but if this guy is in there I'm not sure he's going to answer the doorbell, commander."

"No, but I can get a better look at the inside of the house, Mr. Walker."

"Go ahead. I'll wait a few seconds then I'm going to use my key to the back door."

"I wouldn't advise that," Spiedel said, in a slightly firmer tone.

"Maybe not, but General Walker said you're supposed to follow my orders. So go on and ring the doorbell. Right after you do, I'm coming in. Keep this connection open."

The overcast sky looked like it would bring rain soon–though in southern California such skies were often only a teaser of rain. The gray and black clouds provided for an unusually gloomy afternoon, but it was a darkening that Kit welcomed. It made him feel he was more difficult to see as he crept from the garage to the backdoor, cell phone in one hand and wrench in the other. He heard the ring of the front doorbell and froze. As he heard it ring a second time he turned the handle on the back door. It wasn't locked.

"The door's open; I'm coming in," he whispered into the phone.

"Abbott! Jane! Anybody!" Kit felt silly calling out but would feel maybe dead if Abbott suddenly popped out from somewhere and attacked Kit. Calling out might just cause Abbott to make a movement that Kit could hear. But he heard nothing. The house was still until the clocked chimed, reminding Kit of the chiming he'd heard over the phone when talking to Abbott– was it an hour or days ago?

"Are you alright, Mr. Walker?" Kit heard from the phone in his hand.

"Oh, yes", he said, then walked to the front door and opened it for the commander– who promptly pushed his way in and said, "Please let me go first, Mr. Walker."

Spiedel was not a big man but appeared to be a strong one. Kit had been expecting someone in uniform but Spiedel wore a polo shirt stretched by muscular arms and in his hand appeared a pistol of some sort, quickly drawn as he entered the house. He held one arm up to keep Kit back and silently and with cat-like quickness went from room to room, assuring that there was no one in the house.

When he was finished he spoke to Kit. "General Walker says you have reason to believe your wife has been kidnapped, and was held here. But now you think the kidnapper has moved her. Do you have any idea where he might have taken her?"

Kit shook his head. "Not off hand. My wife's car is in the garage, so I assume he took her in his car. But when I last spoke to him, it sounded like he was outdoors. Of course, he could be at a house somewhere."

"Well, sir, you know your house better than I do. I suggest you look around and see if there is anything that might give you a hint. Anything at all. I am going to call General Walker."

Kit began to look at the house and its belongings in a way he hadn't looked at them in years. It was like he saw things he'd forgotten they had. But nothing seemed out of place or in any way gave him an idea of where Abbott might have taken Jane. He looked in the garage and in Jane's car. He walked in the yard looking for what he couldn't say. He went behind the garage, again, looking for something that he couldn't even began to guess at. Then he saw something that didn't belong.

Not that it was a big deal, but he knew his yard and he knew that only a few months ago he had repaired the back fence. Beyond the fence that was on his property was a chain link fence that separated his yard from the field beyond. He wasn't sure whose fence that was, his or the city or whomever owned the empty land that formed a buffer between the mountains and the residential area. But stuck to the top of the fence was a piece of cloth, like from a shirt. He couldn't reach it because the ground rose up at a steep incline. But he knew that cloth had not been there very long.

Now how would a piece of cloth get caught on that fence, he asked aloud.

Surprisingly he got an answer. "Do you think someone climbed over?"

He turned around to see Commander Spiedel.

"Hmmm. I wonder. People use to ask me if I feared coyotes getting into the yard. I always told them that because of the angle and the difference in elevation between the field and the yard, anything trying to get over would skewer themselves. But I remember now, a few days ago...or maybe a week; hard to keep the time straight lately with all that's happened. Anyway, my wife and I and the dog went for a walk. When we got back the dog became agitated. He went around the house smelling things like there was strange scent. I didn't think too much of it at the time, but later I wondered if Abbott hadn't been in the house.

"Now I see this and I remember when Rick and I met him. He had a cut on his arm."

Kit pointed at the cloth on the fence. "He might have snagged his shirt. He probably misjudged how difficult it'd be to get over, and caught his shirt and cut himself.

That means he came from the field side and it could mean he's been watching our house from out there."

Kit pointed in the direction of the field and the mountains. It was getting seriously dark now and the mountains formed a long and jagged, purple shadow.

"What's out there?" asked Spiedel.

Kit pointed in the direction of a grove of trees. "From here, commander, you could hike and climb all the way to the Mohave Desert, if you didn't kill yourself trying.

"For the local people, there are hiking trails, streams to camp at when the water is flowing, and picnic grounds. But it gets rugged if you go very far in there and in the dark, it's impossible."

"You've been there often?" Spiedel asked.

Kit nodded, thinking a bit before he answered. Thinking that Abbott was out there, holding Jane, in some canyon or culvert. He could even have set up a tent. There are a thousand places a person could set down and not be seen by another hiker for days or weeks, or ever, if he really worked on finding a secluded niche in the hillside.

"Sure, I've hiked there a lot. So has Jane. Abbott must have scoured the area in the last few days, maybe found a place to hide out."

Kit looked at his watch, panicky that by now Abbott had tried to contact the bank and found that there still was not any money awaiting him.

"I should call him; see if I can stall him some more."

>>TWENTY-TWO<<

"As I was saying... "

When Abbott had finished his last conversation with Kit Walker he clipped the phone onto his belt, as he normally did. But he forgot that inside the cave itself cell phone reception would be iffy. So when Kit tried to call him next—unbeknown to Abbott from a few thousand miles nearer than Abbott realized—the connection wasn't made.

Abbott hadn't had much sleep so he decided to wait inside the cave, after double-checking that the woman was still tied down securely, and try to nap until Walker called again. Jane, too, was tired and knowing she could not continue now to dig at the chains with Abbott so near, lay back as comfortably as she could and instantly fell sleep.

Outside, the clouds blackened, and no longer able to contain the water a drizzle began, gaining strength every minute. It was the time of year that southern California can get a storm; despite what the Mamas and the Papas said, most years it does rain in California, at least once in awhile.

When Kit tried to call Abbott his phone rang several times before a curt message came on: "leave a short message," was all it said. At first surprised by the message Kit recovered to leave the excuse he had ready this time.

"Abbott, there was some confusion on the first attempt to transfer, so now they have to re-confirm my ID, which means meeting with another, ah, higher mucky-muck, but it should only take another hour or so. Ah, but don't call me now because I'll be with these people, so, ah, wait for me to call you...it'll be real soon, I promise."

"God, I hope he'll let me stall a little longer," he said, talking to himself, forgetting that Spiedel was there.

"Don't shut off your phone yet," Kit heard.

He looked over at the commander and saw that the man had a device, about the size of a cell phone but looking more like a gadget out of Star Trek. A yellow light was beeping on the screen amongst a series of numbers.

"What is that you..."

Spiedel held up his hand to silence Kit. A few seconds later the beeping light turned to a solid green.

"Affirmative; I've got it," Spiedel said. "You can shut off your phone now. I suggest you don't call him or answer the phone for the time being."

Kit looked at Spiedel, then looked at the device, waiting for an explanation.

"This locked in the location of the phone you called. As we move closer to him it will give us an approximate distance and direction. It looks like he's less than a mile from here. Is it possible there is a place as near as a mile where he could be holding your wife?"

Kit said nothing as he tried to see in his mind the various trails that led into the mountains and could provide a place within a mile that Abbott would feel was secure enough to hide out. Kit knew there were lots of small clearings in the bushes and side trails where someone could secrete themself for a short while, but it would take days to scour them all. Then again, maybe not, if Spiedel's contraption really worked.

"We can't get over this fence," Kit told Spiedel. "We have to drive around and up to the park. We can hike in from there."

Spiedel grabbed Kit by the arm. "It might be best if you let me go myself, Mr. Walker."

"Not a chance," Kit said as he brushed the commander's hand away. Kit started to walk, then trot, towards the house, then he stopped and looked back at Spiedel. "Do you have any other weapons?"

"Just the one," Spiedel answered, which was not true. "Best if you show me the way and let me handle this man when we find him."

Kit nodded as he dashed through the back door of the house. He came out with his foot-long Mag-Lite, which in itself could be a formidable weapon. He jingled the car keys and hustled into the garage. "Let's go then."

As the crow flies they only needed to travel about a hundred yards to get to a point from which they could began a hike into the brush that covered the foothills. But they had to drive down the street and around and back up another city block. Kit parked on the street and they walked towards the fence that shut out traffic from what became a fire road at this point. The gate to the public area, which afforded easy entrance to the authorized hiking trails, plus fire pits, tables and other facilities to allow for picnicking in a woodsy environment, was already locked up. The police must be wary of a heavy storm and decided to close the park early as long as there were no cars around or other signs that any people were still in the area, Kit thought. Better for us; less chance of anyone seeing us or getting in the way of our search.

Kit led Spiedel around the fence that guarded the fire road and squeezed through the opening, the same one Abbott and Jane had used several hours ago. The sky over the mountains was darkening and the drops falling were larger and heavier than before, but it was not yet a heavy downpour.

"Is your gadget still working?" Kit asked, pointing to the device Spiedel carried in his hand. The green light was still solid.

"Yes. It appears the man is not moving around and is roughly a mile to the northeast of us. Do you have any idea what's there?'

Kit thought a moment. "Well, the reservoir is that way, and between here and there is a creek, though it's pretty dry now. There are lots of little culverts and vernal ponds and ditches; no large features nearby other than the reservoir, and he can't be in there. Kids play all around when it's dry, but it can be dangerous in a sudden rainstorm. If you go in farther there are canyons that could swallow a Boy Scout troop, but I don't think any are within a mile of us."

"Would he be able to watch us as we approach?" Spiedel asked.

"Dunno; there are plenty of places along the trails where you can look down on the entire valley. And I know my house is visible from several spots. But it's getting darker, and even if he saw us leave the house, for the angle we are coming to now, I don't think he'd be able to see us. But– I can't say for sure."

Spiedel nodded, then said in a lower voice: "As far as his actual distance from us, it could be within a hundred yards or so, one way or the other, from my readings. So from now on let's try to keep our voices down. No sense helping him."

They had now traversed the high brush that separated the fire road from the main trail. Technically, hikers were not supposed to enter this way, but locals knew this entrance and used it frequently. From here on in they were entering a true wilderness.

"My reading shows we are moving to the north of his location," said Spiedel.

Kit, in the lead, turned back and said, "This trail will split shortly. One branch will continue north, the other will meander off to the northeast. That may be where they are."

Kit found that he was beginning to assume *they*, Abbott and Jane, were really out there somewhere. It made sense now, although without the commander's high tech toy I'm not sure where I would have started looking.

They continued on silently, trying to walk softly and avoid stepping on branches, until they came to the split in the trail. Spiedel stepped off to the right and kept going for several yards while Kit waited. Still watching the device Spiedel waved to Kit to come his way. He nodded to Kit, indicating the directional relay was tracking the signal from Abbott's cell phone, and it was to the right, a direction that a short distance off became darker as they entered a thick grove.

Kit began to imagine all kinds of dire scenarios. The cell phone was lost by Abbott, and while it is lying in the mud somewhere out here, Abbott and Jane are miles away. Worse, Jane is injured, lost, and unable to call for help. I wonder if I'll be of any use to Spiedel?

At the cave Abbott was awake, angry that he'd slept longer than he'd intended. He immediately checked his phone and cursed when he got Walker's message. He began to get a nagging feeling that the time to clear out was near at hand. Stepping deeper into the cave he checked on the woman, who seemed to still be asleep and secure.

As he step up to the mouth of the cave he could hear the soft split-splat of raindrops, though with the thick brush it would likely require a very heavy rain to break through the surrounding canopy. Well, rain or not, Abbott thought, it was time to move to a more open area where I can get decent reception and also be in position for an easier getaway. I don't want to be stuck up here with no way out except the way I came in.

The weary mercenary was confirming what he had already believed to be true: life in the field is for the young and the hungry– he was no longer either. He took inventory: he had his phone, and he picked up the flashlight and a rusty crowbar he'd found in the cave and stashed outside the entrance. Once more he checked on the woman, for whom he'd left food within reach, and in a noble gesture unlinked one of the chains so that she could more easily reach the cans he left for her toilet needs. Abbott exited the cave, struggled against the shrubs and felt the first heavy drops of rain as he stepped out into the open, just a few feet from the treacherous cliffside that angled down into the reservoir.

Jane had pretended to sleep while Abbott undid one of the chain links that held her prisoner. She wasn't sure what he was doing but decided to feign sleep. As soon as she heard him step away she began to dig at the hole she had begun earlier. The dirt and rocks came away easier now and she scraped away furiously, aware that her manicurist would be very unhappy with her.

The piece of metal her eager fingers had felt earlier suddenly came loose in her hands; it was a piece of pipe, about eight or nine inches long. Perfect! She almost shouted aloud. She immediately pulled herself up, stopped to listen, heard noises she could not at first identify, then recognized the rhythm of raindrops. Would the rain send the man back into the cave? She stood still in the blackness, listening for other sounds.

Impatient now, Jane groped towards where the chain that led from her wrist was encased in the rock wall. She began to hack at the rock with the pipe, and then tried to pry the link. This won't be easy, she worried, nor quiet. But what have I got to lose? If he comes back, so be it. She started to chip into the rock hoping to find a weak spot that would loosen and release the chain and link.

It was almost dark enough to use the flashlight, but Abbott felt a reluctance to turn it on just yet. He pulled the collar of his shirt around his neck and wished he brought a jacket or sweat shirt. In a panic he smacked at his pocket to assure himself that the car keys were there. Good, although I could probably go back to the Walker house and find keys for their car, but at this point I don't want to return there.

"It appears he's moving, slowly, but steadily and in our direction. He may be only about five hundred yards away—right there." Spiedel pointed to the east of where he and Kit stood at the west side of the rickety bridge that spanned the creek.

"If it is him, or them, they'll have to come this way to cross the creek," said Kit. "We can wait here and see if they show up. But what will you do, Spiedel? If there's shooting ...well, remember my wife may be with him."

"I understand the risk." He recalled his orders: from General Walker, to assure at the utmost the safety of the Walkers. From the man he knew only from his voice or his electronic transmissions by the initials 'SS', and who Spiedel knew was beholden to others, the names of which Spiedel was not privy to: to terminate the man known as Abbott or Antonio. Ideally he could work his magic to make for a happy ending for all parties concerned.

"I'll wait on the other side of the bridge," Spiedel ordered. "If he has your wife with him he'll surely make her cross ahead of him so I can come up from behind and you can grab her when she reaches the other side. If he's alone, all the better."

"You're forgetting something, commander."

Spiedel waited for Kit to enlighten him.

285

"I'm not forgetting that Abbott is a killer, and won't hesitate to kill again if he feels he needs to, but if my wife's not with him, and you kill him before he tells us where she is, and in this storm…"

"I understand, Mr. Walker."

The bridge was narrow, which was why Spiedel was sure that if Abbott and the Walker woman were together he'd have her go ahead of him, single file. Spiedel began to cross while Kit looked around for a tree big enough to hide behind. The commander held his pistol in one hand and his directional device in the other. As Kit gauged the prospects for a place he could secrete himself yet still be able to speedily get to Jane when she crossed the bridge, he heard a cracking sound. His heart skipped as he feared a gunshot.

Then he heard "Uh!" and turned to see the bridge give way and Spiedel flip crazily up and then sideways. The fall wasn't far; this was a mere creek, but as Spiedel tumbled he first hit a rock on the bank of the creek and then landed on a jagged remnant of a broken bridge span.

"Spiedel! Kit yelled.

A couple hundred yards away Abbott heard the crack, not as loud to him, but it also sounded at first like a gunshot. He stopped in his tracks and listened. He thought he heard human voices.

It must be hikers out late and now caught in the storm. No one else could be here that would pose a danger to him, he reasoned. He decided to risk turning on the flashlight, figuring the better to see what was up ahead and confident he would be better off even if the light gave his presence away. Even as he began to creep forward fanning the light ahead of him Abbott went over his plans—his latest change of plans in this scheme he now was ruing.

Once he got to his car he would drive to the shopping mall a few miles away. There he would call Walker if he hadn't yet heard from him. Then, whatever the result of that call, he would head south. He had saved one of his collection of forged passports for just this purpose; one in a name he hadn't used in recent years and this should serve to get him across the border. He would drive to Mexico City and from there fly back to Europe. He'd either have millions in the bank or he wouldn't, but he just wanted to end this.

Kit scrambled and slid down the bank of the creek to where Spiedel lay sprawled in the mud. With the flashlight Kit could see that the man's leg looked to be injured and his face was bloodied.

"Commander! Can you hear me?"

Spiedel grunted, groaned, and let out the slightest yelp as he tried to reposition himself. "Help me up, Walker."

It was near back-breaking for Kit to pull Spiedel up the side of the creek as the wounded man grimaced and ground his teeth to combat the pain of being moved. The rain was coming down harder now and for every two feet Kit pulled Spiedel up, he slipped back a foot.

"I don't think it's as bad as it looks," Spiedel said, when Kit had finally pulled him up to level ground.

"Easy, Spiedel. I know you Special Forces guys or whatever you are think you're supreme macho men, but we need to be careful before trying to move you."

"No, really," he said. "The leg's not broken, just cut, but my ankle is badly sprained, and I think my arm is what's broken. You'll have to take charge this side of the bridge."

"Yeah, well with all the noise we've just made Abbott's probably heard us."

"Maybe not; the rain is getting heavier and may have covered up some of the sounds. You need to look for my gun."

Kit nearly fell as he skid down the bank and searched with the Mag-Lite. His hands reached down into the muddy puddles that were rapidly becoming a living creek again.

"Walker!" The commander called out in a hushed tone. "I held on to the directional; it looks like he's still moving. He's very close now. Help get me up."

Kit climbed back up the side of the creek, his feet sinking deeper into the mud, and grabbed onto Spiedel, who was attempting to stand up.

"Help me to the other side," he said. "Here, take this." Spiedel gave the directional finder to Kit. Then he wrapped his good arm around Kit's shoulder while his damaged arm hung limply, and took a tentative step.

"Oh!"

"Not so macho, eh?" said Kit, immediately regretting it.

"Just help me across."

They had to get down the bank, sliding mostly, while the injured man tried to keep his ankle in the air so it didn't hit hard on the ground, then hobble the ten yards across the creek bed, and then crawl up the other side.

"Okay, leave me here and you go after him," said Spiedel as he lay down, too exhausted at the moment to care that rain was falling on him as if shot from a fire hose.

Abbott knew he should be getting close to the bridge. Again he was sure he heard voices and he decided to shut off the light and listen, but the rain was so loud now that other sounds were not distinct enough to identify.

As Kit began again to search the creek for the gun he thought he glimpsed a light out of the corner of his eye.

He immediately shut his flashlight off and stared in the direction from where the blip had come. He looked at the directional device and, if he was reading this correctly, it indicated that the cell phone it was locked onto was only fifty or so yards away. Kit stared into the dark; the rain now pelted down on him though the overhead trees blocked some of the precipitation.

A shadow moved, large enough to be a man. He strained to see if there was more than one shadow. Then his foot felt something hard underneath. He poked around in the mud and found the gun. But whether it would operate after being sunk in the water and mud was anybody's guess. Though I can't imagine shooting at a shadow not knowing who it might be.

Abbott figured that something wasn't right; even if there were hikers out here who had gotten caught in the storm they wouldn't be trying to cross the creek to come this way. Despite the rain and the wind and the dark Abbott could hear, could sense, that there were people nearby; he thought he saw movement—it was impossible to tell. Now he was fearful of switching the flashlight back on lest he give away his position. Could they—whoever they are—be on to him? Could Walker have stalled him enough to get a line on where he was?

Abbott turned and began to step lively back in the direction of the cave. He would get the woman; she was still an asset to him, if only to give him a bargaining chip if he needed one. After fifty yards or so in the dark, fearful that at any step he would slip on the leaves or mud, he turned on his light to help him find his way back to the cave.

The more Jane chipped away at the link in the stone that kept her prisoner the less she worried about making noise. By now, if Abbott was near, he would have heard her. He must be gone. She couldn't see but she could feel the chain loosening. Suddenly she fell backward as the chain and the ring of iron that had been locked in stone gave way along with a shower of chipped stone, knocking her back on her behind. But she was loose!

The chain on her wrist was still there but the several feet of chain that had held her stuck like a wild animal was free. She gathered it up and realized it might be too heavy for her to drag. So now she stuck the pipe between the links closer to her wrist and pried with all her night. She strained until she thought she would burst; stopped for breath then pried away again. This time the links began to spread open; tough as they were, the old iron was weakened by time. The chain snapped again sending her sprawling down but now she was free except for the link around her wrist and several inches of the chain, a souvenir she could live with forever if she had to, just to get free of this cave, and to get back to Kit again.

The sound of the rain led her to the front of the cave. She tried to remember the way they had come and how near the edge of the reservoir was. She had no light and all she could see as she peered out through the brush surrounding the rim of the cave opening were distant specks of light. The she thought she heard a rustling in the brush—oh God, no, he's coming back!

Abbott was beginning to shiver now, the rain having turned cold and coming down in a torrent. He might just have to take his chances and stay in the cave until it lets up.

Inside the cave Jane saw a flicker of light at the entrance and she stepped back, deeper inside, wary of the deadly fissure she knew was nearby. Down on her hands and knees she crept forward, thinking she understood a little what it was like for a blind person to enter a place they'd never been before, having no idea of where objects might be. Suddenly her hand was in empty space. Gingerly she stood up feeling around her for some hint of where the caves walls extended and where the gap began and how wide it was. She heard a noise behind her.

"Damn!" It was Abbott; he had seen the remnants of the chain and realized that Jane had escaped. "I can't believe she's out there in that storm," he spoke aloud. Wondering if she might still be in the cave he sprayed the flashlight around and then, remembering the gaping hole he seen earlier, wondered if she had fallen in. One less problem, he thought, but that'll be a murder charge on me anyway.

Had Abbott not spoken aloud Jane might not have been a hundred per cent sure that it was him returning; there was always the chance it was some other hiker looking for shelter. The possibility of that might have slowed Jane's reactions a split second and made a difference.

Abbott stepped toward where he sensed the hole would be and his foot scraped pebbles, which he heard trickle down– he was right at the edge. He flicked the light to his right, then his left. The light caught the gleam of something…it was the woman's eyes! At the same instant he felt the crack of something on the side of his head and dropped the flashlight. He reached for support and found none.

Jane had wound the remaining links of the chain still attached to her wrist and unleashed them with all the might she could elicit from her weary body. All she hoped to do was knock the man down so she could run out of the cave. In the dark she might be able to elude him. She knew of a small canyon nearby, in the opposite direction of the way they had come, where she could hide and wait for help.

She heard a grunt from the man, both in surprise and pain and heard him fall to the ground. The beam of the flashlight shot out onto the floor of the cave, but a part of it caught the black hole where fingers frantically scraped at the ledge, begging for a grip.

It wasn't what Jane had expected. "Oh God," she gasped as she reached down to grab the hand that desperately flayed at something to hold unto.

She felt the desperate man's fingers mesh with hers for the briefest moment before they slipped away and there was nothing there anymore. From the blackness she heard a curse and a groan, then a sound like a bag of dirty laundry landing on a well-watered lawn; then nothing.

"My God, I didn't mean to kill him," Jane said in a gasp, shocked and relieved at the same time. She hadn't intended nor anticipated such brutal action on her part. Desperate or not, it was a sobering thought to have killed someone, even in self-defense. She began to shake and forced herself to step safely away from the hole and sit back on the floor of the cave to catch her breath. Despite what the man had done a faint wish that he wasn't dead existed in Jane's mind.

Standing in the rain, soaked, tired and scared, Kit examined the directional finder and tried to interpret the readings. Suddenly the green light went red and the readings disappeared. "Oh no!"

The last blip of a reading had been slightly to the right of where he had been walking and less than a hundred yards away. He continued in that direction, scarcely daring to breathe. The Mag-Lite gave out a powerful beam even in the rain. It lit his way past the end of a trail to an area where he'd never ventured before. The brush was thick here and there was always the chance of poison ivy, so he'd never seen a reason to hike this area. He knew the reservoir was near and wondered if Abbott had accidentally fallen; or maybe just dropped his cell phone and broken it.

But Kit kept on, now in thick shrubs and tangled, vine-like bushes that scratched him and sprayed water in his face as he tried to deflect the branches. He knew he was making noise even as he tried to tread carefully, not wanting to alert anyone of his presence.

Inside the cave Jane had regained her composure. She used Abbott's flashlight to shine down the hole. It barely reached to the bottom but she could see just the slightest portion of the back of the man who had fallen, and knew he would never trouble anyone again. Now she stood at the entrance to the cave, gauging whether she should stay here or go out into the rain. This place is not easy to find she reasoned, so there is no sense staying here expecting help to arrive. Despite the fact that this cave is certainly unknown to most of the people who live nearby and doesn't appear on any of the maps of the area, I'm only about a half hour's hard walk from my own home and a well-populated area. The worst that can happen now is I get wet and scratched up from the brush. Hell, I look a fright already, anyway, so let's get going. I need to get to a phone to call Kit and Rick.

As she worked her way out she heard what she feared was a bear looking for shelter. Why she would think of a bear, of all things—she wondered later—could only be because she was still stressed and fearful of what might happen next. When she saw a beam of light she knew it wasn't a bear, and she no longer had to dread that it was Abbott.

When she saw a shape of a man that even through the brush and the rain and the darkness could only be Kit she nearly fainted from joy.

"Kit? Kit!" she screamed. "How...is it..." No, it couldn't be, could it?

"My God, Jane! Are you..." Kit couldn't finish because Jane had grabbed onto him so fiercely and hugged him so tightly to her that he couldn't speak.

"I'm safe", she said. "And you, oh Kit I thought you were still..."

"It's okay...what about Abbott?"

She looked towards the cave. "In there...he fell...I hit him and he fell. I think he's dead. Let's get out of here Kit, please."

"Yes, but let me see...I need to be sure."

Just before they reached the creek, which was flowing quite nicely now, Kit explained to Jane about Spiedel. She had not yet wanted to talk about what happened, other than that she was sure Abbott was dead, so they had moved as fast they could, adrenalin keeping them going.

The rain began to ease off a bit. They found Spiedel where Kit had left him; he too soaked to the bone. He had managed to rip an adequate bandage off his shirt to use on his leg cut and had found a long branch to use as a staff.

"I don't think the arm is as bad as I thought at first, and I can probably hike out of here with this staff. What about Abbott?"

Jane told him what happened; Kit assured the commander that he had seen the body at the bottom of the hole and there was no chance Abbott had survived.

"We need to be absolutely sure," Spiedel said.

"I'm am sure," said Jane, "and you don't look like you're in any condition to check on him anyway."

The commander nodded but his look was one that showed he needed the proof of his own eyes. "You take your wife home, Walker. I'll manage." "Just wait here, Spiedel. I'll get Jane home and I'll call an ambulance."

"No!" the commander shouted. "Absolutely do not do that!" He was so forceful he scared Kit and Jane. "General Walker wouldn't like that; please, leave me your flashlight and come back for me if you can."

"Sure, commander. I'll be back in less than an hour. I'll bring you a coat and something to make a better bandage."

"Yeah, thanks. Oh, Walker...my gun?"

Kit looked at the gun in his hand. All this time, while hugging Jane at the cave and the hike back to the creek where Spiedel waited, Kit had carried the weapon but had forgotten it was there. And he was glad he hadn't had to use it.

"Sure, here. I didn't even need it." He grinned at Jane.

"Now go, hurry."

The rain had slowed to a mere spit and from this side of the creek the Walkers knew their way home, even in the dark. Tired as they were it took longer than it usually would to cover the distance. Kit refused to go back until Jane had showered and changed into dry clothes. She was surprised to see he had packed an overnight bag.

"What's this?" she asked

"I want you to go to a hotel for the night."

"Are you kidding? After what I've been through I want my own bed. And I want a drink, first."

"Jane...please. I'm probably being overly cautious, but what if Abbott had someone else with him? Just for tonight, please."

"What about that man out there, Spiedel?"

"He's tough, he can wait for me."

Jane reluctantly agreed and Kit drove her to Pasadena where he got a room, got her settled and sternly commanded her not to open the door for anyone. "Not even me; I've got second key and I can get in myself. Now, I'll call you when I get back home after I help Spiedel."

"Kit, I'll be asleep. I'll be alright now. And be quiet when you come in."

In Bangkok it was mid-morning when Rick's phone rang. Kit rattled off the story while Rick listened with a bit of amazement. He was glad Kit couldn't see his smile.

When Kit gave him a chance to speak Rick said, "I'm truly sorry for all this, but what you did, well, it's amazing." "Me? Hell, Jane's the one. Hey, your man, what do I do with him?"

"He can take care of himself."

"I told you he was hurt."

"Unless he absolutely can't walk out of the woods, he'll somehow be okay, Kit. Those people...well, they're beyond me."

"I guess I shouldn't ask you who he works for."

"Kit, I'm not sure myself who pays his salary, to tell you the truth. But listen, about Abbott; Kit, where we left him; you need to do something if Spiedel hasn't."

Before going back to help Spiedel, Kit stopped at his house, timid going in at first, half expecting somebody to be there. What he didn't expect was the note on the table. It was from Spiedel.

'Mr. Walker: Sorry I wasn't more help to you and your wife but am glad you are both OK. I managed to find the cave thanks to your directions. Yes the man is dead. But it was too difficult for me to finish what should be done.'

The note continued with instructions from Spiedel similar to those Rick had given to Kit. It ended by saying, 'destroy this note, and forget my name.'

Thinking at how tired he was, Kit couldn't imagine how the commander had dragged himself to the cave on a sprained ankle. And where had this mysterious ally of Rick's gone to?

Kit changed into his hiking boots and took the trench tool that he still used around the yard for digging holes for plantings and for cleaning up after the dog, and the flashlight Spiedel had left on the table, and work gloves.

Kit then retraced the route he'd taken when he and Spiedel had begun the evening's adventure. Before he cut around the fence he made sure there was no one out for a late night walk now that the rain had stopped and the air had a refreshed aroma to it.

Again he fought through the brush into the cave. *I can't believe this is here. I wonder if anybody else has found this place in recent years. Well, I'm not going to tell anyone.*

Kit shined the light carefully around the cave and anything he found– the cans Abbott had set up, the bag of supplies he brought, the remains of the chain that Jane had been tied up with– he threw everything down the hole. Then he put the two cell phones he and Jane had received from Rick, smashed them with his foot until they were in several pieces, and threw those down the hole. But first he shined the light down to see that Abbott's body was still there; it was.

What Kit couldn't see was that the body had been violated by two bullets that had been fired by Spiedel, after he had painfully dragged himself to the cave. To do his job right, he had to have his own, positive, visual verification. As he'd looked down the shaft before firing, Spiedel had said to himself, *He's dead, alright, I can see that; but now I know he is.*

Now came the hard work. Kit made numerous trips through the brush to an area fifty yards away and filled his shovel with dirt which he then carried into the cave. On each trip some of the dirt fell off the shovel as he struggled with the branches that slapped at him as he went back and forth. Once inside the cave, Kit tossed the dirt down the hole.

He repeated this again and again, not taking too much dirt from any one spot, and always from at least fifty yards from the shrubbery that covered the entrance to the cave. His one fear was that all the traffic would damage the area enough so that another hiker might notice and think there was a path. But, it's unlikely anybody would come this way in the first place.

The job was tedious and took over an hour. Eventually Kit could look down the hole and see nothing but dirt. He decided he'd dump another five shovelfuls down. *I've never been so tired in my life.*

Before he left Kit got down on his hands and knees and brushed the floor of the cave, eliminating all footprints. He did the same as much as he could at the entrance.

"Oh my, Kit. What if someone finds the body anyway?" Jane asked later when Kit related to her about his evening's work.

"It's not likely, and Rick assures me that if it ever is, his fingerprints will never be identified."

"Yeah, well…assurances aren't worth what they use to be. So what did you do when you finished? You never called, which is fine because I was asleep two minutes after you left the hotel."

"Well, after I had finished with the body…"

>>TWENTY-THREE<<

"End Notes"

To Ed Jones the office seemed too large. Syd Swanson's former office contained a desk as large as the cubicle Ed had become used to working in; the kind with no door and sides that only went up about five feet. Now Ed had his own coffee pot and a secretary, though he did have to share her with several others. He decided he could get comfortable with this life despite the reduction in field time the promotion meant. Now he was truly one of the suits. The price of fame never comes cheap, he mused.

Kerry came in with a stack of papers for him to review and sign. "You need to check your e-mail, Ed, because I've got some upgrades to do on your computer, and I need to get them done this morning."

Ed started to object then caught himself. Don't complain–up until recently he had a machine that constantly cut out on him and lost messages. With Kerry around he now had the latest stuff—that's about as technical as he could described the machinations she frequently performed, always insisting Ed now had the fastest and best and latest software and hardware. Ed believed her but swore he would find the time to learn more about how this damn thing worked. He was still bugged about the idea that information had leaked out of Swanson's department.

One of the envelopes Kerry brought in was an unopened red envelope—not urgent or top secret, but meaning a message of some importance and not something to be spread around to anyone lower in security than himself. That meant Kerry, too, and she knew it but as she pushed the envelope towards Ed she stood there as if she expected him to open it and share the message with her.

"Who's this from?" Ed asked, knowing she already knew even though the envelope was unmarked and would have been delivered by a courier into her hands for immediate delivery to Jones.

"Cairo." She looked Ed straight in the eyes and he returned the look as he reached for the envelope.

"Swanson?" He said, not expecting an answer. Kerry thought it was taking him a long time to read the message on the inside of the envelope but that was because he read it three times before he handed it to Kerry.

"Oh!" she gasped, and for once Ed was sure she was truly surprised.

"A heart attack! I can't believe it; he wasn't old enough!"

Ed sat down slowly, raised his hands in a display of helplessness. "How old do you have to be, Kerry? Guys his age often have heart attacks, and if they're alone and too weak to call for help, sometimes they die."

"But found at his desk, early in the morning? You'd think there would have been people around, someone to notice he was ill. This is too much."

Ed was equally shocked by the news, but his sadness was hidden first by the sudden and unlikely news, and second, by his suspicion. This whole stupid affair, this 'Antonio thing', he'd taken to calling the recent events.

Thinking out loud, he said, "I never understood why Syd was sent to the Middle East in the first place. Didn't sound like a promotion to me."

"The way I heard the scuttlebutt was that it was some special assignment Syd was considered especially qualified for. And after it was over he'd come back here," Kerry offered.

Ed rose from behind his desk, feeling weary, and walked over to the window. He remembered how nearly every day he would tell Syd that it was too nice a day to be inside. That they should be in the fresh air playing golf. It had been their daily ritual, even if it was raining cats and dogs. Now Ed looked out at the blue sky and the green grass and thought that it wasn't such a nice day so far.

Jones felt foggy, unable to think about the paperwork on his desk. He turned to Kerry and said, "Kerry, you want to play with my computer, go ahead. I'm going out for a long walk."

"Okay, Ed. Remember to be back by eleven for the meeting."

"Yeah, the meeting, sure. I'll be back in time."

Conner Patterson walked down a hard-dirt path that led into a woodsy bower a short ways off the main road. Not that the main road from the village of LeDione was much to speak of. His curiosity had gotten the better of him ever since the visit from Ed Jones. No word had have ever been returned to Patterson and when he had called Langley, he was told that Jones would get back to him later. Patterson wondered if Jones ever got the message at all. Rather than reveal his curiosity by insisting on a response he decided to justify his desire to get out of the office by making a courtesy call on a man who was thought to have at one time been on the Agency's payroll, among the payroll of many other agencies.

He had found LeDione easily enough but had difficulty getting directions to the house he was looking for. No one seemed to have heard of anyone called

Antonio or Antonini, which seemed unlikely. When a lad came peddling by on a bicycle Patterson waved him to stop. The boy played dumb until Patterson pulled out an American twenty-dollar bill. Then the bicyclist spoke hastily and was rolling away even before he finished giving the directions, but Patterson managed to interpret enough to get his bearings.

The agent drove south until the main road veered sharply to the west and a dirt road, barely wide enough for a car, slashed into the woods. He was able to drive forward a few hundred yards until the road became too narrow so he got out and walked. It was a pleasant walk of nearly fifteen minutes, accompanied by birdcalls and the buzz of insects. When the trees thinned he could see a structure in a clearing. It looked dark and abandoned. As the scent came to him he understood why it looked so forlorn.

Once it must have been an attractive cottage, wooden with a stone façade, a low rock wall running all around it, pale green shutters and maybe even lace curtains, though he never thought of hired killers as caring about window coverings other than for how much protection they afforded.

Now there was rubble that still smoldered in place and gave off the aroma of burned wood and paper and all the things that go into a house. His shoes kicked up the dust of ashes as he approached what had been the front door. After a few steps inside he decided there was no reason to look for anyone or even for anything that might tell him something of its recent occupant.

Patterson hiked back to his car cursing himself for wearing a new pair of shoes on this outing.

It wasn't to be exactly another vacation—after all, they'd been to Hawaii after a quick trip to Switzerland to finish up the money business, but the Walkers decided they night go over to Mt. Vernon and maybe Monticello while they were in the vicinity. The purpose of the trip was to visit with Preston and Meg Volkers. Preston had been a little mysterious about something he wanted to show Kit and Jane, and would not under any circumstances talk about it over the phone or via e-mail.

"Come when you can; it doesn't have to be immediately, but the sooner the better."

The Preston house was built of brick and wood; the bricks were old but much of the wood on the porch and railings had been replaced over the years. The inside had been remodeled extensively and while trying to keep a comfortable feel to the inside compatible with the exterior, Meg Volkers had a top class contemporary kitchen and the bathrooms were so spiffy you hated to use them.

"And your uncle, the guy who got us in all this trouble, lived here once, is that right?" Jane asked.

Laughing, Preston acknowledged. "Yes, then I inherited it, rented it out for awhile, then I moved back in because I couldn't afford anything else. When we got married Meg and I moved in thinking it would be temporary."

"We got used to it," said Meg. "It's comfortable, plenty big, and once we were here awhile we didn't want to go anywhere else. But parts of the house hadn't been upgraded in years; decades actually."

After dinner Preston came back to the reason he'd asked the Walkers to visit.

"Kit, remember when Fears and Ed Jones and I showed up at your house, and a packet had been delivered to you?"

Kit nodded. "Sure—there were some pictures in the packet. I never saw them again; have you?"

"No. I even called Ed Jones about them. He says he doesn't know what happened to them, though when I suggested he probably couldn't confirm for me if he did know where they were, he laughed and agreed. But I kind of think he was telling the truth about not knowing."

"And the other guy, Ed's boss; I never met him but I thought…"

"He's dead." Preston told Kit and Jane what he'd heard about Syd Swanson's sudden demise.

"I did get one good look at the pictures and I'm sure my uncle was one of the guys. He was much younger then; this would probably have been in the sixties, from the look of him."

"Anyway, to try to make a long story short, when Meg decided to do some redecorating we noticed, or she did, that some floorboards in one room– the room my uncle had used as his bedroom when he lived here after his divorce– were kind of loose. I figured it was from age and we could tighten them up. The wood itself looked pretty good.

"I had to pull some of the boards up to work on them and beneath the floorboards there was a piece of plywood, which seemed odd. I took that out and the slab underneath looked like… well, it looked different. Like if it had been broken up and repaired. Well, why would that have been done, I wondered."

Preston sipped his wine as he put his thoughts in order. "I can't remember how much you knew about the notes we found that my uncle left me."

"I never read them," said Kit. "I don't think my cousin, General Walker did either."

"I remembered something about a file; *The File*, my uncle had emphasized. With everything else was going on with the money and so forth I had forgotten about that. I don't think Jones and Swanson did, but I never heard anymore about it.

"So I start digging away at the floor. Meg thinks I'm crazy, but now I'm getting obsessed because, well you can see what I'm thinking."

"I wanted to whack him," said Meg. "I'm eager to get new carpet in there and he's breaking up the floor."

"Yeah, well when I found this metal box she got more interested."

"Hey, buried treasure, maybe, why not?"

"Some treasure." Preston walked over to a desk and opened a drawer from which he pulled out a brown binder. From out of the binder he pulled a batch of standard office file folders. He handed it to Kit.

Kit looked at it, looked at everybody else in turn, and said, "Is this going to get me in more trouble, Preston?"

Everybody laughed, just a little nervous laugh.

Jane moved closer to Kit to look with him as he opened the file. Each file had several sections with headings. Kit flipped slowly, not reading anything in detail, just getting a feel for the categories and scanning some of the pictures. The sections included 'Chile'; 'Iran'; 'Dallas'; 'Op. Phoenix'; 'Ethiopia'; 'Afghan.'; and several others.

"Anything about the sections you notice?" asked Preston.

Kit shook his head at first, not yet seeing anything. Then he said, "I don't know, vaguely they sound like places the CIA was probably involved."

"They're all in other countries, aren't they?" said Jane. "Even Operation Phoenix was in Vietnam wasn't it? Except for Dallas; what operation would the CIA have been working on in Dallas?"

www.ingramcontent.com/pod-product-compliance
Lightning Source LLC
Chambersburg PA
CBHW070304260626
47160CB00003B/713